Going Under

ALSO BY BARBARA L. CLANTON

THE CLARKSONVILLE SERIES
Out of Left Field: Marlee's Story (Book One)
Tools of Ignorance: Lisa's Story (Book Two)
Going, Going, Gone: Susie's Story (Book Three)
Stealing Second: Sam's Story (Book Four)
Out at Home (Book Five)
Tools of the Devil (Book Six)
Going Under (Book Seven)
Stealing Hope (Book Eight)

THE WHICKETT SERIES
Art for Art's Sake: Meredith's Story (Book One)
Dani's Story (Book Two) ... <Coming Soon>

THE GRASSE RIVER SERIES
Quite an Undertaking: Devon's Story (Book One)
Rebecca's Story (Book Two) ... <Coming Soon>

THE GIRLS' SPORTS SERIES (Children's Books Ages 9-12)
Bases Loaded
Side Out
Live, Love, Lacrosse

Going Under

BOOK SEVEN IN THE CLARKSONVILLE SERIES

BARBARA L. CLANTON

Paperback ISBN   978-1-953734-26-6

Revised First Edition 2022
9 8 7 6 5 4 3 2 1

Cover design by Sarah (Forcoverservice)

Published by:
Bibi Books Publishing Company, LLC

Dedication

For my amazing group of friends from high schools other than my own that I had during my formative years: Jerri; Gina; Donna, Laura, Sonnie, Janine, Alison, Kathy; Jackie, Susan, Donna, Jude, Grace; Diane; Erin; Eileen who all took this quiet shy kid under their protective collective wings and helped me figure out how to be myself.

Acknowledgments

Big honking special thanks go out to my amazing beta readers Andrea Danak, Erin Saluta, and Angela Muir, who not only helped me with copy edit stuff but who also helped me rethink and reimagine critical parts of "Going Under." I am indebted to each of you. Thanks also go out to my ever-supportive family and network of friends. I am grateful for your continued support and encouragement. Thanks to the folks at Regal Crest, who continue to make me look good! And, lastly, thank you to my wife, Jackie. I'm proud to be your "W."

Table of Contents

Author's Note to the Revised Edition

It has been a labor of love to dive back into my earlier writing and do some light editing. "Going Under" is Book Seven in the young adult Clarksonville Series, initially published in 2018. It was written from Susie Torres's point of view. Susie has a lot of changes happening all at once in her life. Her best buddy went off to college and basically forgot her, and then her parents' rocky marriage started shaking apart at the foundation. She tries to keep things together for her younger brother, Miguel, but she just ... can't. Naturally, the rest of the Clarksonville gang is on hand to help her find a good balance. Her struggles to find relief are common among teenagers and mirror some of my own youthful struggles. I am proud to now be 20 years, 10 months, and 21 days sober!

And just a note that this is a *revised* edition, not a second edition. Nothing major has changed in the story plot. Only the grammar, punctuation, and awkward stuff (to my current eyes and ears) have been changed, updated, or eliminated.

I'm confident that the emotions and situations will stand the test of time and that you will root Susie on as she navigates a very difficult time in her life.

Cheers,
Barb
Central Florida (October 21, 2022)

Chapter One
Round Nineteen Thousand

Susie Torres scraped the food into the disposal. She kept her head down, trying to ignore her mother's rising voice on the other side of the kitchen. She rinsed the plate, hoping the rushing water would drown out her mother's ranting at her father over the phone. Poor guy, he just couldn't do anything right.

"Eduardo, I don't understand. Sunday dinner is sacred. You're the one that insisted on that." Susie's mother listened for a while and then burst. "No, I refuse to accept it. The weather in Vermont is the same as here. Upstate New York is on the same—" She held the phone close to her body and snapped her fingers at Susie. "What's the word, Susana?"

"Latitude, Mami." Susie went back to her dishes.

"Latitude. We're on the same latitude and have the same weather. So, you will get yourself back home by Sunday dinner." There was a pause, and then she added, "No. I will not 'listen to reason.'"

Her parents' fights were a regular occurrence. Susie hated it. At least it was early February, and all the doors and windows were shut tight. Susie hated their summer fights more when the entire neighborhood heard every infamous Torres family battle. Susie's mother cradled the phone under her chin and went back to the dining room to wipe the table. Susie's fourteen-year-old brother was doing his homework at the table, and he lifted his textbook so his mother could wipe underneath. How he could concentrate with their mother screaming on one side of him and their *abuelita* blasting the television on the other was beyond comprehension. Apparently, Miguel had adapted.

Susie caught her brother's eye and shrugged as if to say, "Here we go again." Without speaking, she used gestures to ask him if he wanted to do his homework in her room. It was the least she could do because even when her mother hung up, she would continue the storm by cursing her father as if trying to get him to hear her clear in Vermont.

"Mami," Miguel said as he gathered his books, "I'm going to Susie's room. She has to help me with math."

"No video games."

"We won't," Susie said as she washed the last of the pots in the sink. "Go ahead, Miguel. It's unlocked. I'll be up in a few minutes."

Miguel slung his backpack on his back and hurried past their mother. He stopped in the mudroom long enough to put on his shoes and coat. The front door slammed behind him.

Back in the kitchen, Susie's mother rinsed out the rag and hung it to dry. "Eduardo, it's Friday night," she said into the phone. "Why can't you get back here in time?"

Susie was trying to catch her mother's eye to gesture that she was going to head up to her room but jumped when her mother growled, "Who was that? Don't play stupid. I heard a woman's voice. Do you have a woman with you?" She scoffed at Susie in disbelief, but Susie looked away. "The television? Well, turn it down; it's too loud. I can't hear you." There was another pause on her end, and she leaned back against the countertop. "Eduardo, I'm done with this stupidity. It's Friday night, which means you have almost forty-eight hours to get home. Vermont is not that far away. And I'm sure your mother, who sits on that living room couch every day, and who I take care of, would like to see her son once in a while." It sounded like she interrupted him when she blurted, "Just get here, Eduardo." She slammed the kitchen phone into its cradle.

Susie knew she shouldn't. It was suicide, but she said it anyway. "It could be different, Mami."

"What? What could be different?" The edge in her mother's voice made Susie's stomach knot.

"Um, the weather in Vermont might be different than here. Sometimes Nor'easters skirt up the eastern coast and hit Vermont and New Hampshire, but not us."

"Nor'easter," she repeated and shook her head with a smirk. "The only Nor'easter he's going to get is the one here if he doesn't get home on Sunday. And you know what else, Susana?"

"What?"

"Don't take his side."

"I wasn't." As soon as the words came out, she remembered. You never contradicted Isabella Maria de Fatima Torres. Ever. "I'm sorry."

She gestured to the now-empty sink. "The dishes and pots are all done. I'm going to go do homework."

"No video games."

"We won't."

"I can see the light from your room. I will be able to tell."

"Mami, we won't. I have an AP Enviro test on Monday, and I want to get a jump on studying."

"*Ve hacer tu tarea.*"

"Thank you, Mami." Susie tried not to make it seem like she was fleeing, but she threw on her shoes and coat in record time and then flew across the driveway toward her room above the detached garage. Once inside the stairwell, she brushed the snow flurries from her coat. Oh, wow. Maybe there really was a snowstorm coming.

She ran up the stairs and opened the door to her room. Amazingly her brother was actually sitting at her desk doing homework.

She plopped down on her bed and kicked her backpack onto the floor by her desk. She did have a ton of homework, but it was Friday. No one did homework on Friday. Except maybe Miguel. What was that all about? "What's shaking, *Jefe*?"

Miguel didn't look up from his textbook. "Papi calls me that."

"I know. I wish he were home."

"I don't."

"Why not?" Susie sat up.

"Because all they do is fight." He turned around to face her. "And how can *Abuelita* just watch TV through it? They get so loud, and they're mean to each other."

4

"I don't know. She's hard of hearing and all, but those two can blast through anything." Susie smiled at her brother, knowing their parents' constant bickering was hard on him—it was hard on all of them—but he didn't smile back.

"It's gonna be, like, round nineteen thousand when he gets home," he said.

Susie chuckled. "Yeah, I know. I don't know what sets Mami off."

"I know he has to leave home for work, but what if he could stay home more?"

Susie nodded. She missed her father, too. Softball season was coming, and it would be nice if he went to some games. It was her senior year, after all. But she knew that probably would never happen.

She and Miguel sat silently for a few moments, lost in their own thoughts. She pointed to his homework. "Please tell me you're done with that ridiculousness on a Friday night."

He grinned and slammed his book shut. "I didn't know if she would come up here."

Susie opened her closet and pulled out two game controllers. "Super Mario Brothers or Tomb Raider?"

Miguel scoffed. "Tomb Raider."

"Fire it up while I turn on the lights." After turning on the overhead lights, she leaped to her feet and dug out the black blanket.

"Susie, you're sure she can't tell what we're doing?"

Susie grinned. "We'll find out, won't we?" She tucked the blanket over the console, and they scooted underneath.

Miguel laughed and hit the start button.

After an hour of gaming, they stashed the forbidden system in her closet, and then Miguel grabbed his backpack and headed to the main house. It had been nice spending time with her brother, but it was kind of sad, too. The only reason they were hanging out more was to get away from their mother's temper and her father's refusal to let their mother win. Win what? Susie wondered with a sigh.

"You know who's winning?" Susie asked her empty room. "Me. That's who. Because I have Marlee, and we would never yell at each other the way Isabella and Eduardo do."

She dug her cell phone out of her backpack, but before telling her phone to call her *querida*, she took a quick bathroom break. As she washed her hands, she caught her reflection in the mirror and was startled by how tired she looked. Her dark skin had taken on the natural pale of a North Country winter, but to her own eyes, she looked paler than usual. She had dark circles under her eyes, and her hair was completely limp and lifeless. Marlee loved her hair. She called it "brownish auburnish." Susie took a deep breath and smiled. It was her favorite time of day. Time to call Marlee.

She plopped back on her bed and commanded her phone to call Marlee.

"Hey, love of my life," Marlee answered in her sweet voice.

"I miss you." Susie settled back into her pillows. "Guess where I am."

"Mmm," Marlee purred, "your room."

"Warm."

"Your desk?" Marlee teased.

"Getting warmer, but not hot."

"Hot? Hmm, where would you be that's hot?" Marlee growled low into the phone. "I wish I was on that bed with you. I have some fond, very fond memories of you there."

"Me, too. Maybe we can find some alone time tomorrow?"

"It's snowing."

"I hate snow. It keeps me away from you." She pouted even though Marlee couldn't see her through the phone.

"But if the roads are clear, you and Sam have to get out here." Marlee's voice perked up. "I'm getting my bass guitar tomorrow. Sam knows what kind I should get. Even though she plays the violin and not the bass guitar, she'll still…" Marlee stopped talking and blew out a sigh. "I'm rambling. I'm sorry."

Susie chuckled. "*Aay, mi vida*, you're excited. And it's what makes you *you*. I love every rambling minute. Continue."

They chatted for over two hours and could have gone on longer, but Susie's energy drained as thoughts of her parents' constant bickering crept unbidden into her mind. Would she and Marlee end up like that? Snarling at each other over the stupidest things? Never, Susie vowed. That would never happen. She couldn't keep the thoughts about her parents at bay, and she grew increasingly tired until she had to tell Marlee she needed to go to bed. Marlee seemed disappointed, mainly because it was still relatively early for a Friday night, but eighteen-year-old Susie Torres was exhausted for some reason.

Chapter Two
North Country Music

Susie always got a tingle in her stomach when she approached the Clarksonville sign. It meant Marlee. And the sign underneath that read, "Clarksonville. Home of the New York State Softball Champions," made her so proud. Marlee had been the pitcher and MVP of the state tournament that had won Clarksonville High School its title. Okay, it stung a little bit that Marlee's team had eliminated her own East Valley High School team from contention, but Susie had to admit that Clarksonville had been the better team last season.

Susie pointed to the State Champions sign as they went by. "What do you think, Sam? Our turn this year?"

Sam took her eyes off the snowy road to shoot her friend and look of disbelief. "Are you kidding, Sus? We have no pitching—"

"Mary can pitch."

"What are you smoking? Mary is no Christy. Christy is the best."

"Marlee is the best," Susie corrected firmly.

"Well, yeah, that goes without saying. But Marlee pitches for the enemy. I mean at East Valley."

"You're right. But let's at least try to come in second place. We can't let that stupid Southbridge team beat us this year."

"Yeah, if we came in third, Coach Gellar will blame the co-captains for the fail."

"Us."

"Exactly." Sam turned her Mercedes onto Main Street.

"Hey, there it is." Susie pointed to the Northern Music storefront. "Ooh, I see a certain white van." She spun in her seat to face Sam. "Do you promise to make this guitar-buying escapade go fast? I haven't seen Marlee since, like, forever." She stuck out her bottom lip.

"Forever? You mean since my eighteenth birthday party at the youth group meeting on Tuesday?"

"Yeah, like I said. Forever!"

Susie leaped out of the car before Sam had even turned off the engine. She shut the door to the sound of Sam laughing. Marlee and Lisa had gotten out of the van, and Marlee braced herself for Susie's approach. Susie wrapped her arms around Marlee and spun her around. She hugged her tight and said, "I missed you."

"I missed you too, sweetie."

Susie felt her cheeks get warm. She pulled away a fraction of an inch. "I love it when you call me 'sweetie,'" she whispered. "And those crystal blue eyes of yours? They suck me in every time." Susie reached up and stroked the black-dyed ends of Marlee's short blonde hair. "And your hair. Did I tell you how much I love it?"

Before Marlee could answer, Sam called back, "Get a room, you two."

"You spoil all the fun, Samantha Rose," Susie called back. Despite not wanting to pull away, she did and said, "C'mon. Let's go spend all your money on a bass guitar."

"Let's do it." Marlee linked elbows with Susie, and they skipped into the music store. They followed the sound of Sam and Lisa's laughter.

Apparently, Sam had called ahead, and a salesman had set up a selection of bass guitars and amplifiers in varying prices in a private sound room. Susie's and Lisa's jobs were to weigh in on which bass sounded best with which amp. The job was in title only because neither of them really knew what they were listening for. As an accomplished violinist, Sam was the real expert when it came to music.

"Hey, guys," Sam said, "Lisa and I are heading to the accessories section to pick out some essentials." She turned to Lisa and ticked off items on her fingers. "She'll need a music stand, headphones, sheet music, picks, and extra strings. And, well, whatever else I find interesting out there." The salesman followed them out, probably with a dozen or more suggestions that would increase his commission.

As soon as the door shut behind them, Marlee whispered urgently, "Susie, I can't afford all of this. This bass is amazing." She played a quick scale that the salesman had shown her. "It's amazing, but it costs over a thousand dollars. Susie, I can't buy this. Or the amp. Or all the other stuff Sam's out there looking for. Oh, my God, how do I get out of this?"

"I know, I know, *mi amor*. Sam sometimes forgets that no one, and I mean no one, has the money that she and her family have. I mean, come on, did you get a Mercedes for Christmas?"

Marlee shook her head.

"Me, neither. Rust is the only thing holding my car together."

Marlee smiled.

"Ahh, there it is, that smile I live for. Listen, I'll pull Sam aside and talk some sense into her, okay?"

Marlee nodded. "I don't want her to get mad at me."

Susie pulled a stool up next to Marlee. "She won't. I'll take care of it."

Marlee pulled Susie closer and kissed her. Susie moaned and whispered. "Mmm, more of that later?"

"Count on it," Marlee growled.

"Yee-haw!" Susie leaped to her feet and headed to the door. "You practice those scales on that amazing guitar, *mi amor*, and I'll go talk some sense into that blonde-headed rich girl."

Susie was shocked at the pile of accessories they had placed on a flatbed cart. "Sam," Susie said, "can I talk to you?"

Sam was knee-deep in bass guitar strings. She pointed out five packs for the salesman to wrap up. "What's up, Sus?"

"All this stuff?" Susie gestured to the cart. "Marlee can't—" She leaned closer and said in a low tone, "She can't afford all of this."

"She can if I'm the one buying it for her."

"Sam. No, you can't—"

"I can," Sam interrupted. "She already told me her budget was five hundred dollars, so she's going to pay for half of the bass guitar. I'm picking up the other half and all of this." She gestured to the ever-growing cart.

"But it'll take her years to pay you back, Sam. I don't know if she—"

"Consider it a birthday gift."

"Marlee's birthday isn't until June."

11

"Groundhog's Day, then. Sus, it's okay. I like helping out my friends. I'll tell her about the arrangement. And, besides, every now and then, I like to thank you guys for being my friends."

"*Dios mio*, nimrod, you don't have to buy our friendship. We like you, weirdness and all."

"I know." Sam looked down at the carpet for a moment as if gathering her thoughts. "Let me go talk to her." She headed back to the soundproof room.

Lisa put a few books of sheet music on the cart and said to Susie, "You can't stop her, you know. She bought my sister Lynnie an expensive electronic violin and all kinds of stuff. It makes Sam happy. And we all saw how bonkers Marlee went over the bass player in that band. Sam's excited to have someone to share music with."

"I guess, but Marlee's uncomfortable." Susie took a deep breath and resigned herself to her friend's generosity. "Sam will be Sam, won't she?"

Lisa nodded in agreement.

They headed back to the sound room and found Sam and Marlee laughing together. Apparently, they had agreed to a monthly payment so Marlee could pay back Sam. Marlee seemed happy with the arrangement, and that's all that mattered to Susie. Susie volunteered to pull Marlee's van around to the front door to make loading easier, mainly because she didn't want to see the final cost. It was bad enough that Marlee would see it. Once the van was filled, Marlee jumped into the driver's seat, and Susie jumped into the passenger's. Lisa and Sam followed in the Mercedes as they convoyed back to Marlee's house.

The long gravel driveway led to the old white farmhouse that Marlee lived in with her mother. They had something like thirty acres of land, too, but Marlee's parents had never gotten a chance to do anything with it since her father died when Marlee was eleven years old.

Marlee pulled the van up to the side door leading to the kitchen. This was the door Marlee and her mother used as their main entrance.

"Hey, where are we setting up all this stuff?" Susie asked as she stepped out of the van.

"I wanted to set up in the basement. You know, make it my jamming space, but Sam said the temperature varies too much down there, so my mom and I made some space in my bedroom."

"Up the stairs it is." Susie pulled a couple of bags out of the back of the van. "Hey, I don't see your mom's car."

"She's working and won't be home until late this evening." Marlee leaned closer. "Late. Like after dinner late."

"Ooh, la la. We've got the house for the whole day, then?"

Marlee waggled her eyebrows. "Yep. We've got the whole day for you to listen to me fumble around with my new bass."

"Joy," Susie said with a grimace. She knew the smile in her eyes would tell Marlee she was teasing.

Susie followed Marlee to her room right at the top of the stairs. Susie knew instantly something had changed. "Wait? What's different? I can't…" Then it dawned on her. "No, Marlee, you didn't."

Marlee nodded just as Sam and Lisa made it to the doorway.

"She didn't what?" Lisa asked.

"It's okay," Marlee said. "It's down in the basement now."

"Oh, phew," Susie said. "That was your father's recliner. I was hoping you hadn't thrown it out."

13

"Never. But now I have room for my bass and amp and whatever else Sam got me."

Sam beamed. "Oh, I can't wait to get you set up." She dropped the bags of accessories onto Marlee's bed. "Let's go get the rest of the stuff. And I call that Lisa and Susie bring up the amp. You guys are the strongest."

"Hey," Marlee protested but then smiled. "Nah, you're right. And you're the fastest, Sam, but what does that make me?"

"The smartest," all three friends said in unison and then laughed.

"Okay," Marlee said. "I'll take it."

One more trip to the van was all they needed to get the shiny new music equipment piled into Marlee's room. It was obvious that both Marlee and Sam were dying to set everything up, so Susie said, "How about I go downstairs and fix something for lunch?"

Marlee's eyes lit up. "Grilled cheese?"

"And chicken noodle soup."

Susie laughed as Marlee faked a swoon. She knew Marlee's penchant for this particular lunch combination.

"I'll call you guys when it's ready."

Lisa stood up from Marlee's desk chair. "I'll come down and help. These two won't even know I'm gone."

Susie rolled her eyes. It was kind of true. Sam and Marlee were already engrossed in unpacking the amplifier from its box and didn't even notice them. The excited grin on Marlee's face gave Susie mixed feelings. She was glad that Marlee was so happy, but at the same time, she wondered if anything in her own life would ever make her that happy. She couldn't remember when she'd had an enjoyable day like this at home. At least she had Marlee. Marlee made her happy. Susie

14

hoped to get into Rockville University. It was far enough from home that she would be away from the madness. September. Yep, that's when she'd be able to breathe again.

Susie took a deep breath as she walked down the stairs to the kitchen. She had to get her game face on and pretend she was okay.

Susie was an old pro in Marlee's kitchen, having cooked many a meal there for Marlee and Marlee's mother. She whipped together the sandwiches and the soup while Lisa set the table.

"Hey," Susie said, "can you put out a Coke for Marlee? I'll just have water. Grab whatever you guys want to drink."

"You got it," Lisa said. "Geez, I love this kitchen. It's so big, and the light is perfect coming in the windows like that."

There was, indeed, a soft early afternoon glow to the room.

"One day, I'd like a country kitchen like this," Susie said. The sound of laughter brought their attention upstairs.

Sam and Marlee were headed down.

"You picked up those scales so quickly, Marlee," Sam said.

"Thanks. I have to work on that four-finger reach you were showing me." She spread her fingers wide apart on her left hand.

Sam stopped at the bottom of the stairs and said to Lisa and Susie, "You guys? She's a natural. She's got good rhythm and pacing, and she's only been playing for fifteen minutes." She turned back to Marlee. "I can't wait to jam with you."

"Don't make me nervous, Sam. Eee," Marlee squealed.

"Well, let's keep your strength up." Susie gestured for her friends to sit. "Lunch is served."

After devouring everything Susie had prepared, the friends cleaned up the kitchen, and then Sam and Lisa announced that they were going for a ride to parts unknown for a while. A wink from Sam made it crystal clear what they were up to.

Sam helped Lisa put her coat on. Lisa was one-inch shy of six feet tall and had to bend down and hold her long black braid out of the way for the much shorter Sam to be effective. They didn't seem to mind the height difference, so nobody else did either.

"I'll text you when I'm on my way back here to pick you up, Sus, okay?"

"Good idea," Marlee answered for her. "You don't want to, uh, interrupt anything."

Everyone laughed, and Lisa said, "I didn't expect that from you, Marlee." She turned to Sam and said, "See? It's always those quiet intellectual ones you have to watch out for."

"No kidding." Sam smirked. "Oh, hey, do you guys want to do something tomorrow? I'm going to church with Lisa and her family, but after that, we were thinking about going bowling or to the movies or something."

Before Marlee could answer, Susie mumbled, "I can't. I think I need to be home." Papi might actually make it home from Vermont. And, although she didn't really want to be there for round nineteen thousand, she kind of had to be. Maybe she could help smooth things over with her parents.

The silence in the kitchen grew to an uncomfortable level, so Susie added, "My mother wants to have this big Sunday dinner tomorrow, and my father..." She couldn't figure out what to add, so she let her unfinished sentence hang there.

Susie caught the concerned look Marlee exchanged with Sam but pretended not to notice. Sam shrugged as if to say she didn't know what was going on. And, no, Sam didn't know anything because even though Susie's parents didn't mind shouting their problems all over East Valley, Susie did mind. Some things she could handle on her own. And this was one of them.

Once Sam and Lisa left, Marlee turned to Susie. "You okay?"

"Yeah, why wouldn't I be?" Susie needed an immediate change in subject. "They had everything you needed and then some at North Country Music, didn't they?"

Marlee didn't answer. She stepped closer and gently stroked Susie's face. Susie felt her body relax the tiniest of bits. Marlee had a gentle way about her that made Susie feel loved and protected. She hadn't realized how wound up she had gotten herself, but Marlee must have. Marlee stepped closer and locked eyes with Susie. "I've got candles ready for lighting, soft music ready for playing, and a couch ready for, uh, frolicking. How about we make our own North Country music?"

Susie nodded and let Marlee lead her to their private couch in the basement.

Chapter Three
What Was It Like?

On Monday afternoon, Susie sat at her usual table in the school cafeteria. She had basically gone through the motions in her classes that morning. For some reason, she just didn't feel like doing school. She would have bet money that her father would have made it home for Sunday dinner because her mother always got what she wanted. Well, almost always. Susie wouldn't turn straight and marry a doctor anytime soon, but Isabella Maria de Fatima Torres usually got what she wanted. Not this time. Susie's father hadn't made it home on Sunday. He was still in Vermont.

Formal Sunday dinner at the Torres household had gone on despite his absence, and Susie's mother had been eerily and uncharacteristically quiet. She barely spoke a word the entire meal. After a few futile attempts, Susie stopped trying to get any kind of conversation going. Susie's mother left the cleanup to Susie and went upstairs to her bedroom. The master bedroom door was often slammed shut when her mother was mad, but the door closed quietly this time. Was it the calm before the storm?

Susie wouldn't let her seventy-year-old *abuelita* help with the cleanup but enlisted Miguel to clear off the table instead. When they were done cleaning up, Susie asked him if he wanted to play Tomb

Raider, but he said he had homework to do and went up to his room. Yes, things were definitely weird in the Torres household.

"Hey, dork," Sam said as she sat down at the cafeteria table next to Susie. Her lunch tray held a plastic bowl of East Valley High School's version of a chef salad. "What's shaking?"

"Not much." Susie faked a smile. She pulled a ham sandwich and an apple out of her brown paper lunch bag.

"Your life sounds exciting," Sam said sarcastically. "Hey, guess what?"

"What?" Susie didn't look up.

"Softball starts exactly four weeks from today, and it can't come soon enough. I am over this winter. This Arctic cold needs to go back to the Arctic already! Florida. That's where we need to go."

Thoughts of softball and spring should have cheered her up, but Susie couldn't find the energy.

"Preseason workouts shouldn't be too bad," Sam continued. "Weights and cardio. The usual."

"Fun," Susie said without enthusiasm.

"What's up with you, Sus?" Sam said. "Cat got your tongue?"

Alivia and her boyfriend Karl sat down at the table. Karl's six-foot frame should have dwarfed Alivia's petite five-two, but somehow it didn't. They sort of form-fitted together even though they had only been going out for a few months. Her long chestnut hair complemented his dirty blonde boyish cut. They were a cute couple.

"What does that mean, anyway?" Alivia asked. "Why would a cat have someone's tongue? Do you know?" she asked Karl.

"No clue."

19

Susie didn't know either but probably wouldn't have spoken up even if she did know. She wasn't in the mood.

"I know, I know," Sam said. "A witch's cat steals your tongue, so you can't tell anyone what the witch is doing."

"Ooh, don't piss off any witches," Alivia said and brushed a lock of her long hair behind her shoulder.

"Hey, where's Sir Ronnie?" Sam asked.

Karl laughed. "Where do you think? Hungover again. He said he was going to try to get here in time for your Strings class."

Sam laughed. "Oh, that's nice. The second-to-last period of the day." She shook her head.

"He said Mr. Auerbach gets cranky when your quintet doesn't rehearse."

"That is spot-on true," Sam said.

"You know Ronnie and Mondays," Alivia added, "they don't go together. Hey, honey," Alivia turned to Karl, "can you go get my lunch?" She pulled her wallet out of her backpack, opened it, and handed Karl a ten-dollar bill.

"The usual? Ham and Swiss?"

She nodded. "I love you, studmuffin."

His cheeks turned pink as he got up to get on one of the ever-increasing lines.

Susie put her hand on Alivia's wallet. "You have two driver's licenses?"

Alivia grinned and, without a word, handed them both to Susie.

They looked pretty much the same, from Alivia's flattering picture to the New York State emblem and seal, but there were two huge differences. The one printed vertically was Alivia's actual license. Susie tapped the other one printed horizontally. "This one makes you twenty-one."

"Very observant. Sometimes you need to be twenty-one. Know what I mean?" Alivia snatched her licenses back and stashed them in her wallet.

Susie nodded. She did know. Before she'd met Marlee, she used to party with her friends and teammates every weekend, sometimes during the week. Those parties usually included Genny Cream Ale or Saranac Adirondack Lager. But after meeting Marlee, she didn't drink much. Not at all, really, except maybe a couple of times when Sam snagged some wine from her parents' wine cellar or at one of Ronnie's infamous parties. Marlee's father had died in a car crash caused by a drunk driver, and Susie didn't want to upset Marlee in any way by drinking in front of her. But she kind of missed it. Drinking a few beers had always let her forget about whatever random shit was happening in her life.

She knew she shouldn't, but she couldn't stop the words that came tumbling out. "I want to be twenty-one."

With raised eyebrows, Alivia nodded her approval. She kept her voice low when she said, "That's Karl's domain, so I'll let him know you're interested." She had kind of instinctively understood that Sam shouldn't overhear their conversation. "He can give you details, but I think it costs about $150. Just so you know."

Susie nodded and tried not to react to the price tag. That would decimate her meager savings. *Aay*, whatever. She decided not to worry about it and settled in to eat her lunch. The dull headache that had started during first-period English intensified with the ever-increasing noise in the high school cafeteria.

21

When the bell rang to end lunch, Sam, Susie, and Karl headed down the first-floor hallway to their sixth-period AP Environmental Science class.

"You and Alivia had your heads together," Sam said. "What were you two cooking up?"

Susie was surprised at how easily the lie came. "Nothing. She was telling me about some party they went to. Some college kids had a keg or something." The lie felt kind of weird because Karl was walking right behind her.

"Yeah, those guys like to party," Sam said with a wink at Karl.

"Yes, we do," Karl said in proud agreement.

Susie opened the classroom door to allow Sam and Karl to enter first, but then a slew of other kids took advantage and slid into the room, blocking her own entrance. By the time the last of her classmates made it through the door, the late bell rang.

"You're late, Ms. Torres," Ms. Armstrong said. She winked at Susie to let her know she was teasing.

Susie found her smile and slid into her usual seat behind Sam and in front of Karl. She liked her science teacher. She was pretty much no-nonsense and made learning the boatload of AP material seem easy.

After taking attendance, Ms. Armstrong asked for attention. She was a young teacher but definitely knew how to teach and command a classroom. She wore glasses, but they didn't make her look nerdy, and she usually wore her honey-brown hair pulled back into one of those teacher buns.

"Let's continue our notes about water." She flicked on the projector and a PowerPoint presentation slide shined on the whiteboard in the front of the room. Susie loved PowerPoint days because Ms. Armstrong dimmed the classroom lights, making it easier to text Marlee.

"Water is kind of important," the teacher said. The students laughed in agreement. "But did you know that only about three percent of all water on this planet is fresh water, and most of that is caught up in glaciers or deep underground?" She clicked to the next slide depicting the natural life cycle of water.

Susie grinned. As a geology geek, she had seen this chart so many times that she had it memorized. And that meant it was safe to text Marlee. She slowly pulled her phone out of her front pocket and kept it under the desk. Like most kids in school, she had gotten good at seeming attentive—notebook out, pen in one hand as if taking notes—and phone under the desktop in the other hand. Texting one-handed was sometimes a trial, but Susie did it easily. She made sure the volume was completely turned off.

"Miss you," Susie's text read. She hit the send icon.

Waiting for the reply, Susie wrote down the keywords on Ms. Armstrong's chart. Precipitation, condensation, infiltration, evaporation. The list kept coming, and Susie deftly wrote them down until a quick vibration told her Marlee had responded.

"Me, too. How's AP Enviro? AP Java is slow today."

"Water cycle today. Know it already." Susie glanced down now and then to make sure her one-thumb texting was hitting the correct letters.

"Smarty-pants."

Susie smiled.

"So, uh, Susie," Ms. Armstrong said, "can you please explain the process of percolation to us?"

Shoot, she'd been snagged. She turned the phone over on her thigh so the glow wouldn't give her away, just in case she hadn't been caught. "Sure. Percolation is when water moves through rock and soil down to the aquifers."

"Good answer," Ms. Armstrong nodded once. "Now put that phone away, please."

Susie nodded and slid the phone back into her pocket. Marlee knew that if a reply didn't come back, Susie had either gotten caught or gotten caught up in the lesson. She'd explain later.

When Ms. Armstrong looked down to click to the next slide, Sam whirled around in her seat and smacked Susie on the arm. "Slacker!" she whispered.

Embarrassed at getting caught so publicly, Susie scrunched her face in reply.

Karl patted her on the back, teasing her about her misdemeanor.

With five minutes left, Ms. Armstrong finished the class notes and then reminded them to work on their third-quarter research paper due in March.

When the bell rang to end the class, Susie stashed her notebook in her backpack and stood up. It was time to head to her Ethics class with Mrs. Sherman. Her last class of the day, thank God. She was kind of tired of school at the moment.

"Hey, dork," Sam said, "are you lifting with the team and me later? You never said."

"No, I'm going home. I don't feel so great." And besides, she wanted to get home as soon as she could in case her father came home.

"Yeah, you do look a little weird today, um, I mean pale."

Susie didn't even smile at Sam's teasing as they headed into the already crowded hallway. "I'll lift at home or whatever." She said it without real conviction, but the more she thought about it, maybe that's what she needed to do to get herself out of her funk—some good ole sweat therapy. "I'll do squats, too. That'll be my cardio."

"You're voluntarily doing squats?"

Susie nodded.

"Whacko," Sam said and smacked her friend on the arm. "I'm off to Strings. Hey, wanna bet on whether Ronnie makes it or not?"

"Nah, that boy is way too unpredictable."

Sam nodded her agreement. "Okay, see you later." She headed down the hall and disappeared into the sea of high school kids.

After school, Susie raced home without breaking too many laws. Her heart sank when she didn't see her father's car in the driveway. Luckily her mother's car wasn't there either. She was a nurse at Dr. Webster's office and often worked until five or six o'clock.

Miguel wasn't due to be home yet, either, but Susie ran in to check on her *abuelita* to make sure she was okay. After a quick hug, she refreshed her grandmother's water glass and then bolted to her room. She threw her backpack on her desk and then changed into workout clothes. She loved having her weight set right there in her room. One entire corner of her room was dedicated to working out. She had a rack of hand weights and a bench. She kept one part of the workout mat clear for stretches, crunches, and jump-roping. The best

25

part about working out was when Marlee came over and worked out with her. It was so intimate watching Marlee get strong. It was nice and private.

It usually only took three deep breaths to get her relaxed and into workout mode, but this time she needed more. Still not quite settled, she did two minutes of squats. She was always amazed at how out of breath she'd get after squats. Not to be deterred, she meticulously went through her weights workout as well. Today was chest, shoulders, and triceps. Tomorrow she'd focus on her back and biceps, and the next day would be legs. Every day was core day, though, and Susie ended her workout doing several hundred crunches before exhaustion flattened her on the workout mat.

After a minute of recovery, she stood up and walked over to her desk. She took a healthy swig of water and looked out the window, hopeful. Nah, he wasn't home. What had she expected? She stared at his empty parking spot for a while and then looked down the street to see if she could see him coming. Nothing. Her mind imagined all the ways her mother was going to explode if he was still stuck in Vermont and didn't get back. Then her mind imagined her father in a car wreck on the back roads. What if no one saw his car go into a ditch? What if he was bleeding?

Susie groaned and took several deep, cleansing breaths. There was no sense in making herself sick. Her father would get home when he got home. *If* he got home, her mind countered.

Susie flung herself on her bed and called Marlee. Marlee sometimes had free time during her after-school job at Aldwell's Auto Repair. Hopefully, today was one of those times.

"Hey, girlfriend," Marlee answered the phone. "You left me hanging during sixth period."

"Sorry," Susie answered. "Ms. Armstrong kind of caught me."

"Oops. That sucks."

"Yeah, I know. Sam gave me grief about it."

"That's her job."

Susie chuckled. "Do you have time to talk now?"

"Yeah. Mondays are usually dead. Especially when it's cold like this, no one wants an oil change or brake work, so I'm hanging in Paulie's office filing paperwork."

Susie groaned. "That sounds like fun."

"It's orderly, and I enjoy order."

Susie laughed. "True. True." Yes, her girlfriend definitely did like things a certain way. Susie was quiet for a minute, trying to get her brain to chill out.

"Hey, are you still there, Susie?"

"Yeah, sorry. I was thinking."

"About what?"

"Can I...can I ask you a question, Marlee? I mean, you don't have to answer if it upsets you or anything. Oh, wait, is Paulie or anybody else there with you?"

"No, I'm alone. You have me worried now. Go ahead and ask."

Susie stammered, trying to find the best way to phrase her question. The direct approach was best, she decided. "Marlee, what was it like when your dad didn't come home? You know. That night when..."

"When he was in that car crash? The night he died?"

"Yeah."

"Why? What's going on? Is your dad okay?"

"Yes, yes. He's fine." *I think.* "He just…he hasn't…he isn't home from his business trip yet, and he was supposed to be here yesterday."

"Did he call? Do you know where he is?"

Susie's chest tightened as tears threatened. She tried to keep the tightness out of her voice. "My mom does, I think. She would have said something if he was missing or whatever."

"Missing?" Marlee's concern was clear.

"No, he's not missing. I just…" Susie punched the comforter. It was completely unsatisfying. She made a mental note to punch something of substance later. "I just miss him. And my parents fight all the time. And…"

"And what?"

"And I hate it, Marlee. I hate it. I hate them." She couldn't stop the tears and didn't care.

"Oh, sweetie, do you want me to come out there?"

"No, no, no." Susie took a breath, trying to stop her sadness. "It's going to be World War III here when he gets home, and I don't want you anywhere near it."

"I'd come if you wanted me to."

"I know." Susie closed her eyes and pictured Marlee's smile. "And I love you for it."

Susie sat bolt upright when she heard the crunch of tires on the driveway. A quick peek out the window told her that her father had made it home.

"Marlee, he's home."

"I'll let you go. And Susie?"

"*Sí, mi vida?*"

"I love you."

"*Te quiero tambien. Te quiero mucho*, Marlee. Bye."

Susie hung up the phone and watched her father pull his suitcase out of the trunk. "Papi," she said quietly to the empty room, "did you and Mami forget how to love each other?"

Chapter Four
Papi

Susie threw her coat on and raced across the driveway to the main house. Her father had just removed his shoes in the mudroom and was heading into the house, so Susie ripped her own shoes off and darted after him.

"Papi!" Susie said, wanting to throw herself at him for a hug but held back. "You're home."

He turned at the sound of her greeting and smiled. "*Cómo está, mi hija favorita?*"

"I'm fine." There was so much more she wanted to say, like why did he have to take so many business trips away from home, for one, but she held her tongue. "How was Vermont?"

"Snowy."

"That's why you couldn't get home." It wasn't a question.

"Right. When is your mother due home?"

Susie checked the clock. It was approaching five. "Any minute now, probably, but you know she sometimes stays later to finish paperwork." You do know that, Papi, don't you?

"Let me get unpacked, and then you can tell me all the awful things your brother has been doing."

Susie would have loved the chance to rat out her brother for something, but she didn't want to upset the already teetering apple cart. And, besides, she couldn't think of a single thing to rat him out for. Okay, that was weird.

Her father greeted his mother in the living room and then headed upstairs to the master bedroom. The door clicked closed quietly.

In a rush, Susie realized that her grandmother hadn't started dinner. She hustled into the living room and said, "*Abuelita*, what's happening with dinner? Should I get something started? Did Mami have a plan?" Susie was a good cook in her own right, but no one told her that she needed to prepare dinner for the family.

Susie's grandmother muted the television and turned to face Susie. She patted a spot on the couch next to her. "*Ven a sentarte conmigo.*"

Susie sat as bidden. "What's going on? Are we going out to dinner?"

Her grandmother shook her head. "No, no. *No tengo permitido cocinar comida.*"

"Why aren't you allowed to cook? Did your doctor say you shouldn't?" Her grandmother's arthritis had been particularly gnarly that winter.

"*Tu madre me dijo que no. No mas.*"

"Why?" Susie said, confused. "Why would Mami tell you not to cook anymore? You're the best cook in this house."

"I think she want *tu padre* to have lesson," Susie's grandmother said in broken English.

"What lesson?"

Her grandmother shrugged. "*No sé.*"

31

"Should *I* make dinner?" Susie knew she would be treading on dangerous ground either way she went. If she hurried into the kitchen to throw together a meal, then her mother might think she was taking sides with her father. On the other hand, if she didn't get dinner started, then her mother might accuse Susie of being selfish and lazy. This was a no-win situation.

Abuelita shrugged and patted Susie on the leg affectionately.

Caught between a rock and a hard place, Susie decided to at least look around the fridge, freezer, and pantry and see if she could throw something simple together. Maybe she could make *arroz con gandules*. They had pigeon peas, but making fresh rice would take forever. There was white rice leftover from Sunday's dinner, but her father insisted on no leftovers. Not even leftover rice.

There were frozen chicken quarters, and she could thaw them out in the microwave, but what could she make to go with it?

With a sigh, Susie pulled her cell phone out of the pocket of her sweats and was just about to call her mother when her father bounded down the stairs into the kitchen. He seemed happy to be home.

"She's still not home?" her father asked.

"No, I was just about to call and find out what we're doing for dinner."

He nodded and then pulled a beer from the refrigerator. Susie did her best not to gasp. Her mother never allowed him to drink beer before or during dinner. What was going on in this house?

He sat at the kitchen table and poured his beer into a glass. He poured it so perfectly the one-inch foamy head looked really inviting. Too bad she wasn't twenty-one yet. They wouldn't be able to stop her from grabbing a cold one from the fridge any time she wanted.

"You know," he said, "your mother makes small things into *montañas*. There truly was a snowstorm in Burlington."

"Papi, you don't have to justify yourself to me."

"I know, *mariposita*, but I want you to understand that I take my responsibility to you and Miguel seriously. You two are my life." He stopped for a moment, and Susie wasn't sure if she saw tears in his eyes. "I'll need you to take care of things when I'm gone."

"Where are you going?"

He took a long drink from his beer. "I mean for work. When I have my trips. I need you to make sure the driveway is shoveled or the lawn is mowed in the summer. I need you to help your mother in the kitchen."

"I already do that."

His countenance relaxed. "You do, and I thank you for that. You are a faithful daughter even if Mami is hard on you about your chosen lifestyle."

Susie decided not to challenge him on his choice of words. She had the same *lifestyle* as any other kid her age—go to school, do homework, maybe get a job, help out at home, have a social life which, luckily for Susie, included an adoring girlfriend, sleep, and then do it all over again the next day.

"And I, for one," he said, "keep telling her how good Marlee is for you, but she doesn't listen. She won't hear anything except the noise that comes out of her own head." He swirled his beer and mumbled, "It has to be her way or no way at all."

Susie had always believed him when he said he was okay with her liking girls. But was that only because her mother was diametrically opposed? Was it only because whatever her mother thought, he chose the opposite? Her heart sank. Now she didn't know what to think.

"And," he continued, "Miguel is going to be doing more around here. A *lot* more. Your mother babies him too much. Her version of reality isn't very realistic. Miguel is fourteen and old enough to help around the house and yard."

Susie hoped her grin conveyed the fact that she one thousand percent agreed with her father. Gleefully, she couldn't wait to hear what his chores would be.

He took a drink from his beer and said, "I want you to keep track of your mother's car and take it in for maintenance and oil changes at the proper times. Your own car, too, but I think you already do that, right?"

"Yeah."

"And you'll need to make sure the furnace for the main house and the furnace for your room are working properly. Check the filters. I'll write out a list, okay?"

"Papi," she said tentatively, "are you going away?"

He stared silently at his beer glass for so long that Susie forgot to breathe.

"Work, Susie. You know my sales territory covers the entire North Country of New York and most of Vermont. Some of my trips take longer than others." He looked up from his glass and smiled. "I can't be in both places at once, and I need your help."

Susie jumped at the sound of her mother's car pulling into the driveway. She frowned when she noticed how tightly her father clutched his beer glass. She wanted to disappear, but there was nowhere to go, so she stood up from her chair and headed to the sink to wash the few remaining breakfast dishes from that morning. It was a good strategy because her back would be to the kitchen door when her mother came in.

Sounds of her mother hanging up her coat and setting her bag down in the foyer only ramped up Susie's nerves. When would the yelling start? Or would it be complete silence? Maybe her mother wouldn't even come into the kitchen. She had obviously seen Papi's car and knew he was home. Maybe she would go right up the stairs and hide in her bedroom all evening.

Susie jumped again when her mother spoke. "Susana, pull last night's leftovers out of the fridge and start heating them up." Susie spun around to face her mother. Her father was sitting at the kitchen table with his second beer, but they hadn't greeted or acknowledged each other in any way. "After that, wipe the table and set it."

"Yes, Mami." Susie hurried to the fridge and pulled out the food from their Sunday dinner the day before—the dinner that her mother demanded her father get home for but didn't.

Susie's mother turned to her father at the kitchen table. "Eduardo," she said simply. His only response was to raise his glass in greeting.

"I'll be upstairs," Susie's mother said to the kitchen, turned on her heels, and headed up the stairs.

Clever, Mami, clever, Susie thought. Her mother, grandmother, and she had gone out of their way to prepare a big spread for Sunday's meal, but her father hadn't showed. And now her mother was punishing him by serving those leftovers. Her father always demanded freshly prepared meals, refusing to eat leftover food. Serving leftovers flew right in the face of her father's usual demands.

35

Serving leftovers was her mother's way of serving him an ultimatum—he would either acquiesce and relinquish power to her mother for this round, or he would fuss, and the match would continue indefinitely.

Susie pulled out the container of roasted *pernil* and the leftover bowl of *arroz blanco*. She put the pork dish in the microwave to heat it and grabbed a rag to wipe the dining room table. Papi, she thought as she passed him on her way to the dining room, the ball's in your court. What's it going to be?

Once the table was set and the food warmed up, Susie called her brother down from his room. Her grandmother turned off the television and sat in her usual spot at the table. Susie got her a big glass of ice water and asked her father what he wanted to drink. He held up his beer glass and said, "I'll get myself another. Want one?" At any other time, his grin would have been playful, but now she knew it was an evil grin—one that was gleeful to be pushing her mother's buttons. He grabbed another beer on his way to the head of the table. That still didn't mean he was going to eat. Maybe he was waiting for Susie's mother to come back down before starting a rampage.

Susie was about to sit, but her mother was still upstairs. Susie wasn't sure what to do, so she acted as if this was any other typical weeknight. Which it completely wasn't, but if she used her imagination, maybe she could fake her way through the evening. She headed to the bottom of the stairs and called up softly, "Mami? *La cena está lista.*"

Getting no response, Susie wondered if she should repeat it but louder. She decided it was better not to poke the bear and headed back to the dining room. Her heart warmed hearing her father and brother engaged in a friendly but animated argument over who would win in a fight between Captain America and Iron Man.

Her mother finally came down and sat at the table. Susie tried not to hold her breath, waiting to see what her father would do. It was up to him to either serve himself the reheated food or serve a feisty opening volley for the continuation of round nineteen thousand. All eyes were on him.

He said grace, and to her amazement, he pulled the platter of *pernil* to him and dished some on his plate. "Smells good," he said, putting a smaller portion on *Abuelita's* plate. He then passed the pork dish to Susie's mother.

Susie let out a quiet sigh, dug into the rice, and passed the bowl to Miguel. Maybe dinner would be normal after all.

The conversation at the table that evening centered mostly around Miguel and—school, sports, and homework. Her father even asked her how Marlee was doing. That was nice. No one except *Abuelita* ever did that. So even though there was no yelling, things were *not* normal. There was absolutely no communication between her father and mother.

After the meal, Susie's mother supervised the cleanup, which miraculously included Miguel at her father's insistence. Her mother didn't protest, but Susie knew she would blow up about it later. After being released from kitchen duties, Susie hugged her abuelita and then headed to the mudroom to put on her shoes and coat. Once outside in the frigid February night air, she inhaled deeply and looked at the stars. Her father would say the angels had thrown glitter onto the black canvas to brighten the winter night sky. A wave of sadness overcame her. When would things go back to normal?

Despite the freezing temperature, she closed her eyes and took another slow breath. She let it out slowly, opened her eyes, and headed to her sanctuary over the garage.

Chapter Five

Latin Lover

After more than a week of her parents' silent treatment toward each other, Susie was glad to have the youth group meeting as an excuse to get out of the house on a weeknight. Sam pulled into the Clarksonville Community College parking lot and barely had the engine of her Mercedes turned off when she scrambled out of the car and leaped into Lisa's arms. It was clearly something she often did because Lisa caught her deftly and spun her around easily. Oblivious to everyone, they kissed like they hadn't seen each other in months.

Susie rolled her eyes at her friends and headed toward Marlee, who was leaning against the back of her van, waiting.

"Hey, stranger," Marlee said to Susie. Whatever she had been about to say next was lost as Susie pressed herself against her girlfriend and kissed her. Susie sighed as soft, eager lips met hers. It didn't take long for the kiss to escalate and flood her body with warmth.

"Mmm," Marlee moaned. "Better stop," she said between kisses, "you're turning me on."

"That's the idea," Susie whispered in Marlee's ski-cap-covered ear.

"It's working." Marlee pulled Susie tight against her and sighed.

"Lesbians on the loose," a male voice called jokingly in the parking lot.

Susie groaned. It had just been heating up nicely.

"Shuddup, Ronnie," Sam called over to him from a similar embrace with Lisa.

Ronnie laughed and pulled his boyfriend, Jordan, toward Sam. "Susie, my God. Give that girl some air!" While Ronnie was a dark-haired Italian, Jordan was slightly taller with a ruddy complexion and flaming red hair.

"Shuddup, Ronnie," Susie echoed but stepped back from Marlee.

"Come back," Marlee whimpered. "It's cold." She jogged in place to warm up.

Susie put her arm around Marlee and led her to Ronnie and their group of friends. On the way, she whispered, "Let's blow this youth group meeting. Let's go somewhere, you and me, and you know, finish what we started."

"After," Marlee whispered back. "It's Lisa's birthday."

"Oh, yeah." Susie clapped Ronnie and Jordan on the backs in greeting and then said, "Happy seventeenth, Lisa!"

"Thanks," Lisa said. "I'm finally catching up to all of you guys." Her cheeks were bright red from the cold. After hugs and a series of happy birthdays from the boys, Lisa added, "I'm taking my driver's test on Friday. If it doesn't snow, that is."

"Good luck," Jordan said. "We'll be rooting for you." He gave her another quick hug, and Susie wasn't sure why Lisa made a sour face at Sam when his back was turned. Sam frowned back at her and shook her head in disapproval.

"Hey, guys?" Marlee said, rubbing her arms. "Can we go inside? It's winter out here."

"Let's go," Sam said and linked arms with both Ronnie and Jordan. "Guys, you gotta wait until after the meeting to start drinking. I can smell it on your breath."

"Aww," Ronnie whined, "but Jordan wanted me to try a new IPA he found. It's called Deathtrap IPA. It's from a small craft brewer in Vermont. We only had one."

"One six-pack?" Sam joked.

"No, dearie, one, okay, maybe two, each. It's really good. You should try one. *After* the meeting, of course. I saved one just for you, Samantha Rose." He rubbed his shoulder against hers.

"Thanks, but no thanks, Ronnie. I'm driving." Sam stopped suddenly, causing the boys to stumble. "And which one of you, pray tell, is driving tonight?"

Susie burst out laughing when each one simultaneously pointed to the other. The frown on Marlee's face made her instantly regret laughing. Marlee must have been thinking about her father. She squeezed Marlee's gloved hand with her own.

Sam was not to be deterred. "One of you had better sober up before I let either of you back in that car."

They mumbled something, and Susie jumped when Sam barked, "I mean it, Ronnie. You're not going to kill yourself or someone else on my watch."

Whatever they mumbled back must have satisfied Sam because she dragged them by their linked arms up the steps of the Student Union.

Once inside, they found their usual meeting room decked out in streamers, balloons, and other birthday decorations. A gorgeous two-layer sheet cake sat majestically in the center of the table. Sam had paid for all of it, of course, but had asked Anne Foster, the Rainbow Alliance Youth Group's adult leader, to decorate the party's room.

"Happy birthday, Lisa!" the crowd of youth group members shouted at once. It wasn't a surprise party, but it had that feel.

Lisa beamed. "Thanks, everybody. I've had the best day today. This is the icing on the cake."

"And Sam'll be the cherry on top later," Ronnie said, using his patented stage whisper.

Anne clucked her disapproval of Ronnie's off-color joke while both Lisa and Sam covered their faces. Apparently, they had plans to leave the meeting early for some quality alone time.

"Gather 'round, everyone," Anne said. "Before we start our birthday celebration, I want to get some nuts and bolts out of the way." She glared at Ronnie warning him not to make any inappropriate remarks. Sufficiently chastised, he twisted an imaginary key over his lips and threw it over his shoulder. "Our next meeting is canceled because—"

A chorus of boos interrupted her sentence.

"No, no, you'll like the reason. All schools, including this one, will be closed for mid-winter break."

A chorus of cheers filled the room.

"I forgot that was coming up," Susie said to her friends. "A whole week of vacation. I can't wait."

Her friends nodded in agreement.

"So, we'll meet again the week after the break. I'll send an email reminder, but that isn't to say I'm not available to all of you." She let her gaze find each one of the students present to let them know she was serious. "You all have my phone number and email address. I can meet you here in thirty minutes if needed."

"Thanks, Anne," Sam said. "We're lucky to have you."

"And the Rainbow Alliance," Jordan added.

A murmuring of agreement spread through the group, and then Anne announced it was time for cake.

Once the birthday song was sung and the cake was cut, the students drifted off into small groups to socialize.

"Hey, Ronnie," Susie said, "what the hell is an IPA?"

"Ask Jordan," Ronnie said and pointed to Jordan. "He's the beer snob. I just drink them."

Jordan turned around dramatically. "I heard my name?" His flaming red hair was dyed with green highlights. He had his own unique style, for sure.

"What's an IPA, Jordan?" Susie repeated.

"India Pale Ale. The story goes like this," he said with a dramatic flair. True to form, a crowd gathered around him whenever he started a story. The crowd included a junior named Jessica Myers, who went to Marlee and Lisa's school. Jessica was kind of butch with her black leather jacket, silver-studded leather bracelet, and dark eyeliner. Susie had sized her up pretty quickly and felt no threat from her in terms of stealing Marlee away. It was just cool for Marlee and Lisa to have someone else at Clarksonville they could be themselves with.

"Apparently," Jordan continued, "there were a lot of Englishmen stationed down in good old India way back in the day, the 1700s or so.

43

You know because the sun never set on the British empire and all that?"

"Pip, pip, and cheerio, Governor," Ronnie said in his best English accent.

"Would you like a spot of tea?" Jordan answered.

When the chuckles died down, Jordan continued. "So, these Englishmen wanted to drink some good old English brew from home, but it was too far to ship and too hot in India to brew. Somebody finally came up with a way to add lots and lots of hops to the mix to make it last on its long journey from England to India. It was a hit."

"It's actually a tad bitter from the hops," Ronnie added, "but it's good. And it beats Genny Light."

"Phht," Jordan spat. "Light beer. Blech. That's like dishwater."

With the crowd around them, the conversation took a turn, and Susie wondered if she'd like IPAs. She wanted to ask Jordan the difference between an ale and a lager, but Marlee was headed their way with two slices of cake and two cans of Coke stuffed in her pockets. Maybe she'd ask Ronnie in school the next day. If he didn't know, she could text Jordan for an answer.

"Hey, Marlee," Sam said. "How are those DVD bass lessons going?"

Shit, Susie thought to herself. She hadn't even thought to ask Marlee about her new obsession. Note to self: be a better girlfriend.

"Great," Marlee gushed. "I'm still working on the four-finger spread—"

"Shuddup, Ronnie," both Sam and Susie said simultaneously, even though Ronnie hadn't said a word.

44

"Oh, come on. It was right there for me." He grimaced. "She left it wide open."

"Ronnie!" Sam and Susie admonished.

"Go on, Marlee," Sam said with a shake of her head, waving Ronnie away.

"Anyway," Marlee said, oblivious to Ronnie's suggestive teasing, "music is all about patterns. Music is basically math, and it's amazing. The whole notes, half notes, major scales, minor scales, octaves. It's basically base eight." She looked up and to the left and wondered out loud, "Why isn't it base ten? Or is it base twelve with all the sharps and flats?"

"Good questions," Sam said. "Let me know when we can play a duet."

Marlee's cheeks tinged red. "Don't make me nervous, Sam. I haven't even let my mom hear me play yet." She pointed to her ears. "I wear headphones."

"One day, you won't want to," Sam reassured her.

The meeting that evening was basically a social event, so after Lisa opened the presents that people had brought her, Sam and Lisa excused themselves, saying they had a few errands to run. Everyone knew that was code for finding a private spot to be alone, but no one, not even Ronnie, teased them about it.

"Happy anniversary, you guys," Marlee said.

Susie felt her face flush again. Again, she had forgotten something important. "Nine months, right?" At least she knew that. She made another note to herself: be a better friend.

Sam and Lisa nodded, and then Sam said to Ronnie, "Who's driving?"

"Me."

"Really?"

"Yes, Mom," he said. "Jordan really wants to taste those beers, so I'll quit."

"I'm gonna believe you, Ronnie." Sam blew him a kiss.

To Susie and Marlee, she said, "We'll see you guys later."

Once they left, Susie said low in Marlee's ear, "How soon until we can leave, too?"

"How 'bout now?"

"Really?" Susie's whole outlook on life brightened. "I'll get our coats and get you another Coke for the road. You say goodbye to whoever needs saying goodbye to."

Five minutes later, they were in Marlee's van heading to a dark private parking lot they'd recently found in the middle of nowhere. They left the engine running for the heater. Marlee had brought two full thermoses of hot chocolate and two blankets for their expected private time.

A while later, Susie collapsed. "That was incredible, *mi vida*." Susie zipped her sweatshirt closed over her bare chest. "I hate winter. All these clothes get in the way. I want to get to all of you." She unbuttoned the top of Marlee's jeans and pulled down the zipper in one yank.

"Wait, wait, wait." Marlee put her hand on top of Susie's. "I need a rest. You know? Gather my strength?"

"Nope," Susie said and began a series of kisses from one side of Marlee's exposed neck to the other.

"Susie, come on. Seriously, I need a break for a minute." Marlee chuckled when she said the words, but Susie detected a serious tone and let up.

"*Aay*, but your Latin lover can't keep her hands off you."

"I know. I know." Marlee sat up. "What does that mean, anyway?"

"Lover?" Susie narrowed her eyes mischievously. "Let me show you." She leaned down and kissed Marlee's collarbone.

"No, dork." Marlee laughed and nudged Susie off of her. She sat up and leaned against the back of the driver's seat. "Latin. What is a Latin, uh, person?" Clearly, she was trying to avoid the word "lover."

With a sigh, Susie sat up against the passenger seat, leaving a foot or more gap between them. "You take Latin; you know what Latin means."

"A language developed in ancient Rome, but what does that language have to do with lovers?" Marlee took a sip of hot chocolate from her thermos, licking her lips afterward.

The action jolted Susie dead center, so she forced herself to look down at her own unopened thermos. Her current need for Marlee was overpowering her ability to think. Marlee was clearly serious about taking a break, so Susie decided she'd better do the same, or she might end up doing something she'd regret.

"Um," Susie stammered, "Well, any country that speaks a language derived from Latin is considered a Latin nation."

"Spanish, Portuguese, French, Italian," Marlee said. "Countries like Brazil, Mexico, and French Guiana are all Latin countries. Latin *American,* to be exact."

"See? You knew everything already, Marlee. You just have to put all the pieces together."

Marlee grinned. Warmth spread through Susie's chest. She lived for that smile. When Marlee took another sip of her hot chocolate, Susie quickly looked away so she wouldn't be distracted. She opened her own thermos and took a sip. It wasn't hot anymore, but it was warm enough.

"So, you're Latin," Marlee said, "but what's the difference between Latin and Hispanic? Are you Hispanic, too?"

"Yep. Hispanic basically means the entire Spanish-speaking world. Latinos is the term for Hispanics born in the United States, so every Latino is Hispanic, but not every Hispanic is Latino."

"You were born in Puerto Rico?" Marlee said with a clear question at the end of her statement.

"Which is part of the United States."

"Oh, yeah, right. So, you are both Hispanic and Latino."

"Latina," Susie emphasized the *a*. "Spanish is a gendered language."

"I know. It's weird and sexist."

"So," Susie cleared her throat, "have you learned everything you wanted to know about Latinas?" She put her thermos off to the side, hopeful.

Marlee grinned. "Does my hot-blooded Latin lover need round three?"

Susie nodded, ready for anything Marlee offered.

Chapter Six
Mami

Susie checked the clock in the living room as she dusted the bookshelves above the piano. She had already worked at the college that morning, like she did every Saturday, setting up science labs for the various science professors. Most of her paychecks went toward gas, and most of the gas was used driving to Clarksonville, which is exactly where she wanted to be headed in about an hour. She had to pick up Sam, buy flowers, and then head to Marlee's house to celebrate Valentine's Day, but that could only happen if her mother were satisfied with her cleaning job. Yes, her mother was on a rampage—this time, it manifested as a cleaning tear. And it had started the day before. Late Friday afternoon, right after Susie got home from her pre-season softball workout, her father pulled his car out of the driveway for another weeklong business trip. He hadn't even stayed for dinner, which threw her mother into a rage as he left. The worst part was when he closed his car door and didn't look at his wife as he went. Susie could never imagine Marlee driving away like that or Marlee screaming angrily at her. Never. It hurt her heart to see her parents do it.

Even *Abuelita*, who usually seemed oblivious to the fights, had started going to her friend's house on Saturdays to play cards to get

49

out of the house. Susie had driven her the couple of miles that afternoon but didn't stay because she had strict orders to return home immediately.

"*Buenas suerte,* Susana," her grandmother had said with a frown as she got out of Susie's car that morning.

"I'll take all the luck you have, *Abuelita.* I just hope she lets me go out tonight."

"Ahh, to see your *cherubin,* Marlee." The frown turned into a teasing smile.

Susie nodded and said, "I'd better get back. Don't let them cheat in there, okay?"

Her grandmother grinned and headed up the walkway to the front door. Susie waited until her grandmother was in the house and sped home to begin her Saturday career in cleaning.

Susie had the dusting down to a good rhythm. She pulled out a stack of books, dusted the shelf, and then dusted each book in turn before putting them back. She had to be efficient. Her mother would check. She always did. Susie worked from the top shelf to the bottom, dusted her way around the furniture and the lamps, and then finally cleaned the piano. She straightened up the sheet music and framed photographs in the process. She'd learned to clean the piano last because the dust from the shelves seemed to take its time settling down on it, and her mother always had a fit. Susie would swear up and down that she had dusted the thing, but her mother never believed her.

After a quick but thorough vacuum, Susie checked the piano one last time. The family photographs displayed on top had been there for so long that she didn't notice them much anymore, except to dust them. Of course, there wasn't one picture of Susie with Marlee on the piano or hanging on the wall. Not even one of the thousand pictures her mother had taken when Susie and Marlee went to the winter formal at Marlee's high school. Susie hadn't seen a single one of those pictures. Her mother was probably hoping Susie's attraction to girls was just a phase and that she'd grow out of it.

She picked up the picture of her entire family. Susie had been twelve and Miguel eight. She smiled at her father's handsome good looks—from his thick dark hair, and stylish sideburns, to his precise eyebrows. They had all looked happy back then. Even her mother looked happy with her long dark auburn hair, dyed, of course, draped over both shoulders. She even sported a genuine smile. Wow, that had been six years ago. What had happened in those six years to make her parents bicker so much?

She put the picture down carefully, did a triple-check for dust, and picked up her cleaning supplies. She knew better than to put the stuff away, just in case her mother found something else for her to do.

"Mami?" Susie called up the stairs. Her mother was in the master bedroom cleaning out her closets and dressers, usually a springtime chore, but for some reason, it had become a mid-February one. "I'm done in the living room if you want to check it over."

"Come up here," came the curt answer.

Susie's stomach clenched. Now what? She set the cleaning supplies on the dining room floor and headed upstairs.

"What's up, Mami—Whoa!" Susie couldn't believe the mounds of her mother's clothes piled up on the bed, dressers, and the two bedroom chairs. "Mami, what are you doing?"

"Cleaning out the deadwood," her mother said without emotion. "Take what you want, most of this is going to Goodwill, and then I'm going shopping."

"Mami…" Susie paused, trying to figure out what to say. What was going on in her mother's head? No, it was best never to try to figure that out.

"Here, I pulled these blouses out for you." Susie's mother handed her a stack of folded shirts and gestured to the pants pile. "These pants won't fit you. You're too tall. And too hippy."

"My hips aren't big," Susie protested.

"Bigger than mine. You've got your father's hips." Her mother looked at her father's side of the bed near the front window. She walked over and picked up an empty water glass he'd left on his bedside table and turned to look out the window. After a few moments, she said quietly, "Who has a business trip on the weekend, anyway? Monday through Friday. Those are business days. What could he possibly be doing right now?"

Susie knew enough not to answer but stood still near the bed, holding the stack of her mother's discarded shirts.

Her mother's voice increased in volume as she added, "It's his rules or nothing. Why do I slave and make fresh meals for him every night? Why this obsession with no leftovers?" She turned to face Susie. "Do you know how much money we would save by making bigger batches to have over the next few days?"

Susie didn't get a chance to answer because her mother kept going. "A lot. That's how much. And his mother? Who takes care of her every day? Is she my responsibility? I didn't even want her to live with us. Did you know that?" Her mother's eyes flashed with anger.

"Oh, no. It didn't matter that I had a baby to deal with. No, he didn't care about that, did he? He said his mother would help me take care of the house and the baby, but that's not what happened, is it? No, I ended up having to take care of her, too. That damn television blasting all day and night."

Susie thought that was a little unfair since her grandmother usually did most of the cooking and seemed pretty self-sufficient.

As if reading Susie's thoughts, her mother said, "She caters to him. Fixes his favorite meals. Whatever *I* suggest, whatever *I* want to prepare, she ignores. Ignored in my own house, Susana, in my own house!" Her mother smacked his bedside table with her open palm. Susie jumped at the impact. "To be disrespected in my own house."

Susie didn't respond. Anything she said might have made things worse, and she had to stay on her mother's good side if she had any hope of giving Marlee flowers later.

"He lives in his own reality. And the rest of us have to live there with him. You know what he needs, Susana? He needs a reality check. That's what he needs. He doesn't do anything around the house if I don't tell him what to do. I have to tell him to take out the trash. I have to tell him to mow the lawn. I even have to tell him to shovel the driveway. How hard is that to figure out, right? It's snowing, and the driveway needs shoveling. Easy. You and that blonde friend of yours do more shoveling than he does."

Susie blanched at her mother's impersonal reference to Marlee. But she had come to expect that from her mother and let it go. She had to if she wanted to keep her own sanity.

Her mother picked up a shirt from the mound on the bed and folded it with sharp, quick movements. Susie put her own stack of shirts down by the door and helped her mother fold clothes.

"And it's Valentine's Day," her mother said. "You'd think he could bring his wife some flowers or a card. Something."

They folded in silence until her mother said, "Aren't you going out to see your friend today?"

"Yes, Mami, I need—" Susie amended her sentence quickly. "I'd like to leave in a little while. I'm picking up Sam first."

"Go, go. I can do this alone."

"Thanks, Mami. Don't forget to pick up *Abuelita* at five."

"As if I'd be allowed to forget," Susie's mother said sarcastically.

It hurt Susie's heart to hear her mother malign *Abuelita*. She turned to go without saying a word, picked up the big stack of shirts, and headed out of the room. Before she reached the stairs, Miguel popped his head out of his room.

"Is she mad?" Miguel whispered.

Susie nodded.

He blew out an exasperated sigh. "This blows. I was supposed to meet Scott at the rink."

"I don't know what to tell you, *Jefe*. Is your room clean?"

He frowned as he shook his head.

"Dude, I wouldn't ask her for anything until your room is cleaned."

Miguel rolled his eyes and sighed again. "Whatever." He sulked back into his room.

Susie sped down the carpeted stairs as quietly as she could, put the cleaning supplies back in the hall closet, and was just about to head to the mudroom to put on her shoes when she saw the refrigerator. Now was as good a time as any, she thought. During the rampage deep clean of the kitchen the night before, Susie had been assigned to clean out the refrigerator. She noticed that her father still had five beers left from the Saranac 12 Beers of Winter gift pack *Abuelita* had given him for Christmas. Among them were two Tropical Snow Storm IPAs.

Without giving it much thought, Susie stashed the two IPAs and the three Big Moose Winter Ales into a bag and headed to the mudroom for her shoes and jacket. If her father fussed about the missing beer, Susie would tell him that her mother asked her to throw them out. Once back in her room, she stashed four of the beers deep in her closet, keeping one of the IPAs out. One beer wasn't going to affect her driving, right? What was the harm?

She made sure her blinds and curtains were closed so her mother couldn't see what she was doing and twisted the cap off the bottle. She sniffed the fragrant brew and smiled. "Smells good," she said to her room. She took a tentative sip and immediately understood what Ronnie was talking about when he said IPAs were bitter. It was bitter, but it was kind of good, too. It was way different than the Genny Cream Ale Christy always got. She took another sip. It was nice and cold, too. Despite being the middle of winter, the cold beer was hitting the spot.

Susie took a shower and got ready for her night out with her friends. She was disappointed that she didn't have time for a second beer after she'd drained the first, but she had to get moving if she was going to pick up Sam on time. Sam used to be notoriously late for everything, but ever since she'd started going out with Lisa, she was

Ms. Punctuality. Susie knew the feeling. More time spent with Marlee was more time off the front lines.

The ride out to Clarksonville seemed to take forever. Sam kept up a constant chatter about some new piece her strings quintet was playing, but Susie heard little of it. She said the appropriate *wow* and *oh, really* at the right times, but her mind was on the hurtful things her mother had said about Susie's father and grandmother. Susie hadn't realized how unhappy her mother had become.

As Susie drove past the gas station just outside the Clarksonville town line, she noticed the neon beer signs in the convenience store's window. If she had that fake ID, she could walk right into that stupid store and get a six-pack of Genesee Cream Ale. Wait, that was old thinking. Maybe she'd get a six-pack of IPA or try some of that Brooklyn Lager her cousins from Brooklyn were always raving about. Ronnie, using Jordan as his source, told her that the main difference between lagers and ales was the type of yeast used. Ale yeasts fermented at the top of the brewing tank, while lager yeasts fermented at the bottom at lower temperatures. She was curious to see if she could taste the difference between them. Ooh, her father liked Corona with lime. Maybe she should try that, too. Although she doubted the convenience store had limes. And was Corona an ale or a lager or something else? She'd have to check next time she was in a store near some actual beer.

"Where are you?" Sam said and put a hand on Susie's forearm.

Susie glanced over. "What?"

Sam laughed. "Wow, I asked you a question and got no reply. You were a million miles away, Sus."

"Sorry, bestie. I was just…" Susie couldn't come up with anything. How could she tell Sam she was daydreaming about beer? Alcoholic much?

"Hey, it's okay, Sus," Sam said. "Just know that if you ever want to talk about anything, you can talk to me, okay?"

"Nah, I'm fine. Just tired. Mami's been on a cleaning rampage since yesterday, and I'm cleaned out."

"Yikes. I won't even ask why."

"And get this," Susie added. "She even had Miguel working, too!"

"No! Really? Your mother's only-begotten son had to actually do manual labor?"

Susie nodded as she turned into Lisa's neighborhood. "Believe it."

"No wonder you're tired."

"So, what question did you ask me?"

"I asked if you'd talked to Christy lately."

"Nah," Susie said. "Last I heard, she had a new boy toy at UCLA, so she's probably too busy to check in with her old softball buddies way back here in northern New York."

"I guess."

Susie sighed. She missed her friend. She'd hung out with Christy since she was fourteen years old and Christy was fifteen. Christy could always be counted on to throw parties for the softball team, sometimes every week. The team would hang out, and usually, the order of the night would be drinking. It was at Christy's that Susie had learned to drink. Christy's parents always traveled, so they always had the place to themselves. As she thought about those parties, Susie realized she had cut her drinking down severely since she'd been in a relationship with Marlee. With Christy gone, those good old days

Barbara L. Clanton

were gone, too. Sure, nowadays, she might have a couple of beers at
Ronnie's parties, but that was nowhere near what she'd have at
Christy's. She'd usually drink at least a six-pack all on her own,
sometimes more. And the night Marlee had come to one of Christy's
parties for the first time, Susie would only have three and then
stopped abruptly. And it was right there in Christy's backyard that
she had kissed Marlee for the very first time. A flutter of desire settled
low in her belly.

Susie pulled into Lisa's driveway but waited in the car while Sam
went in to greet Lisa's parents and siblings. She went in loaded with
several flower bouquets and boxes of candy, the biggest ones for Lisa
and the smaller ones for each member of Lisa's family. It wasn't long
before they came back out and headed to Marlee's house. Apparently,
Marlee's mother had gone out and wouldn't be home until late that
evening. They'd have the entire house to themselves.

Finally, at Marlee's house, Susie knocked on the kitchen door but
didn't wait for an answer. She let herself in and called, "Yoo hoo!
Your valentines are here." She held the dozen red roses they'd picked
up in East Valley behind her back.

Marlee popped her head out of the living room and raced into the
kitchen. "Hi, you guys."

"Happy Valentine's Day, Marlee," Sam said.

"Thanks for cooking dinner for us," Lisa added. "Whatever it is,
smells really good."

"Meatloaf, mashed potatoes and gravy, and dinner rolls," Marlee
said. "You'll all be happy to know that no one'll be poisoned because
my mom helped me make the entire meal."

58

Everyone laughed, and then Marlee added, "I even made a green vegetable because my valentine loves them more than me." She wrapped herself around Susie and kissed her hello.

Once Marlee extricated herself, Susie gave her the flowers.

"They're amazing. Thank you, sweetie."

"Happy Valentine's day, *mi amor*."

"You, too. Where did you guys find roses in the middle of winter?" Marlee smelled the flowers and smiled.

"Flower shop," Susie said with a laugh.

Sam reached out for Marlee's bouquet. "Here, let me put those in water for you."

Marlee handed over the flowers.

"Hey, you guys," Lisa said. There was excitement in her voice. "Guess what?"

"What?" Marlee said.

Lisa reached into her back pocket and pulled out her shiny new driver's license.

"Nice," Susie said. "Good for you. It sucks taking your road test in the winter, doesn't it?"

"No kidding," Lisa agreed. She got hugs all around and then tucked the license safely in her pocket.

Susie hung up her coat and said, "And Marlee, I'll have you know that I do *not* love vegetables more than you, *mi vida*."

"Yay!" Marlee said and clapped her hands three times. "Marlee: one, Broccoli: zero!"

Susie chuckled and asked what she could do to help.

"Nothing, except maybe put the Cokes and bottled waters on the table."

"Will do." Susie opened the fridge. She knew she shouldn't do it, but she couldn't help it. She rooted around the refrigerator to see if Marlee's mom had any beer. She didn't remember Marlee's mother ever throwing back a cold one, but you never knew. Striking out, she wondered if the McAllisters had a backup refrigerator anywhere. Nah, she'd been seeing Marlee for almost ten months and didn't remember a second refrigerator. And, besides, what was she going to do if she found beer? She couldn't very well drink it in front of Marlee. She was driving, anyway, so forget the whole thing.

Susie put the sodas and waters on the table and patted her pocket. The necklace she was giving Marlee later for Valentine's day was safe. The matching earrings were back home on her dresser. She'd give those to Marlee on Wednesday for their ten-month anniversary. If she got to see Marlee, that is. At the Torres household, you never knew when round nineteen thousand and one would erupt.

Chapter Seven
You're Wanted

Susie was stoked as she, Sam, and Karl left the cafeteria after lunch. Only two more class periods to go until school was over, and she could zip home and get ready for Marlee to pick her up for their ten-month anniversary dinner. Sam recommended an intimate Italian restaurant in the heart of East Valley, so Susie went ahead and made reservations. Marlee loved Italian food, so that should put her in a good mood for what Susie hoped would become an intimate evening later. She loved that van of Marlee's.

Sam reached the door to the AP Enviro classroom first and opened it for Susie to enter first. "After you, anniversary girl," Sam said with a sweep of her hand.

"Oh, no, no. I insist. You first." Susie also swept her hand in invitation.

"Oh, I just couldn't," Sam said, still holding the door open.

By then, a couple of kids were waiting to get in the room behind them.

"You were here first, Sam. I insist."

"It would be rude not to let you in before me," Sam said.

"Somebody go in," a classmate called good-naturedly from the hallway.

"I am indebted to your kindness," Susie said as she walked through the door. The herd of classmates followed her in.

"I win!" Sam said over the din of moving students. "I out-Canadianed you!"

Susie burst out laughing as she took her seat. "That Canadian nanny of yours has rubbed off on you, Sam." Susie instantly regretted the words. Sam's nanny of eighteen years had moved out recently to live with her sister in Quebec, and it had devastated Sam, who thought of her as a second mother.

Sam leaned in and whispered in a baby voice, "I'm all growed up now. I don't need my nanny anymore." Her smile let Susie know she wasn't upset by Susie's faux pas.

The bell rang to start class just as a ting came in on Susie's phone. She glanced down as Ms. Armstrong took attendance and smiled. Marlee sent another anniversary greeting.

Susie sent a quick text back to Marlee. "H.A. to you, too! I love you!"

"Hey, what's the diff between Great Britain and the United Kingdom?" Marlee texted.

Susie smiled. Marlee's text almost sounded like the start of a joke, but Susie knew it wasn't. Marlee was always thinking, thinking, thinking. The girl was a walking brain. Curious about everything. But Marlee wasn't the only curious one. Susie herself had recently become obsessed with the different types of beer. She had been peppering Ronnie and Jordan about the differences between lagers and ales, but now she wondered what the heck a pilsner was. Or how about malt liquor? She wanted to share her curiosity about beer with Marlee, but she couldn't. She didn't want to upset her. So instead, she researched privately. She didn't like having secrets from Marlee, but it was kind of necessary.

Susie started texting back. "The UK is—"

"Ms. Torres?" Ms. Armstrong interrupted. "Put that ever-lovin' phone on my desk, please."

Susie cringed as the class oohed at one of their own getting caught with a forbidden cell phone in class. She did the walk of shame to the front of the room.

"I have repeatedly given you the benefit of the doubt, Ms. Torres, but it stops today. If I see that phone out in class again, I will write you up for insubordination."

"Yes, ma'am. Sorry." Susie felt her entire face flush from embarrassment. She turned around and grimaced at Sam as she made her way back to her seat.

Karl, who sat behind her, clapped her on the back as if to say, "Way to mess up, Torres!" Susie didn't dare turn around and stick her tongue out at him or give him a withering glare. She couldn't risk it. No, for today and probably forever, she would be a dutiful student who took excellent notes. She would be such a model student that Ms. Armstrong would beam at her every day and give her nothing but A-pluses.

Ms. Armstrong turned the lights off and then began the PowerPoint lesson on the screen. She pointed to the opening slide and said, "Today's lesson is mainly about cause and effect. The word effect describes what happened. Cause describes why the effect happened. We'll be discussing rivers as the vehicle." She flicked to the next slide, which had the simple question, "Why are rivers important?" She looked at the class and said, "Karl, what do you think?"

Karl cleared his throat and said, "Uh, you can cool off in them in the summer? Oh, and you can go fishing, too."

"Sure, you've hit on ways humans use natural water for recreation and sustenance. Why else are rivers important?"

Students volunteered various reasons—drinking water for animals, habitats for fish and other water creatures, and habitats for plant life.

"All good answers, and don't forget that rivers provide a means for draining land after rain and snow." Ms. Armstrong clicked to the next slide. "So we've determined that rivers are important. Now tell me how we, as humans, mess up the rivers?"

"Pollution," Susie offered.

"Go on," Ms. Armstrong said.

"Factories dump chemicals into the water."

"Good. They also dump hot water into the river, completely messing up the natural temperature. What else?" Ms. Armstrong looked out over the class, signaling that she wanted another student to pick up the thought.

"Fertilizers from farms," said a shy girl in the back row.

"Yes, indeed," Ms. Armstrong said. "Not to mention animal waste washing into the water. And then there's human waste."

"Eww," Susie groaned. She wasn't the only one.

"And what about good old-fashioned household garbage?" Ms. Armstrong asked the class. "Cans, bottles, Mylar balloons, cardboard, kitchen waste, kitty litter, dog feces, old cars…" She showed slide after slide of garbage-polluted rivers. Dead fish floating in the slime made Susie's stomach knot. *What a waste*, she thought. *How can we let this happen?*

Just then, her phone lit up on Ms. Armstrong's desk. Sam must have seen it, too, because she turned slightly in her seat and wagged one slow finger at Susie. It was probably Marlee texting her back.

"So, Karl," Ms. Armstrong said, "how inviting do these rivers look for swimming or fishing now?"

"Not so much," he said grimly.

"C'mon, Karl, let's go fishing."

"No, thanks," Karl said with a laugh.

"But what if you depended on that river for food and water? What then? Clearly, there is a cause, and there is an effect. A big effect is on the environment. The cause? Pollution. But then pollution can also be considered an effect. What caused the pollution? Humans. Humans affect so many things, but collectively we don't seem to realize the impact our decisions make, and if we do, we're completely apathetic." She clicked to the next slide, which simply read, "Humans Destroy the Natural Order."

Ms. Armstrong paused for a moment. "Humans are starting to wake up, though." The next slide showed a mound of garbage collected by a bunch of high school students doing a river cleanup project in Massachusetts. "Prevention and cleanup do not have to come from big government," she said. "Prevention and cleanup can come from us using a grassroots approach."

Ms. Armstrong was about to say more, but there was a knock on the classroom door. Without saying a word, one of the front office assistants walked in and handed her a note. The assistant then spun on her heels and left. Ms. Armstrong read the note by the light of the PowerPoint slide and said to Susie, "You're wanted in the front office."

"Me?" Susie sat up taller. "Why?"

"I don't know, but it says you won't be returning to class, so you should bring your backpack with you." She walked over and handed Susie the note. Susie read it, but all it said was that Susana Torres was to report to the main office immediately. Scrawled underneath, it read, "Will not return to class." Why not?

Sam looked at her with questions in her eyes, and Susie shook her head to convey she had no idea what was happening. She stashed her notebook in her backpack, stood up, and headed for the classroom door.

"I'll call you later," Sam said.

Susie barely registered the words but managed to nod as she went out. Was everyone all right? Was her father okay? Had there been an accident? Her mother? Miguel? Oh, no, was it *Abuelita*?

Susie picked up speed and ran to the main office, her backpack bouncing as she went. She had never been in the office before, so when she walked in, she wasn't sure where to go. When none of the office assistants looked up, she went to the long counter. "I got a note to come down here," she said to the woman closest to her. She held up the pink slip of paper.

The woman, engrossed in typing something into her computer, didn't move or acknowledge her existence.

Susie wasn't sure what to do. She looked around and caught the eye of a woman near the windows. The attendance lady. "I got this slip?" Susie said again weakly.

"Maureen," the attendance lady thundered to the super-engrossed woman, "you have a customer."

"Hmm?" Maureen looked over at the attendance lady who was pointing at Susie. "Oh." Without getting up, she asked Susie, "What do you need?"

For the third time, Susie held out the office pass. "I was told to come down here."

The woman made a few clicks on her computer and then stood up, obviously not in any hurry. She reached for the pass and read Susie's name on it, "Susana Torres." She rifled through a stack of papers and finally found what she was looking for. She handed a note to Susie and sat down to resume typing.

The note read: "Call Dr. Webster's office immediately." The phone number was scrawled at the bottom.

"Oh, no," Susie mumbled, "that's Mami's boss." Did something happen to her mother? Why didn't her mother just text her?

Susie reached into her pocket for her phone. Her anxiety skyrocketed when it wasn't there. She put her backpack down and patted all of her pants' pockets. Nothing. Her phone wasn't even in her sweatshirt pocket. Backpack? She never put her phone in her backpack. Just as she unzipped the top compartment to check, realization hit her. Her phone was sitting loud and proud on Ms. Armstrong's desk.

"I don't have my phone," Susie said to the woman named Maureen. "Can I use the office phone?" Susie heard the panic in her voice as she tried not to freak out.

She got no response from the woman named Maureen. Maybe she was hard of hearing or something. Susie didn't care. She reached over the countertop for the nearest office phone. She noticed it said to punch the number nine before making a call. She hit the nine and waited to hear what would happen. There was a click and then another dial tone. She quickly punched in Dr. Webster's number.

Just as the phone began to ring in Susie's ear, Maureen stood up and said, "This phone is for office use only, young lady." She pressed the hang-up button with one hand and reached for the receiver with the other.

"It was ringing," Susie protested. "I don't have my phone. How am I supposed to—"

Maureen pointed to a pay phone in the lobby outside the main office.

"But I don't have any change."

Maureen didn't seem to care as she hung up the office phone and continued to point outside the office.

Susie glanced toward the attendance lady, who seemed oblivious to Susie's plight. Susie groaned and muttered, "Fine. Whatever." She fumed out of the main office and navigated the halls back toward Ms. Armstrong's room. Just as she turned the corner toward the cafeteria, the bell rang to end sixth period. The swarm of students flooding the hallway blocked any attempt at speed. Once she finally reached the classroom, the door was locked, and the lights were turned off. She looked in and saw that her phone wasn't on the desk anymore.

Susie smacked the classroom door with her hand. It stung nicely for a second, but then she had to try and remember where the science teachers' prep room was. She merged into the sea of kids and headed back the way she'd come toward the south wing. She reached the door in record time and saw her teacher inside with a coffee cup in one hand.

Thank God, Susie thought as she knocked. Ms. Armstrong turned her head and then looked surprised to see Susie at the door.

Before her teacher could say anything, Susie blurted, "Do you have my phone?"

Ms. Armstrong opened the door. "No, Samantha Rose took it when you didn't come back. She said she'd give it to you after school. Was that okay? Maybe I shouldn't have—"

"No, that's okay. Sam's my best friend. It's just that they wouldn't let me use the office phone, and the note said to call my mother's work, and …" Susie couldn't stop the tears from forming. She hated crying in front of her teacher, but she couldn't help it. She wiped at them in frustration.

"Susie, come in here." Ms. Armstrong held the door open and gestured for Susie to enter. "We have a phone right here. I'll punch in my code. Make your call from here."

Susie reluctantly stepped into the small shoebox of a room but said, "No, that's okay. Sam has Strings now. I'll just go there and get my phone."

Her teacher had already headed to the prep room phone and was punching in her code. "It seems important, Susie. Just do it now. I'll be in the chemicals room right there to give you some privacy. Okay?"

"Okay. Thank you." Susie plopped herself down on the hard chair in front of the phone. It felt kind of weird being alone in a teachers-only space but calling Dr. Webster was infinitely more important.

As soon as the doctor's receptionist answered, Susie blurted out who she was and that she'd been told to call.

"Yes, yes, Susie," the receptionist said. "Your mother has been taken to East Valley Hospital."

"The hospital? Why?" Susie leaped to her feet, ready to run.

"Dr. Webster thinks she'll be okay. It's just precautionary."

"What happened?" Susie squeezed the phone line.

"No one's sure. She was in the break room when Marcy found her—"

"'Found her'? What does that mean?"

"Stay calm, Susie."

"I can't 'stay calm.' What happened to my mother?" Susie felt a reassuring hand on her shoulder. Ms. Armstrong stood next to her.

"Dr. Webster thinks she might have fallen and possibly hit her head. Marcy found her lying on the break room floor. Her cell phone was on the floor next to her. Dr. Webster thinks she may have fainted or had a seizure."

"A seizure?"

"She was just coming out of it when Marcy found her."

"She's at the hospital now?" Susie paced back and forth as far as the phone cord allowed.

"Yes. They sent her there in an ambulance."

"An ambulance? Alone?"

"Yes."

Susie slammed the phone down and said to her teacher. "Big favor?"

"Sure. What do you need?"

"Can you find Sam and tell her to meet me at East Valley Hospital after school? Emergency Room?"

"Yes, Yes. Yes, of course," her teacher said. "Anything you need."

"Thank you." Susie flew out the door and sprinted for the senior parking lot.

Chapter Eight
Come Back to Bed

Snow started falling as soon as Susie turned onto County Road 62 toward the hospital. It was a light flurry, but she barely noticed except for the fact that she had to turn on her windshield wipers. Another thing she barely noticed was that she'd left her coat in her locker at school. It didn't matter. None of it did. Her mother… no, she couldn't think about her mother yet. She had to think about driving and blinking back the tears blurring her vision.

She pulled her old Toyota into the first open spot in the hospital parking lot and threw the gearshift into park. She bolted out of the car and ran into the Emergency Room entrance. Once at the front reception desk, she gave her mother's name and was instantly given a treatment room number and vague directions. As she headed into the curtained-off area, nothing registered except the numbers above each room. After several agonizing moments, she finally found the number seventeen and took off in a run.

"Mami!" Susie whipped open the privacy curtain. Her breath caught in her throat. She wasn't prepared for what she saw.

Her mother looked small and limp in the hospital bed. Her eyes were closed. An IV tube ran out of her arm to a bag of clear fluid hanging on a metal pole. Machines blinked silent messages she didn't know how to interpret. Although she barely remembered to breathe, the only reason she didn't freak out completely was the rhythmic sound of her mother's heartbeat coming from some kind of monitor. It was oddly reassuring.

"Susana," her mother said in a raspy voice.

Susie rushed to her mother's side. "I'm here." She placed a hand on her mother's arm. "Are you okay? What happened, Mami?"

"Not sure." The voice was stronger. Susie's mother closed her eyes and was quiet for so long that Susie thought she might have fallen back to sleep. "Water," her mother said, breaking the agonizing quiet.

"Okay," Susie looked around and took note of her mother's purse tucked underneath a small table. Then she saw a plastic cup of water with a straw on top of the table. The clear liquid looked like water, but she took a whiff just to be sure. "Here you go. It's got a bendy straw, so you don't have to sit all the way up."

Her mother leaned forward and let Susie place the straw in her mouth. She took a small sip and lay back down.

Susie put the water cup down and rubbed her mother's arm over the sheet. She glanced past the edges of the curtain, hoping to find a nurse or doctor passing by. Where was everyone? Anyone?

She turned back to her mother and asked again, "Mami, what happened? What do you remember?"

Susie's mother's eyes fluttered open. "Susie, I'm so tired. *Déjame solo.*"

"Okay, but I'm right here if you need me." Susie's next words were so faint that her own ears barely heard them. "I love you, Mami."

Susie breathed in slowly, held it for a moment, and then released it. Christy had taught her that calming trick, saying she'd learned it from one of her therapists. Susie took a few more slow, calming breaths until her nerves were somewhat in check. But barely.

Susie opened the curtain of her mother's room and looked out onto the bustling emergency room. She tried to catch someone's, anyone's attention. The nurses were running around with purpose, and Susie couldn't get any of them to see her. She didn't want to leave her mother's side to demand answers, so she kept her faith in the audibly rhythmic heartbeat.

She wondered why her mother was so tired. They couldn't have given her a sedative or anything. Dr. Webster's receptionist said she'd either fainted or had some kind of seizure, and Susie was pretty sure they didn't sedate you for those things.

Susie continued her vigilant attempts to flag down a nurse or a doctor and was just considering leaving her post to find someone when Sam appeared physically.

"Sam," Susie called in a loud whisper, "over here."

Sam saw Susie and picked up speed. She carried Susie's coat and cell phone.

"How's your mom?" Sam asked while giving Susie a quick hug.

"She was awake and coherent when I first got here, but she's sleeping right now. Other than that, I have no idea how she is. And nobody's been back here to help."

"Nobody? No doctor, no nurse, not even a tech?" Sam looked furious.

"No. I mean, obviously, somebody must have examined her when she first came in." Susie gestured to the IV and the heart-rate monitor.

"I'll be right back." Sam put Susie's coat down on a foldup chair and handed Susie her cell phone. She flung the curtain open and flew into the hallway.

Susie heard Sam's voice in the distance but couldn't make out what she was saying. After a few moments, Susie heard the distinct words, "Right away, Ms. Payton. I'll send a nurse in immediately. I'll page Dr. Roth, the attending physician. We're sorry you had to wait."

Susie knew Sam rarely played her "I'm from a rich and influential family" card but was grateful for her friend's influence.

Within seconds, Sam was back. "Hopefully, that'll do the trick. Hospitals are so understaffed."

Susie hugged her friend.

"So, seriously, Sus," Sam said, "what do you think happened?"

Susie shrugged. "No clue."

"She wasn't sick?"

Susie shook her head. "Not that I know of."

"Drinking? Drugging?"

"No way, Sam. My mother hates that kind of stuff. You know how much she hates when my dad drinks beer."

"True." Sam looked out the curtain and sighed. "What are these people doing? Maybe being *Samantha Rose Payton* doesn't matter to anyone anymore."

"Sam, you matter to me," Susie said.

"That's not what I meant, but thanks for the ego boost."

"No worries. Oh, shoot," Susie blurted. "I never checked in with Papi or Miguel or *Abuelita*." She pulled her cell phone out of her pocket.

"No, no," Sam said. "Give it here. I'll call them, okay?"

"You will?"

"Of course." Sam looked out the curtain again and then pulled it wide open. A nurse and doctor team were heading right for their room. "The cavalry is here, Sus. I'll call your family from the lobby, okay?"

"Thanks," was all Susie could get out as emotion choked her throat closed. "Wait," Susie called after Sam. "Can you call Marlee and cancel for tonight? Do *not* let her drive out here, okay? It's snowing, and I don't want to have to worry about her, too. Tell her that I'll call her when I get a chance."

"You got it," Sam said.

"Thanks, Sam." Susie turned away quickly, not wanting her friend to see the tears in her eyes.

The doctor walked in and grabbed the chart at the foot of the bed. The nurse went around and punched buttons on various machines. After what seemed like forever, Dr. Roth said, "Heart rate still looks good." He made some notations on the chart.

"What happened to my mother?" Susie asked, hoping she didn't sound too forward.

He turned toward her for the first time. "Daughter?"

Susie nodded.

"I see the resemblance." He winked and then said, "Well, we're still not sure why she fainted. Her heart sounds great. Her blood pressure is fine. All she remembers is that she was in the break room at work and was just about to have a cup of tea. She doesn't remember feeling sick or lightheaded. She had eaten lunch at least an hour before. Had she had a recent head injury or any kind of injury?"

"No," Susie answered. "Not that I know of."

"Has she ever fainted before?"

"Not that I know of."

He jotted a few notes on her mother's chart. "Does she take medication?"

"Not that I know of," Susie said. "Wait, I think she takes birth control pills." She wasn't sure. "I don't know."

"Noted. No *new* medications?"

"I don't think so." Susie's stomach knotted. Why hadn't she paid more attention?

"Anyone in your family have heart problems?"

"Not that I know of." Susie hated sounding like a broken record, but they were truthful answers. Oh, how she wished her father was there. He would have all the answers.

"Young lady," Dr. Roth said, "why don't you have a seat? You're looking a little pale."

Susie sat as directed. It was a good thing since her legs had started to feel a bit shaky.

"I'm pretty much ruling out a seizure at this point. I think your mother simply fainted. But why? That's the question. Fainting happens when heart rate and blood pressure drop too quickly. Reduced blood flow in the brain results in loss of consciousness."

"That sounds serious," Susie said. She was so glad she was sitting down.

"Vasovagal syncope is most likely the reason for your mother's fainting episode. The body overreacts to certain triggers, like the sight of blood or emotional distress. That's where I'm leaning, but we still have to rule out anything serious that might involve the heart, so we're going to keep your mother overnight for observation."

"Overnight?" Susie sat up tall. This was serious.

A hospital tech came into the room and said, "Transport?"

"Ah, yes," Dr. Roth said. "CT scan first, and then she's to be admitted."

"You got it." The transport tech got to work unhooking her mother from the machines in the room. The beeps from her heart stopped.

"Once she's settled in upstairs, we'll know more," Dr. Roth said to Susie and left the room without waiting for a response.

The transport tech attached her mother's IV bag to the side of the movable bed, unlocked the wheels, and said, "Mrs. Torres, are you ready to go for a ride?"

Susie leaped to her feet when her mother opened her eyes. Susie placed a hand over her mother's. Her mother looked confused for a split second, as if she didn't know where she was, but then a look of pure agony passed over her face, and she closed her eyes again.

"Can I go with her?" Susie's knuckles were turning white from the extreme grip she had on the side rail of the bed.

The nurse handed Susie a clipboard. "We'll need you to stay here and fill out these forms."

Susie regretfully released her mother's hand to take the clipboard and pen. She fanned the thick stack of papers. "Maybe my father should be the one to do this. I want to stay with my mother." Where was Sam? Sam always got people to do what she wanted.

"You can't go into the scanning room with her," the nurse said, "so you might as well stay and at least get a start on it, okay? As soon as she's admitted, we'll let you know what room she's in. We can't admit her until we get all the important information." She pointed to the clipboard.

Susie nodded and sat down on the foldup chair. It was pure agony watching her mother get wheeled away. "I'll see you after your scan, Mami."

Susie took a cleansing breath and started filling in the forms. After writing in her mother's name, address, and telephone number, the form asked for insurance information. She reached for her mother's purse and pulled out her wallet. After jotting down the insurance information, she put the wallet back.

Something Dr. Webster's receptionist told her over the phone wandered into the forefront of her brain. Susie mumbled, "Her cell phone was on the floor next to her."

Susie dug in the purse for her mother's phone. She hit the on button and watched the voicemail screen come to life. It was a voicemail from her father. Susie hesitated for the briefest moments but then hit the play button.

She held the phone to her ear and heard her father's voice. "Isabella, it's Eduardo. I'm delayed in Vermont again. I'll be back on Friday evening. I'll talk to you then." Susie frowned at the curt tone in her father's voice. There was a rustling sound and then a clunk as if the phone had been dropped or set down hard on a table. Susie was about to press the off button when she heard him say in a faraway voice, "I hate this."

It was hard to hear, but another voice, this one distinctly female, said, "You just hung up with your wife?"

"Yes. I hate this."

"I know, Eddie," the female voice said. "It's hard, but you're doing the right thing. Come back to bed."

Suddenly dizzy, Susie reached for the back of the chair next to her. She closed her eyes and took a deep breath. It helped, but not much. Anguish squeezed her heart as she understood why her mother had fainted.

Chapter Nine
Family Tree

On Saturday morning, two full days after her mother was released from the hospital, Susie woke earlier than usual. This would be the first full day she would spend with both her parents. Her father's arrival at the hospital late Wednesday night had softened Susie's heart a little, even though she was still majorly pissed at him for cheating on her mother. It felt like he had cheated on their entire family. And he kind of had, emotionally, anyway.

"Vermont business trip, my ass," Susie muttered. She sat up in her bed. "Monkey business, if you ask me. Affair business." She squeezed her eyes shut against the tears. "Papi, why did you do this?" she said out loud to her dark room.

In the hospital, Susie's mother had barely looked at him. She said she was tired and told him to go home and take care of *his* mother and kids. It was obvious she was reminding him about his obligations. Susie couldn't help imagining what it would be like if Marlee was in that hospital bed telling her to go home. Susie absolutely would have refused. She would have slept in the chair all night just to be near her.

But her father hadn't put up any kind of fight at all. On his way out of the room, he told Susie he'd see her at home. Susie stayed until the official end of visiting hours and basically watched her mother sleep the entire time. Thank goodness Sam had stayed long enough to bring Susie something to eat from the hospital cafeteria. Sam wanted to stay, but Susie told her to go home. Her misery really didn't want company. Sam hesitated but went home after a few more reassurances from Susie.

The sun wasn't up yet, so Susie stretched back against her pillows, eyes wide open, thinking about her parents sleeping in their room. She wondered if her mother had confronted her father yet. If not, was she ever going to? Although Susie wasn't sure what she would have done, her head told her that if Marlee ever stepped out on her, it would be over so fast that Marlee wouldn't know what hit her. But her heart told her something entirely different. Her heart told her she loved Marlee so much she might pretend she didn't know. Was that what her mother was going to do? Another thought hit Susie like a ton of bricks. Is that what her mother had been doing all along? Pretending?

Susie's thoughts were making her miserable, so she distracted herself by thinking about Marlee. They had spent the night before with Sam and Lisa. They had gone to a diner outside of Clarksonville, one of the many properties Sam's family owned. After that, they went bowling, and Susie was proud of herself for staying within twenty pins of Marlee in both games. Marlee was a pitcher, and bowling was right in her wheelhouse. After bowling, Sam and Lisa drove off alone to find a quiet spot to be alone, and Susie and Marlee made themselves cozy on the couch in Marlee's finished basement. The space heater wasn't the only thing heating up the basement, and Susie squirmed at the delicious recollection of their ten-month anniversary celebration. Of course, there was always the danger that Marlee's mother might open the basement door, and even though the well-placed privacy screen gave them a couple of extra seconds to move apart, they had learned to be quick when they were intimate in the basement.

They were very nice memories, but Susie couldn't put it off any longer. She had to get up. Since it was still too early to go in the house, she decided to get a workout in. After a quick trip to the bathroom, she changed into workout clothes and warmed up by jump roping. Feeling good, she plopped down on the mat for a few sets of crunches. She sailed past her usual amount during her first set, enjoying the burning sensation in her abs. It helped take away the numbness. She crunched out another and another until exhaustion finally hit her. She fell to the mat spent. She lay there for a few minutes catching her breath.

Susie couldn't stop the tears from falling as she lay on the floor of her bedroom. The mere thought of imagining Marlee leaving a voicemail with another woman's voice asking Marlee to "come back to bed" agonized Susie's heart. She rolled on her side into a fetal position. It wasn't real, but it still felt like death. She could only imagine how her mother felt.

Susie rolled onto her back and then sat up. She wiped the tears from her face and took a swig from her water bottle. The sky had lightened outside. Maybe it was time to go in and assess the damage. She stood up and looked over to the house. The light was on in her parents' bedroom.

"They're up," Susie muttered. "Time to check in on the war."

Susie took a quick shower and dressed in comfortable sweats and a t-shirt. She threw on Marlee's hooded Clarksonville softball sweatshirt and, before heading to the main house, sent Marlee a quick text that read, "I love you." Simple and sweet.

Entering the main house quietly, she stood in front of the shrine to Mary that her grandmother had set up in the front entryway. Susie closed her eyes and said a silent prayer. "Blessed Mother, please look out for my family and guide us with your love." She paused for a minute and added, "We need it."

Susie stood silently in the front entryway and listened to the sounds of her parents making coffee and quietly talking in the kitchen. It seemed like a normal morning. She knew it wasn't, but they didn't know she knew.

"Would you like an omelet for breakfast?" Susie's mother asked Susie's father.

"That would be fine. Thank you."

It was a simple exchange, a polite exchange. Too polite. And, Susie thought with a sinking feeling, her father should be the one making breakfast for her mother. She was the one that had spent a night in the hospital. After doing a few tests, the doctor concluded that nothing was seriously wrong. He thought she'd simply fainted because her body had overreacted to the emotional distress of watching a YouTube video about the recent execution of children in Iran. At least that's what her mother told the doctor she had accidentally seen on her phone just before fainting. Susie was impressed that her mother had come up with such a good lie, but Susie knew the truth. There was no YouTube video, only the four-word betrayal in her father's voicemail.

Susie hesitated outside the kitchen door before going in. A family picture hung on the wall beside the doorway. In the photo, Susie had been seven or so; Miguel had been three. She smiled at her brother's image. He had been so innocent then, still a baby. Susie had been so protective of him back then. She sighed. She had always watched out for him, but now her protective role was going into overdrive. Susie quietly snuck back to the front door. She opened it slowly and then closed it more forcefully so it would be heard in the kitchen.

"Susie," her mother called, "is that you?"

"*Sí*, Mami."

"You're up early for a Saturday."

Susie wasn't sure how to answer. She didn't want to let on how worried she was for her mother's physical and emotional health, so she simply said, "Yep."

Susie stepped into the kitchen but couldn't look her father in the eye and pretend she didn't know what he had done. She asked her mother, "How are you feeling?"

"There's nothing wrong with me. I just fainted from that stupid video. That's all."

Susie knew better but said, "You have to stay off of YouTube, Mami."

Her mother smiled and added, "I'm fine. Everyone should stop fussing."

"Okay, Mami." Susie got a glass from the cupboard and poured herself a glass of orange juice. She had yet to look toward or even acknowledge her father. If she didn't do it soon, he would know something was up. She turned toward him at the kitchen table and said, "Good morning."

"Good morning," he answered just as simply. "What's on your agenda today? Seeing Marlee?"

"I'm not sure," Susie said. She kind of wanted to stay home with her family, but it was better to keep her options open, just in case the yelling reached new heights.

"Help your mother today," her father said sternly and took a sip of coffee.

"Of course," Susie said. It's what I do every Saturday and Sunday and Monday and… She stopped her retort in mid-thought. Somehow her father might read the sarcastic tone in her head. Are you going to help, too, Papi? Hmm? She just got out of the hospital. She had to go to the hospital because of you!

She turned away from her father and said, "Mami, I'll get the laundry going, okay?"

Her mother nodded. And that was it. Usually, there would be a series of instructions about not using too much bleach on the whites or about not putting her bras in the dryer and hanging them up to dry instead. But today? Nothing.

She chugged her orange juice, rinsed the glass in the sink, and headed up the stairs to her parents' room for their laundry. A quick look at the bed told her what she needed to know. They had both slept in it. Susie threw the used towels and washcloths from her parents' bathroom into the laundry basket and put out fresh ones. She picked up the basket and, before leaving, took one last look around. Her stomach lurched as she thought about the pain her mother must be in. But there was nothing Susie could do except act like she didn't know anything and suffer in silence.

After getting the laundry going, Susie drove her *abuelita* to her friend's house to play cards. Once she got home, she moved the laundry along and then decided to help her mother clean the kitchen, but her mother seemed determined to do it by herself. Not to be deterred from helping, Susie straightened up, dusted, and vacuumed the living room and dining room instead. After putting the vacuum away, an idea came to her. Instead of walking around on eggshells around her parents like she had been doing for the past few weeks, she decided to take matters into her own hands. She was going to remind them what had brought them together in the first place. She was going to remind them what being in love was all about. And most importantly, she was going to remind them that they were a family. A family that was going to stay together no matter what.

Determined, she pulled every family picture off the wall and put them on the dining room table. She pulled the photo albums out from under the TV hutch and then pulled the pictures off the piano. She piled them on the table, making sure her parents' wedding pictures were on the top of the stack.

"What are you doing, Susie?" Miguel said. He had one foot on the first tread of the stairs and one hand on the handrail. He looked at her like she was nuts.

"A school project," she lied. Her brain scanned for an even better lie. One that even her parents would believe. "An ancestry project. A family tree."

"Oh, cool," Miguel said. "And then once you've got it done, I won't have to redo it when I'm in twelfth grade."

Susie laughed. "Good thinking, *Jefe*."

He beamed at her use of his pet name. Apparently, he was becoming used to her calling him that. "See you later, alligator." He bolted up the stairs toward his room.

"After a while, juvenile," Susie called after him. Susie grinned and grabbed some printer paper from her mother's computer in the living room.

She was just about to go into the kitchen to ask her mother to tell her about the family pictures when her mother announced that she was going upstairs to lie down. Susie's heart fell. Fine. She'd start with the enemy, then. Her father was the one who needed the bigger reminder anyway.

"Papi?" Susie called down to the basement, where her father had gone after breakfast. His cover story was that he was down there rewiring an old lamp, but Susie knew better. He was hiding out.

"What's up, *mariposita*?" He looked up from the bottom of the stairs.

She hesitated. She hadn't really thought through what she was going to say to him. "I have this…" She looked at him as her life flashed through her head. Early memories of him holding her hand, going up the front steps into church, playing ball in the yard, lying in the grass, finding shapes in the clouds.

"Susie?"

"Um, I have this project at school?" She hadn't meant to make it sound like a question. "And I need your help. Mami's help, too."

"What kind of project?"

"I, uh, need you upstairs."

He shrugged and said, "Okay, I'm all yours."

After an hour of reviewing family photos and taking notes about various cousins, aunts, uncles, and grandparents, Susie's mother came down the stairs after her nap and joined them at the table. She sat on the other side of Susie.

Susie's father opened one of the photo albums to a bunch of Susie's baby pictures.

"Isabel," Susie's father said, "do you remember this one?" He placed the album in front of Susie so her mother could lean in and see it.

"Susie's baptism."

"Do you remember how she cried when the priest poured the water on her head?" Susie's father smiled at Susie's mother.

Susie laughed. "I guess I didn't want him ruining my hair," Susie joked. A warm feeling filled her as she watched her parents laugh. She leaned away from the table as her mother moved to get a closer look.

"*Aay*, Eduardo, look at your mother. She looks so young here."

Susie's father leaned in, and Susie found herself pushing her chair back to let her parents get closer. Susie stood up and backed out of the dining room, the smile on her face stretched from ear to ear.

Chapter Ten
Phoenix

Sunday after church, Susie ran up the stairs to her room. It wasn't easy to do in a dress and heels, but the faster she got up there, the more time she would have with Marlee on the phone. Her mother wanted her back in the kitchen to help with dinner as soon as she changed.

Susie sent Marlee a quick text, which resulted in an almost immediate call.

"I miss you," Susie said as she answered the phone.

"Me, too," Marlee echoed. "Church today, huh?"

"Yeah, my mom gets in these church moods now and then, and the entire family heads off to mass. We used to go every Sunday, but then it turned into Easter and Christmas only for some reason. Twice-a-year Catholics, you know?" Susie put her cell phone on her desk and hit the speakerphone button.

"Why do you think your mom was in the mood for church today?"

Susie knew precisely why her mother was in the mood for church—her father's disregard for his family obligations—but Susie wasn't sure how much she wanted to tell Marlee. She hadn't even told Sam yet. And that thought alone disturbed her. Why would she want to tell Sam something extremely private about her family before she told Marlee? Marlee was her girlfriend. Marlee should be the first one she told everything to. Sure, she'd known Sam longer. But something didn't make sense.

"Susie?"

"Oh, sorry, *mi vida*," Susie said. "I'm trying to change while I talk to you."

"You're undressing while you're on the phone with me?"

Susie laughed. "Mmm. I wish it were more enticing than it is." She unzipped her dress and shimmied out of it, letting it drop to the floor at her feet.

"I'll be the judge of that," Marlee purred into the phone.

Susie felt her face flush. Marlee sure had gotten bolder since they'd met ten months before. Susie cleared her throat and said, "Hey, can I ask you a question? You're such a brainiac. You'll probably know this."

"Sure," Marlee said. "What's up?"

Susie threw on a pair of casual but dressy pants and said, "The priest today said something about fire purifying the soul." She sat on the bed and threw on her socks. She had to raise her voice so Marlee would hear her through the speakerphone. "He said fire not only destroys but also creates new growth. Like when a forest fire ravages a forest. Everything is destroyed, including the deadwood..." The instant she said the word, she remembered her mother saying something about cleaning out the *deadwood*. She had been referring to her clothes at the time, but could she have meant Susie's father? "Um, the deadwood is also destroyed, which needed clearing out to

90

make room for new growth. He made a big deal about every ending having a new beginning. Something like that."

Susie went to her closet, picked out a suitable Sunday dinner shirt, and shrugged it on. "Marlee, are you still there?"

"Yeah, I'm here. I'm just trying to figure out what you want from me."

Susie laughed. "I can't remember the name of that thing that rises up from the ashes. It's like a bird or something?"

"It's called a phoenix. One phoenix dies, and then a new one is born from the ashes of the old."

"Right. See? I knew you'd know. You know everything."

"Hey, how's your mom? No side effects or relapse from her hospital trip?"

"No, she's her same fire-breathing self." Which wasn't exactly true. Physically her mother seemed fine, but otherwise, Susie wasn't so sure.

"Your father okay?"

Susie couldn't answer for a moment as emotion squeezed her throat closed.

"That's it then, isn't it?" Marlee said, her voice soft.

Susie picked up the phone, took it off speakerphone, and put it to her ear. She leaned back against her desk.

"Susie, I can tell there's been something on your mind lately. You can trust me, okay?"

"Mm hmm," Susie said with a tight voice.

"You can tell me anything." There was a moment of quiet until Marlee added, "If you want to."

"I want to, but I have to go. My mother is yelling for me from the front door. Hold on." Susie held the phone to her chest and yelled out her window. "I'll be right down, Mami." To Marlee, she said, "I'm back."

"I love you, sweetie," Marlee said. "Call me later."

"I will," Susie said. "I love you, too, *mi corazon*."

"I'll hang up first, so you don't have to."

"Bye," Susie said, waiting for the line to go dead. She and Marlee often spent hours outwaiting the other to hang up first. Susie's heart swelled because Marlee had understood that Susie didn't need the stress of seeming eager to be off the phone or wanting to hang up first. Was that what her father was doing? Hanging up first?

As Susie put on her shoes, it dawned on her. It wasn't that she *wanted* to confide in Sam before confiding in Marlee. It was that she didn't want to upset Marlee. She had involved Marlee and Marlee's mother with her stupid family troubles seven months before on that stupid night in early August—right after their three-month anniversary—right after Susie's own mother told her she was 'unnatural.' She didn't want to confide in Marlee because Marlee might start to see her for what she was—damaged goods. Damaged goods that came from a family who didn't always act with love, understanding, or compassion. Susie wanted desperately to shield Marlee from all of that because Susie desperately wanted to keep Marlee in her life.

But at the moment, she had to get in the house and try to save her family.

After setting the table and helping her mother get the meal together, Susie took drink orders and called everyone to dinner.

Oddly, her brother Miguel didn't help at all. No, not oddly. That was business as usual, even though her father had recently told her Miguel would be helping out more. Whatever, Susie thought. Nothing had changed.

When her father lowered his head to say the blessing, Susie did as well.

"Thank you, Lord, for the food we are about to receive and for the nourishment to our bodies. Bless the hands that prepared it and those that will partake in your name."

That was typically where her father finished his blessing, but he kept going.

"Bless this family, Lord. Help us with our daily struggles. Help us find peace. Help us not create crises where there are none."

Wow, Susie thought. That last one was directed right at her mother. Cheap shot, Papi, cheap shot.

"Also, Lord, help us forgive each other's trespasses," her father continued. "In Christ's name, we pray. Amen."

"Amen," Susie said, along with the rest of her family. She wondered if her father's statement "forgive each other" meant what she thought it meant. A slow smile crept up her face. It had to be. Her father was, in a way, asking her mother to forgive him. Maybe showing her parents all those photographs had helped him see the error in his ways. Maybe he and her mother were on the mend. Maybe there would be no more *business* trips to Vermont.

Susie's mother scooped out a ladle of Fiesta Chicken from the slow cooker and poured it over a mound of yellow rice. She did this for every plate and passed them around. Susie loved her mother's Fiesta Chicken, with the black beans, corn, and the not-so-secret ingredient salsa. But they'd never had it for Sunday dinner. Maybe a few things would be changing in the Torres household from now on. For the better.

"So, Eduardo," Susie's mother said, "what did you think about Father Murphy's message today?"

"What is this?" Her father held up his plate of food. The room grew stock-still.

"Fiesta Chicken. You like it."

"It's Sunday."

Susie exchanged a glance with her brother. They both knew what was about to happen. Susie could not believe her father was picking a fight, especially when he had just asked for forgiveness. Maybe things weren't going to change after all.

"It *is* Sunday," her mother agreed coolly. "And you know what? I went to church this morning just like you did, but I was the one who had to put together this meal for my family. Did you help?"

"This is *not* a proper Sunday dinner meal."

"Oh, because Sundays are so important to you? Because you were home last Sunday? And not in *Vermont*?" Susie cringed at the acid dripping over the word *Vermont*.

He glared at Susie's mother, and she glared right back at him. No one at the table moved. Susie felt herself holding her breath, letting it out slowly while waiting for the gauntlet to fall.

Her father had no response and simply harrumphed. His face hardened as he ate a forkful of the chicken dish without comment.

"Go on, everyone," Susie's mother said to the rest of the family. "Eat. Don't let it get cold."

Susie took a bite. It was as yummy as ever. "This is good, Mami." She hoped her father didn't think she was taking sides, but it *was* good. Everything her mother made was good. Why couldn't he understand that? Was he that arrogant, that selfish, and that self-centered to understand?

Susie stayed lost in thought as the meal went on. Her brother, father, and *abuelita* did most of the talking, which was fine with her. Her parents didn't say much of anything to each other during the meal, and Susie didn't contribute anything, either. It was hard pretending that her world wasn't falling apart. She didn't know what was worse—her parents' yelling matches or this quiet standoff.

Once dinner was finished, her father looked her right in the eye and commanded her to help with the cleanup. She blinked twice as she looked at him. What was he talking about? Did he not know that she helped her mother every night? She turned to bring a stack of dirty dishes to the kitchen, and then it dawned on her. Control. He was losing control over his family and ordering her to help made him feel like he was in control of something. That's it, Susie mused. He sensed that his wife would no longer tolerate him lording over her the way he had always done. Susie couldn't imagine lording over Marlee, making her do things in a certain way, not in a million years.

Had her mother been subjugated to him her entire married life? Susie recalled her father as the king of the castle for as long as her memory reached back. Had her mother ever been the queen? Or was she just his servant?

Susie put the pan she had been washing down with more force than she meant to. She turned to face her mother. "Mami?" she blurted before her mouth could stop her.

95

"Hmm?" Her mother looked up from the Tupperware bowl she was putting the leftovers in.

Dios, Susie didn't know what to say. She wanted to know if her mother was all right. She wanted to know if her mother had had a good life. She wanted to know if her mother still loved her husband.

"Um," Susie began but didn't get a chance to finish.

"Mami," Miguel burst into the kitchen, "Papi's taking me to the movies. We're picking up Scott, too. He wanted me to tell you. Bye." He ran out just as quickly as he had run in.

"So much for *sacred* Sundays," Susie's mother muttered and went back to putting the food away.

Susie was glad Miguel had interrupted the moment because she had no idea what she had been about to say. Susie went back to washing the pots and pans and loaded the dishwasher. Usually, at that moment, Susie would usually ask if she could go to her room to do homework, which would morph into calling Marlee. But since it was mid-winter break and there was no school for the entire week, Susie decided she would hang around to see if her mother needed her.

"Mami?"

"Hmm?"

"Do you want to watch a movie or something?"

Her mother chuckled. She wiped her hands on a kitchen towel and then pulled Susie into a hug. Susie stiffened for a moment but then hugged her mother back. Hugs were not usually in her mother's repertoire.

"You're a good daughter," Susie's mother said. "I know this is hard on you kids. And I don't know where it's going, but…" she pulled out of the hug and turned away.

96

It sounded as if her mother was fighting back tears, paralyzing Susie. What should she do?

"Mami, what do you need?" Susie touched her mother's arm.

Her mother took a breath and let out a big sigh. "Nothing, *hija*." She turned back around, and Susie's suspicions were confirmed. Her mother's eyes were glossy with tears.

"Go to your room and call your friend," Susie's mother said, a genuine smile lighting up her face. "I'll finish up here. Go visit her tomorrow. Get out of this house for a while."

"Okay," Susie said meekly. "Okay. Thank you, Mami." She headed toward the kitchen door but then turned around. "Let me know if I can help. Help in any way at all."

Her mother simply nodded and turned toward the sink.

"I'll be in my room," Susie said, not expecting a reply. She didn't get one.

On the way to her room, Susie filled a small bucket with snow. It would do nicely to chill one of the beers she had stashed in her closet. Back in her room, she put the bottle of beer in the snow bucket and then changed into a pair of sweats, a t-shirt, and Marlee's sweatshirt.

She texted Marlee, "Done with dinner. Call me when you can."

The call came a full five minutes later at the precise time Susie was twisting the cap off one of the Saranac Big Moose Winter Ales. She managed to get in a swig before answering.

"Sorry, sweetie," Marlee said. "I was practicing a few scales and riffs and didn't hear the phone." She laughed and added, "*Riff* is a rock-n-roll word that's in my vocab now. Are you impressed?"

"I love that you love your new bass." Susie turned the main lights off and opened the bathroom door an inch so the nightlight would give her a bit of mood lighting. Just what she needed after the tense situation in the house. She plopped back onto her bed and took another sip from the beer. Not bitter like the IPA. It was nice and smooth with a good flavor. "When are you going to play for me?"

"I'm working Tuesday and Wednesday until four, but how about tomorrow?"

"Sounds great," Susie said.

"Really?"

"Really," Susie said.

"Yay!" Marlee clapped in the background. "My mom's working tomorrow, so come over anytime you want."

"How's six?"

"At night?"

Susie could almost hear Marlee's disappointed frown over the forty or so miles that separated them. "No. Six in the morning."

Ahh, now Susie heard the smile.

"Why wait?" Marlee said. "Come now."

"I wish I could, *mi vida*. I wish I could."

"How was dinner?"

It was a simple question, but it was Marlee's way of letting her know that it was okay to talk about anything that was bothering her. She took a couple of gulps from the beer and blurted, "My father cheated on my mother."

"What?" The shock in Marlee's voice was palpable.

"Yeah, that's why my mother fainted at work. She heard a voicemail—" Emotion choked Susie's throat momentarily. When she got herself back in control, she told Marlee the entire voicemail message, her father's blessing that evening, and her mother's tears.

"Oh, sweets, I'm so sorry to hear about that. It sounds like your parents have some stuff to work out."

"Yeah, Miguel will be devastated if he finds out."

"Like you are."

Susie's heart clenched, and through her tears, she squeaked out, "Yeah."

"This is their deal, you know. They are the ones who have to figure this out. Not you."

"I know, but…" Susie didn't want to admit to Marlee how hopeful she had been after her parents sat for over an hour with the family photographs reminiscing about their lives together. It now seemed so futile and extremely naïve. But these were her parents. Shouldn't she fight to keep them together? Shouldn't she fight to help them communicate better? To *see* and understand each other?

"I can hear you thinking," Marlee said softly. "Is everything going to be okay?"

Tears welled in her eyes at Marlee's question. "I don't know." It was the truth. She didn't know. But she sure as hell wasn't going to let them go down in flames while she watched and did nothing. No way.

"Hey, Marlee?"

"Yeah?"

"The United Kingdom is made up of Great Britain and Northern Ireland."

Marlee laughed hard in the phone. It was the best sound in the world.

"And before you ask," Susie continued, "Great Britain is made up of England, Scotland and Wales."

"Thanks for the clarification. I forgot I asked you that."

"On the day my entire life changed," Susie said.

"When you come over tomorrow, I'll make you feel better."

Susie warmed at the thought. Yes, Marlee always did make her feel better. In every way imaginable.

Chapter Eleven
Tell Me

On Monday morning, Susie was up again before sunrise. Since it was too early to go into the main house and too early to leave for Marlee's, she worked out instead. Softball practices would be officially starting in one week, and she wanted to be strong and ready.

Who knew what Coach Gellar would have in mind for them next Monday afternoon. Everybody knew that Clarksonville and probably Southbridge would be better than East Valley this year, but Susie also knew that Coach Gellar would do everything she could to change that. And that probably meant a lot of squats and running starting Monday.

It was still dark when Susie saw the lights turn on in the main house. Her mother had to be at work by seven-thirty to get the examining rooms stocked and ready to go for Dr. Webster's patients. Her mother loved nursing. She loved taking care of people.

After a shower, Susie got dressed and stashed her wallet in her back pocket. She put her car keys in her front pocket and then threw on her winter coat. She was going to head out to Marlee's for the day after she greeted her parents. She wanted to find out what time her mother wanted her home. She buttoned up her coat as she walked

101

across the driveway to the main house. Even though it was almost March, it was still majorly cold.

Susie prayed her mother wouldn't need her for dinner and would suggest she eat at Marlee's. Especially because Susie knew, just knew, that her mother was going to serve the leftovers from Sunday's meal. And since her father was a stickler about not eating leftovers, it was going to majorly blow up later.

As soon as Susie got to the front door, she realized that *later* had already arrived.

"You're going to *Vermont* again, aren't you?" Susie heard her mother say. Susie took her hand off the door latch, not wanting to walk in on their conversation.

Susie couldn't hear what her father said, but the anger in her mother's voice was thick. "You go to *Vermont* a lot, don't you?" The acid was back. "*Vermont* is very attractive to you, isn't it? *Vermont* takes care of your needs, doesn't she? But what about our family, Eduardo? Don't we take care of you? *I* don't take care of you?" The angry emotion in her mother's voice tore at Susie's heart. "Any time you wanted my body, Eduardo, I gave it to you. For over eighteen years."

Susie physically recoiled at hearing her mother's words. She took a step away from the door. She didn't want to hear her parents' very private conversation.

"Eduardo, I gave you children. Two beautiful children," Susie's mother continued. "What about these children of yours, Eduardo? What about your mother? Your home? Our life together? Have you thought about any of this? Or is *Vermont* the only thing on your mind lately?"

Susie knew she didn't want to hear her father's answer, so she turned around, jumped into her car, and started the engine. She willed her car to warm up fast because she didn't want to face either of her parents. She couldn't believe her father was leaving again. Why? Didn't he love them anymore?

She pushed the thought aside and focused on the temperature gauge. The instant the needle moved off the peg, she put her car in reverse and turned around in the driveway. She glanced in the rearview mirror just to make sure her mother wasn't looking for her and then punched the gas. She'd text her mother later to let her know she was at Marlee's. It was better to go than get pulled into her parents' meltdown.

It wasn't quite seven-thirty when Susie found herself at the convenience mart just outside of Clarksonville. It was still too early to go to Marlee's, and since she hadn't had a chance to eat breakfast, she pulled in. She found a spot near the door and got out. She shivered at the damp cold. Maybe those spring rains were trying to find their way to Clarksonville County. She was ready for spring big time.

She went in and found warm donuts in a self-serve display case. Yum. She knew it wasn't very healthy, but she was hungry and grabbed two—one for her and one for Marlee. Marlee loved donuts and cookies and candy and soda. Susie smiled at the thought of Marlee's sweet tooth. What else? OJ, she needed OJ. Susie walked to the floor-to-ceiling beverage coolers and found what she was looking for, sixteen-ounce bottles of orange juice. She pulled out two.

The next cooler's blue and white Bud Light ad caught her eye. In the next three sections, she noticed the various beers' brightly colored cans and bottles. Oh, look, there was that Brooklyn Lager her underage cousins always bragged about drinking. She wondered how it stacked up to the Saranac Ale she'd had the night before. She found a twelve-pack of Corona and read the label. Oh, it was a lager. So was Bud Light. Interesting. Damn, if she had that fake ID, she'd be able to buy some and do a few taste tests—one of these days.

She paid for her makeshift breakfast, jumped back in her car, and then took her time heading to Marlee's house. She pulled into the long gravel driveway and parked in her usual spot. Although Susie liked Marlee's mother, she was happy to see that her car wasn't there. That meant she and Marlee would have the house to themselves. That was just what the doctor ordered.

Before turning off the engine, Susie pulled out her phone and texted Karl.

"Any word on my library card?" He would know what she meant.

His text came back fairly quickly. "You're in luck. I was going to text you later. My cousin Dirk said he got yours back in the latest batch."

"Cool. When can I get it?"

"Tomorrow? Alivia and I are both twenty-one, you know. Want to hang out?"

"Yeah, definitely." Marlee would be working until four o'clock tomorrow anyway, so why not get her fake ID, have a couple of cold beers for her taste test, and then head out to Marlee's at four? Two beers weren't over the legal limit for driving, were they? She texted Karl about buying her some Brooklyn Lager. She said she'd pay for it when she saw him.

"Will do! Meet us at Alivia's at noon. Dirk will be there, too."

"It's a party!"

She closed her cell phone and was just about to turn off the car engine when a sharp rap landed on her window. She jumped at the sound.

"You scared the shit out of me, Marlee." Susie put her hand to her chest. She yanked the keys out of the ignition and opened her car door.

"Sorry! You've been sitting out here for, like, five minutes. That's way too long for you not to be kissing me."

"Mmm," Susie said as she got out of the car. "C'mere." She pulled Marlee to her and leaned back against the driver's door. She stroked Marlee's cheek as they kissed.

"I love the way you kiss me," Marlee said and stepped back. She fanned herself. "Nope, not cold out here at all."

"C'mon," Susie said, taking Marlee's hand. "Let's go inside, and I'll show you more of where that came from."

"Ooh, let's go." Marlee let herself be led up the steps to the kitchen.

Once inside, Susie threw her keys on the kitchen table and hung her coat on her usual hook. "Your mother's not home?"

Marlee locked eyes with Susie and slowly shook her head. She raised an eyebrow in expectation.

Susie felt her breath quicken. She took a step toward Marlee and, putting both hands on Marlee's shoulders, walked her backward. When Marlee's back hit the door, Susie removed her hands from Marlee's shoulders and pressed them flat against the door on either side of Marlee's head. She inched closer but didn't touch any part of Marlee.

"Oh, man," Marlee groaned, "you torment me."

"You love it." Susie moved closer, feeling Marlee's breath on her lips. Just as she moved forward to kiss Marlee, her stomach growled. "*Dios mio*," Susie took a step back. "I forgot our breakfast in the car." She grabbed her keys from the table. "I'll be right back."

Marlee whimpered. "What a tease."

Susie was back in no time with the now cold but still fresh donuts.

"Ooh," Marlee said as her eyes lit up. "You know a way to a girl's heart, don't you?"

"This girl's heart," Susie said and put a finger directly on Marlee's chest. "The only girl I need."

Marlee's cheeks turned red. She took a big bite of her chocolate-frosted donut to hide her embarrassment.

"You're so cute," Susie said.

Marlee looked down and blushed even more.

"And you can't take a compliment." Susie nudged Marlee and said, "C'mon, let's finish, so we can go upstairs."

"Upstairs, huh?"

"So, I can hear you play bass, silly."

"And after that?" Marlee waggled her eyebrows and blushed even more.

Just then, a text came in on Susie's phone. She groaned. It was probably her mother. She held her breath and glanced down. It wasn't her mom. It was Karl.

"Who was that?" Marlee asked.

"Just my mom," Susie lied. "Let me tell her I got here okay." Susie quickly answered Karl, telling him that no, she didn't want any Jack Daniels, just the beer. Then she truthfully texted her mother to tell her where she was.

After finishing their donuts and juice, they headed up the stairs to Marlee's room. Susie's phone dinged. She glanced at her screen. It was Karl again. She texted him back that, sure, she'd take a twelve-pack. Thanks.

Once in Marlee's room, while Marlee tuned her guitar, Susie kicked off her shoes and made herself comfortable on Marlee's bed. Another text dinged. Susie wanted desperately to ignore it, but she couldn't if it was her mother. Sure enough, her mother wanted her home by 4:00 to make dinner. Damn. She'd have to leave by three.

"Your mom again?" Marlee asked.

"Yes," Susie spat. "Who else?" Her eyes flashed. "Why even fucking ask?"

The hurt look on Marlee's face had Susie on her feet instantly. "No, no, no, *mi vida*. I didn't mean to take it out on you." She didn't dare touch Marlee until Marlee forgave her. "I'm sorry, sorry, sorry." Susie stood there, her arms folded in front of her. When Marlee didn't make a move, Susie's bottled-up emotions spilled over, and she started sobbing.

Marlee put her guitar down and pulled Susie into a hug. "It's okay, sweetie. You just startled me." She rubbed Susie's back. "You're okay."

Susie finally caught her breath and said, "I won't be like that with you. I can't be that way."

Marlee squeezed her tight. "Are you afraid we'll turn into them?"

Her nod made Marlee frown. "We won't. We can't. We're not them. We haven't had their experiences."

Susie took a deep breath and wiped at the tears in her eyes. She looked Marlee straight in the eye. "If I ever," she choked back more tears, "Marlee, if I ever hurt you in any way, let me know immediately, and I will change. I don't want to be like that."

"You won't be," Marlee said again.

"You don't know that. I didn't think my parents could treat each other like they do now." She paused momentarily, searching for the love she knew she'd find in Marlee's eyes. "But if it can happen to them, then maybe it can happen to us. So you'll tell me, right?"

Marlee tried to pull her closer, but Susie wasn't budging until she got an answer. "You're stubborn, aren't you?" Marlee said with a soft smile.

Susie nodded.

"Okay, then," Marlee said. "I will always tell you if you hurt me in any way. Okay? Are you satisfied?"

Susie nodded again, letting herself relax a little.

"And the same goes for me, too, Susie," Marlee said firmly.

"Oh, no, no, no," Susie said, taking Marlee in her arms. "You could never hurt me. Ever."

Marlee hugged her back, and the hug soon turned into something more as Susie focused her attention on nuzzling the sensitive skin on Marlee's neck. She trailed kisses from one side to the other while Marlee moaned encouragement. Marlee opened her eyes and said, "I need…"

Susie's labored breathing matched Marlee's. "Me, too."

Susie lay down on Marlee's bed. She sighed as Marlee's weight settled on top of her. A well-positioned thigh put pressure in just the right place. Marlee lowered her mouth to Susie's, their lips lightly touching. Marlee increased the pressure of the kiss and then began her own trail of kisses from one of Susie's sensitive earlobes down and across Susie's neck to the other earlobe. Susie's body hummed, and she whimpered when the soft lips moved on in search of new delights. Marlee's kisses made their way along the collar of her t-shirt. Susie groaned. *Dios*, why had she worn a t-shirt, not a button-up shirt? That would have been way easier for Marlee to remove. Susie sat up enough to let Marlee remove her shirt. The bra followed instantly after. Susie lay back down with a sigh as Marlee continued to feast on her body. Susie arched up and wrapped her hands around the back of Marlee's head to increase the pressure of Marlee's kisses. Marlee reached lower and popped the button of Susie's jeans with one hand. Susie's abs tightened. Marlee knew exactly what Susie needed at that moment. With agonizing slowness, Marlee unzipped Susie's zipper and then began an entirely new exploration with her fingers.

The bass long abandoned, they fell into a familiar rhythm and forgot about the rest of the world for a while.

Chapter Twelve
To be Twenty-One

After her Tuesday morning biceps and back workout, Susie went into the house to make breakfast for her *abuelita* and her brother. Her mother had already left for work, so they had the house to themselves.

"What do you want for breakfast, Miguel?"

He shrugged. As usual, he was not helpful.

She listed breakfast items hoping one of them would pique his interest. "Cereal? Pancakes? French toast? Scrambled eggs? *Huevos Rancheros*? Cheese omelet? Waffles?" Ahh, there it was, the fourteen-year-old head nod. "Okay, then. Waffles it is."

Susie headed to the living room, where *Abuelita* was watching a morning talk show. "Are you okay with waffles?"

"*Sí, sí*, Susana. *Gracias*." Her gaze never left the television screen. Apparently, some hunky Latino singer was getting ready to perform.

"Okay, coming right up."

Susie liked cooking for her family. It made her feel like she was contributing. Especially with her parents fighting the way they were, any chance she had of keeping things semi-normal for her brother and *Abuelita* made her feel good.

Once breakfast was devoured and the kitchen cleaned up, Susie headed back to her room. She should have worked on her Environmental Science paper but decided to clean her room instead.

After she'd remade her bed with clean sheets, a glance at the clock told her it was time to drive her brother to his friend Scott's house, and after that, she'd go to Alivia's. She couldn't wait to get her new ID. She was trying to stop thinking of it as a *fake* ID, so she wouldn't slip up in front of a store clerk or something.

After dropping her brother off, she headed up two more streets to Alivia's house. She pulled in behind Karl's pickup truck and then headed to the front door. The loud music told her the small party was already underway. When no one came to the door after her knock, she opened it and called in, "It's me, Susie. I'm coming in, okay?" She walked in and followed the music to the TV room in the back of the house.

"Hey, Susie," Karl said and lifted his glass to her. "Ready for a cold one? We put your twelve-pack in the fridge for you."

"Aww, that was nice," Susie said. "Yeah, I'll take one."

She hugged Alivia and then shook hands with Karl's cousin Dirk. There was little family resemblance. They were both tall, but where Karl was lean and lanky, Dirk was broad-shouldered and muscular. Karl had light brown hair and an attempt at a mustache, Dirk's hair was jet black, and his face was baby-smooth clean shaven. He had muscles for days, his tight shirt accentuating that fact. The only thing that seemed kind of out of place was his greasy hair, which made him look sloppy, but it didn't matter. It was just that Karl and his cousin didn't look anything alike.

Susie followed Karl into the kitchen, and after giving her one of the Brooklyn Lagers, he handed her a receipt for the twelve-pack. Susie pulled out her wallet and paid up.

"Do you want a glass, Susie?" Alivia asked.

"Nah, this'll do." Susie twisted off the cap and took in the aroma. There wasn't much of an aroma to it, not like the IPAs she'd had, but it was still interesting. She took a swig and smiled. It was smooth, and it tasted good. She'd have to text her cousins later and tell them they were right.

"C'mon, Susie." Alivia grabbed her arm. "Dirk has your *library card*." She pulled Susie into the other room.

Back in the TV room, Dirk raised an appreciative eyebrow. Her skin crawled as he leered at her. "How old are you, sweetheart?"

"Eighteen."

"No, you're not, gorgeous. You're twenty-one." He whipped the fake ID out of his back pocket and handed it to her.

"Cool." Susie took the ID and said, "Thanks." As far as she could tell, the ID was flawless. Her picture looked just like the original, and it even had the State of New York seal on it. The big difference was that under-twenty-one IDs were printed vertically, and this gem was printed horizontally, and, yep, it made her twenty-one years old.

She turned toward Alivia to show her—anything to get away from Dirk's leering eyes. Thank God she didn't have to deal with him after this.

"How does it feel to be twenty-one, Susie?" Alivia said, looking at Susie's new ID.

"Honestly? It feels weird. How long have you guys had yours?"

Karl put his arm around Alivia and said, "Since school started."

112

"Oh, that's why you've always been in charge of 'special drinks' at Ronnie's parties. Hey, where is Ronnie anyway?"

Karl rolled his eyes. "Where else? Off with Jordan."

"His boy toy," Alivia teased.

Susie knew the feeling. She jumped at any chance to be alone with Marlee.

Alivia had a serious look in her eye when she asked, "Sam doesn't know about your new *library card*, does she?"

"Nah," Susie said. She was going to add something about Sam not understanding her need to unwind, but it sounded hollow. An awkward moment followed since it had been clear that Susie had been about to say something else.

"Nope," Alivia said, "you know what? I get it. You don't have to explain. Right, studmuffin?"

"Right," Karl said and sat on the couch. He took another swig of his drink. "Just know that you can party with us anytime." He raised his glass to her. She raised her bottle in kind.

Alivia and Karl sat on the couch, comfy and cozy. Dirk sat in one of the two recliners, but Susie opted to sit on the floor near Alivia and leaned back against the couch far away from him. Her first beer went down quickly.

Dirk got up to get her another, and in the two minutes he was gone, Karl and Alivia started making out. That made Susie a little uncomfortable, and she was almost happy when Dirk came back. Feeling awkward with her friends kissing passionately near her, Susie turned toward Dirk and said, "So how old are you, Dirk? For real?"

"Twenty-two."

"Seriously?" Susie said. He looked younger than Karl. "What do you do?"

"I'm in sales."

When he didn't elaborate, she found she didn't care. "Hey, you guys, sorry to interrupt, but are there any more musicals in your future?" During the first semester, Alivia and Karl starred with Sam and Ronnie in East Valley's "Fiddler on the Roof" production.

Susie relaxed as they talked about high school and their future plans. Her second beer was gone before she knew it, and Dirk handed her a third before she could even decide if she was ready. Amazingly, the third beer went down so smoothly that she was surprised. However, she shouldn't have been because she could pound down a six-pack at Christy's parties without thinking about it. Of course, at Christy's, she would space the beers out over a longer time frame, but for some reason, she really didn't care about that right now. She wobbled on her feet when she stood up to go to the bathroom.

"Easy there, sailor," Dirk said. "Need help?" He leaped to his feet and offered her his arm.

"Nah, I'm fine." The last thing she wanted was Mr. I'm-in-Sales touching her.

After a trip to the bathroom, Susie checked the clock on the DVR and decided it was time to go.

"Hey, guys," Susie said. "I'm going to head over to Marlee's. She's getting off work in a little while."

"Are you okay to drive?" Alivia asked, a look of concern on her face.

"Babe, she's fine," Karl said. "She only had a couple of beers."

"I'm fine," Susie reassured them, "but thanks for asking." She said the words, yet she wasn't sure she *was* fine to drive. In fact, she felt a little unsteady on her feet. She was, however, in a mostly happy and relaxed state. Mellow even. And that's what she'd been going for.

"I'll get your twelve-pack from the fridge," Karl said and headed to the kitchen.

Alivia walked Susie to the front door. There was a mischievous gleam in her eye when she asked, "I know I already asked you, but how does it feel to be twenty-one?"

"I'm not sure, but I think it feels freeing like life is going my way for a change."

Alivia raised an eyebrow in question but said, "Hey, my parents are away for a few more days, and we've got the place to ourselves. You should hang out with us tomorrow. You make it more fun." Alivia squeezed her arm but didn't let go. She looked up at Susie with penetrating eyes. If Susie didn't know better, she would think Alivia was flirting with her.

"Yeah, sure. I think I will," Susie said. Marlee was working again tomorrow anyway.

"Here you go." Karl handed her the now nine-pack.

"Cool. And thanks for getting me that ID."

"No worries. Glad to do it."

"Same time tomorrow," Alivia reminded her as Susie headed out the door. The cold February air hit her lungs and made her feel light-headed. Dizzy, she leaned against the column of the front porch to steady herself. She blew out a steady, calming breath and then breathed in slowly. It wasn't a deep breath. That might have put her over the edge. After a minute or so, she felt steady enough to walk to her car.

"What a lightweight," she mumbled to herself. "I am out of drinking shape." She balanced the box on her hip and unlocked the trunk. She made room for it next to her softball gear. She'd have to get a blanket or towel to hide her stash better because, right now, it was the first thing you'd see when you opened the trunk.

She got in the driver's seat and started the engine. As she waited for the engine to warm up, a moment of reality hit her as she realized she was probably about to drive impaired. She had to be over the legal limit. Maybe she'd ask Karl about getting her one of those portable breathalyzer things that told you your blood alcohol level. That way, she'd know if she was okay to drive. But right now, she had no choice. And, besides, she felt fine. Nothing was going to stop her from seeing her amazing girlfriend. Susie's heart fluttered as she thought of Marlee. They didn't get to see each other enough. It sucked that they went to different high schools, but maybe, just maybe, they'd get to go to the same college and play softball together. Wouldn't that be amazing? And what would be even more amazing was if they could be roommates in the same college dorm room. Just the two of them. They would be able to lock the door and be alone as often as they wanted to. They wouldn't have to worry that someone's mother was about to walk in on them or some stranger was going to look into Marlee's van when they were being intimate. Yes, that was going to be amazing.

Susie wiped the happy, hopeful tears from her eyes and pulled onto the street. Driving to Marlee's, she thought about whether she should test out her brand-new ID. The convenience mart near

Clarksonville sold beer. And she'd been wanting to see if she could figure out the difference between an ale and a lager anyway, so it made sense to buy some kind of ale to compare to the Brooklyn Lager at Alivia's tomorrow. She could stash it in her trunk alongside the lager.

As she approached the convenience mart on County Road 62, she decided that since she already had some Saranac Ale stashed in her closet, she'd wait another day to test out her new ID. She didn't want to have too much inventory hidden in her trunk.

Even though she'd decided against buying beer, Susie pulled into the convenience mart anyway. A couple of burps along the way told her she needed to do something about her beer breath. Not sure what would work, she grabbed some Altoids and a pack of Tic-Tacs. If one didn't work, the other would. On a whim, she found the aisle with the toiletry items. She felt like she'd hit the jackpot when she spotted the sample-sized mouthwash. "Bingo!" She pulled a few off the shelf and felt weird bringing her items up to the cashier. The cashier didn't seem to notice. That was a good thing, Susie mused. Good for when Susie wanted to buy beer. She tucked the thought away for another day.

Susie got back in the car and took a swig of the mouthwash. She swished it around in her mouth and then gargled for a while. She opened her door and spat on the ground. She felt bad doing that and made a mental note to put a spit cup in her car so she could dump out the mouthwash in a more convenient place. Once she was headed back down the road, she popped a Tic Tac in her mouth. They were so small that it was gone almost instantly. An Altoid was next. Confident that she didn't smell like a brewery, Susie pulled into Marlee's driveway. She was elated to see Marlee's van. That meant Marlee was already home. And, even better, Marlee's mother's car was *not* there.

Susie parked and went up to the kitchen door. She knocked but got no answer. Testing the knob, she found it unlocked and let herself in. Weird. It was the second time that day she had to let herself into a friend's house. She closed the door behind her and heard the shower running upstairs. Susie hung up her coat and stole up the stairs. She would have snuck into the bathroom to surprise Marlee, but fear of Marlee's mother coming home at just the wrong moment sobered her up a little. Instead, she took off her shoes and plopped onto Marlee's bed. She smiled at the still cold but opened can of Coke on Marlee's bedside stand. She sighed as she remembered the beautiful morning and afternoon they'd spent in that very bed the day before. The chemistry between them was incredible. Susie thanked the universe every single day for Marlee. And that bass guitar, Marlee had played it so well. Too well for just a beginner, but then again, Marlee learned anything she tried quickly. Susie smiled at remembering how red Marlee's cheeks had gotten when she first started playing for Susie. It was the first time she had played in front of anyone else. Marlee had a nice touch on the strings and good rhythm, too. There was no doubt about that, Susie thought with a devilish grin.

She closed her eyes and felt herself drifting off. She wasn't sure whether it was the beer or the warm, safe feeling she got being near Marlee. She didn't fight it as sleep overtook her.

Being kissed awake was the best feeling ever.

"Hey, sleepyhead," Marlee said. She was fully dressed and lying on her side next to Susie.

"Mmm, I fell asleep. Sorry." Susie rolled over so she could face Marlee.

"You must have been tired."

"I let myself in. Was that okay?"

Marlee laughed and brushed a lock of hair off Susie's forehead. "More than okay, sweetie. Finding you here in my bed was the best thing ever."

Susie smiled and reached over to kiss Marlee. Marlee pulled back just as things were starting to heat up. She sat up just out of kissing reach.

"You looked so peaceful. I hated to wake you up, but Sam and Lisa will be here any minute."

"Sam and Lisa?" Susie sat up and regretted the fast movement. "We're hanging out with them?"

"Yeah, I was wondering why you didn't respond to Sam's group text. We're going to D'Amico's for dinner and then back here so Sam can play violin with me on bass. Is that okay?"

"Yeah, yeah. Sorry, I just have to wake up. Aren't you nervous? I mean, wow. You're going to play with virtuoso Samantha Rose Payton."

"I *am* nervous," Marlee said quickly, her blush verifying that fact. "I'm nowhere near ready, but she really wants to. I mean, I don't know anything about playing with someone else."

"You'll be fine. I can't wait to hear you guys."

Marlee stood up and reached for her guitar case. "We're moving this operation down into the basement temporarily. There's not enough room for all of us in my room."

Susie scooched over to the side of the bed. As she did so, her stomach roiled.

"Are you okay, sweetie?" Marlee put a hand on her shoulder. "You look pale all of a sudden."

"I'm okay," Susie lied. "I think I'm hungry, that's all. I didn't eat lunch." The third sentence was the only true one.

"Want some water?"

Susie's stomach churned again, so she simply nodded. The instant Marlee left the room, Susie let loose a sour acidy burp. She blew out a sigh at how much better she felt. Marlee came back with a bottled water a moment later, and Susie took a tentative sip, not sure which way it was going to go. When her stomach didn't instantly protest, she relaxed a little. Another swig led to her chugging the entire bottle, which was kind of a mistake since her stomach almost betrayed her again.

"Feel better?" Marlee took the now-empty bottle from Susie.

"Yep." She stood up and felt steady. She didn't feel *good*, but she did feel steady. "So, I assume you want me to carry this bad boy down there?" She tapped the bass amplifier.

"You can wait for Lisa if you want."

"Okay, that's a blow to my ego, but you're right. I'd better wait. I don't think I can navigate all those stairs by myself."

"You and I could move it."

"Lisa will positively kill me if I let Clarksonville's star pitcher tax herself during pre-season."

Marlee smacked Susie lightly on the arm. "You're probably right, and then she'd kill me right after!"

Susie opted to carry Marlee's music stand and binder of sheet music along with a few cords Marlee might need in the basement. Marlee grabbed her bass and a few more things, and soon the only thing left was the large, awkward, and heavy amp.

After setting things up in the basement, Susie and Marlee headed up the stairs just as Marlee's mother was coming in the door. You'd never know that Marlee and her mother were related. Marlee most definitely favored her father, with her lanky build and light blonde hair. Marlee's mother had plain brown hair and a slightly darker complexion.

"Hi, Mom," Marlee said and hugged her mother.

"Hi, honey." Marlee's mother smiled at Susie and said, "Hi, Susie. Enjoying your mid-winter break?"

"Yes, it's nice to have a break from the routine." Except for the headache that had come upon her as they carried Marlee's music stuff into the basement, she had been enjoying it. It almost felt like the start of a hangover. Could you have a hangover on the same day you'd been drinking? Keeping her mind focused, she said, "I just wish I could get a few hours of work at the college, but they're on break like we are."

"Oh, right," Marlee's mother said. "You work for the science department? Setting up labs?"

Susie nodded. "It's fun. It's not even like work. But now that softball season's pretty much here, I'm not going to be able to work much at all."

"Sorry to hear that."

Marlee's mother turned to Marlee, "So that means your youth group meeting is canceled tonight, isn't it?"

"Yeah, but we're going out with Lisa and Sam for dinner. Is that okay? Mom, you'll be okay for dinner on your own, won't you?" It was clear that Marlee was feeling bad about abandoning her mother.

"Actually, I will because I'm only home long enough to freshen up, and then I'm going out to dinner. You remember Bob from my office?"

"Mr. Moore? Your boss?"

"Yes. He and I are going to Le Bistro." Marlee's mother paused for a moment and said, "Are you okay with that?"

Marlee's deer-in-the-headlights expression almost made Susie crack up, but she didn't dare make a sound. Ever since Marlee's father had died in a car accident six years prior, Marlee's mother had been alone. Marlee had recently confided to Susie that she was ready for her mother to find someone new, but Marlee hadn't worked up the courage to let her mother know that. The theoretical possibility of her mother dating had just become a reality.

"Yeah. Bob's nice. Have fun." Marlee then told her mother about their after-dinner plans to play music in the basement.

"My daughter, the rock star," Marlee's mother said with a grin. "Okay, girls, have a fun evening, and Marlee, don't wait up for me. I may be late."

"Okay." Marlee's voice was high and tight.

When Marlee's mother headed up the stairs, Susie pulled Marlee into a hug. "You'll be okay. She'll be okay. Everything'll be okay."

"Promise?"

Susie nodded. Marlee lay her head against Susie's chest.

Chapter Thirteen
Don't Fight It

On Wednesday morning, Susie woke up feeling strong and ready to tackle anything. She didn't have a hangover or even a hint of one. No, her body had taken care of that the day before at Marlee's. Okay, she'd finally had to give in and sneak some aspirin from the bottle in Marlee's kitchen, and that, combined with lots and lots of water at the restaurant, seemed to do the trick. But this morning, she was bright-eyed, bushy-tailed, and ready to face the world.

Her father was still in Vermont, and her mother didn't need her to make dinner since they were going to have leftovers from Sunday and Monday's meals. Susie was free to do whatever she wanted. She loved mid-winter break. Too bad it only came around once a year.

As she made French toast for her brother and *abuelita,* she made sure to drink plenty of water. Christy had always talked about hydrating to reduce the severity of her hangovers, and since Susie was meeting up with Karl and Alivia later, she wanted to be game ready. She planned to have two beers with them and two beers only. Just enough to do her taste test. She didn't want a repeat of yesterday's sudden nap and insta-hangover at Marlee's.

A joyful feeling took over her, and she almost squealed out loud as she did the dishes. She would be going to Marlee's again, and even better, Marlee's mother wouldn't be home until late that night. Marlee and Sam had such a productive music session yesterday that they were eager to do it again. Susie was impressed by how well Marlee had hung in there with Sam. And Sam really drew out the best from Marlee. It was obvious that Marlee was still learning, but watching her drink in everything Sam told her was incredible. But that was Marlee, curious about everything and smart, smart, smart. And Sam? She would make an excellent teacher. Sam's parents expected her to major in business or finance or something along those lines, but Susie thought Sam would be better suited as a teacher. Either way, hopefully, Sam would figure it out.

Susie headed back up to her room and spent a few minutes stretching her sore muscles before dedicating her entire workout to her core. She decided to stick to working her abs because her other muscles needed time to re-knit themselves stronger after all her intense workouts. After the workout and a shower, Susie decided to wear a tight cleavage-revealing top to entice Marlee. Not that Marlee needed enticing, she was a very attentive girlfriend in all kinds of wonderful ways. Susie squirmed at the thought and put on a tight pair of black jeans to go with the top. Satisfied with her look, she decided to be productive and sat down to work on her Environmental Science paper for a while.

She turned the desk lamp on and thought about something Ms. Armstrong had said. "Humans destroy the natural order." It was so true. Collectively, humans sucked when it came to the environment. But how could she turn that into a research paper? She opened her textbook and flipped through the pages hoping something interesting would pop out at her. After an hour, she had a few possible topics written down, but that was it. No thesis. No plan for the paper. She looked over at her rock collection on the shelves next to her desk. She reached up and grabbed her favorite—the rose quartz. Her father knew her penchant for rocks and stones and had gotten her the quartz for her eighth birthday. She held it tightly and said a not-so-silent prayer, "Papi, come to your senses. You're in Vermont now, and hopefully, you're telling that other woman…" A lump formed in Susie's throat. She took a sip of water before continuing. "Papi, tell that woman you're done with her. Tell her you are coming home to your family, that you have to stay here. Be the man Mami married. Be the father Miguel and I expect you to be. Be the father who gives his daughter rose quartz for her eighth birthday. Be the one who defended me to Mami when she had a meltdown over me liking girls and falling in love with Marlee. Papi, don't destroy the natural order of our family."

Completely derailed from anything academic, Susie squeezed the rose quartz one more time and placed it carefully on the shelf. She stood up, pulled the remaining Saranac Ales from the hidey spot in her closet, stashed them in a bag, and then snuck them into her trunk. Excited about starting her day, she went into the house to tell her brother and her *abuelita* where she was going.

After receiving a grunt from her brother, she thanked her *abuelita* for watching him. It was obvious that *Abuelita* knew the Torres family was in "all hands on deck" mode when she gave Susie a heartfelt hug. Susie tried not to think about what her *abuelita* thought about her eldest son having an affair. Or maybe she didn't know.

125

That's right. No one really knew except Susie and her mother. And no one, except Marlee, knew that she knew.

Susie parked in the same spot on the street behind Karl's truck in an almost repeat of the day before. But, no, Susie vowed. She would *not* have a repeat of the day before. She did not want to show up at Marlee's house tipsy or hangovery. Having a hangover in the middle of the day was like giving yourself the flu on purpose! Kind of stupid.

Susie knocked on the front door, and again no one came to answer it. She let herself in and found Karl and Alivia cozying up on the couch. They were so engrossed in each other that they didn't look up.

Susie took her coat off and laid it on one of the recliners. She was relieved to find that Dirk was not there. *Dios mio*, he was kind of creepy.

"A-hem!" Susie said to Alivia and Karl loudly and then laughed.

Alivia pulled away and giggled, "Oh, sorry. We didn't hear you come in."

"Obviously not."

Alivia stood up to give Susie a quick hug. "I love that top," she whispered suggestively in Susie's ear.

"Thanks." Susie felt herself blush. Alivia was definitely flirting with her. What was that all about?

Karl stood up. "What 'cha drinking today?"

Susie showed him her lagers and ales. "They're warm, though."

"Let's put those in the fridge," Karl said, reaching for the box. "I'll put one of each in the freezer, but we can't forget about 'em."

"Oh, Karl, remember the time you left your beers in the—"

"Yes." Karl interrupted and cleared his throat. "Susie does not need to hear that story right now."

Susie laughed at Karl's red cheeks. "Here," Susie said, reaching for the box. "I'll put these away. You two, uh, get your fill until I come back."

"Ooh," Karl said and sat down. "Thanks."

Alivia flew back onto the couch and into his arms before Susie left the room.

Susie made her way to the kitchen and stopped mid-stride when she saw Dirk sitting at the kitchen table. He was focused on sifting a pile of something brown. Her brain finally registered what it was. Pot. Dirk was sifting a pile of pot, sifting out seeds or something.

"There she is," Dirk said, looking up from his work. "Karl told me you'd be back."

Susie cringed. Not only had he made it sound like she was back to see *him*, but the lecherous look on his face made her skin crawl. Yep, the guy was a creep.

"Thanks again for the ID," Susie said, not really wanting to talk to him. Not even small talk.

"Not a problem."

She put one lager and one ale into the freezer as quickly as possible. She stashed the box with the remaining beers in the fridge. It wasn't until she closed the refrigerator door that she wondered why she had brought in the whole box. She was only planning on drinking two.

"Hey, gorgeous," Dirk said. "Do you smoke?" He held up a newly rolled joint.

"Nope."

"Want to try?" He held it out toward her. "Free of charge. And if you like it, I'm your guy for a permanent supply."

"Uh, no." Susie headed toward the kitchen doorway. "I'm gonna head back in." She didn't wait for him to respond and headed back to the TV room.

Thankfully, Dirk didn't follow her, and Susie was able to sit in one of the recliners and hang out with her friends. Their main topic of conversation was how serious Ronnie and Jordan were getting. Apparently, Ronnie rarely hung out with Karl and Alivia these days, preferring to spend all his time alone with Jordan. He even started cutting school to be with Jordan.

Susie had been watching the clock and, after a half hour, said to Karl, "So what d'ya think? Will my beers be cold enough?"

"Oh, yeah. Go for it!"

She stood up from the recliner and headed back into the kitchen. Unfortunately, it looked like Dirk was wrapping up his pot-sorting and joint-rolling project. She didn't make eye contact with him as she flung open the freezer door and pulled out her two beers. She grabbed a bottle opener on the counter and headed back out the door. Her speed would have made a NASCAR pit crew jealous.

"Two-fisted, eh?" Karl said with an admiring nod.

Susie held up both bottles. "Yep, I'm doing a taste test. I want to see if I like lagers or ales better."

"Cheers," Alivia said and raised her drink. "We're drinking Long Island Iced Teas. Karl makes them so good. You should try one."

"Nah. It's beer for me today."

Karl leaped to his feet so fast that Susie jumped. "I know what we can do. I have just the thing." He headed to the kitchen, leaving both Susie and Alivia confused.

Alivia shrugged and said, "Who knows what my studmuffin has in mind."

Susie chuckled and popped open the Brooklyn lager. She had heard Alivia call Karl that before, but it was still funny. And if she had to admit it, Marlee was a bit of a studmuffin, too. Especially when she got that hungry look in her eye.

Susie took a sip of the lager to distract herself from her very distracting train of thought. It was good. Nice and cold and had a good taste. Next, she popped off the cap to the Saranac Ale. She took a sip and noticed a difference immediately. It was fuller in taste and had a really nice flavor. She alternated sips until she finally came to a decision about which she liked better.

Karl returned carrying a tray with four empty beer glasses and four empty shot glasses. A bottle of Jack Daniels also sat on the tray. Jack Daniels? Wasn't that whiskey?

Karl set the tray down, put his hands out, flanking the tray, and announced, "Boilermakers!"

"What are boilermakers?" Susie asked, one eyebrow raised.

"Only the best thing since time began," Karl said. He pointed to the beers in her hand. "What did you decide?"

She held up the beer bottle in her right hand. "Saranac Ale wins. The other's good, though."

"Fantastic choice," Karl said.

Just then, Dirk walked in with four more of the Brooklyn Lagers. He must have grabbed them from her box. "You wanted these?" he said to Karl.

"Yep." Karl turned to Susie. He took them from Dirk and then held them up toward Susie. "You don't mind, do you?"

Apparently not, Susie thought wryly. "No, that's cool."

Karl filled up the four shot glasses with whiskey.

"Susie, you're going to love this," Alivia gushed. "It takes you right where you want to go but quicker."

Alivia held Susie's eye for a second and then smiled. Susie nodded. Okay, she'd try it. The shot wasn't big at all. How bad could it be?

Karl handed everyone a beer and a shot and explained what to do.

Susie said to Karl, "Okay, let's go for it."

"Whoo hoo!" Alivia said. "On three. One, two, three!"

Susie dropped the whiskey shot into the beer. A spike of adrenaline rushed through her as the beer foamed up to the top of the glass. She quickly put the glass to her lips before it could spill on the carpet. She watched as Karl and Dirk chugged their concoctions smoothly. Alivia stopped partway to catch her breath, so Susie didn't feel bad when she had to stop for a second, too. Although she was the last one to finish, it didn't matter. The beer/whiskey combination was interesting. Different.

"Well?" Karl said and then let loose a long and bubbly burp.

Everyone laughed, and before Susie could say a word, her own burp forced itself out. "*Aay, Dios mio*, that was fun, you guys!"

"One more," Dirk called out.

"Oh, God," Susie said and blew out another sigh. "I don't think so." She was already feeling the mind-altering effects of the first boilermaker.

"Oh, c'mon, chicken," Alivia said. "One more, and that's it. Really, life will finally seem like it's going your way, Susie. That's what you want, isn't it?"

Susie nodded and put her glass down on the tray with a clatter. "One more."

A cheer went up in the living room, and Karl sent Dirk back into the kitchen to get a few more of Susie's beers. The second boilermaker went down even more smoothly, and even though Susie still had to stop once, at least she beat out Alivia that time. On the third boilermaker, though, she surprised everybody, including herself, by chugging the entire thing without stopping.

"Phew!" Susie said as she put her beer glass down on the tray. Her world was spinning at just the right speed around her.

She stepped back and reached behind her for the recliner but missed and fell, not very gracefully, onto the carpet.

Alivia was up in an instant. "Oh, my God. Are you okay?"

Susie just laughed and laughed. She laughed so hard she couldn't get any words out. She was already down so figured she might as well stay there. She closed her eyes and sighed. "Pillow?" was all she managed.

"Sure." Alivia reached over to the couch for a pillow and put it under Susie's head. "There you go. Comfy?"

"Yeah." Susie opened her eyes to find Alivia hovering over her. Her long chestnut hair fell forward to frame her pretty face. They locked eyes as Alivia reached and moved a lock of hair off Susie's forehead.

Susie wasn't sure how it happened, but Alivia's lips were suddenly on hers. Alivia's hungry lips were soft but insistent as she kissed Susie passionately.

Susie pulled away. "What are you doing? I don't like you like that. I have Marlee. You have Karl."

"I know, sweet thing," Alivia said and stroked her cheek. "I just wanted to see what it was like." She leaned down and whispered in Susie's ear, "You're fucking hot, Susie."

"That was goddamn sexy," Dirk said.

"Mm hmm," Karl said, his voice low.

Susie smiled at the compliments but closed her eyes, aware when Alivia moved away. The unmistakable sounds of her making out with Karl on the couch made her glad her eyes were closed. Floating in her beer and whiskey-induced tranquility, she barely registered Alivia saying, "Karl and I are taking this party to my room." Susie didn't have the strength to nod as she drifted away on a happy sea of drunken bliss.

Susie woke to the luscious sensation of Marlee massaging her breasts through her top. She moaned.

"Like it, do ya?" Marlee's voice was different. Hard, aggressive.

A knee landed in between her own and nudged her legs apart. Wide apart. Harsh lips kissed her neck and trailed down to feast on her open cleavage. A hand went directly between her now-spread legs and rubbed her roughly on top of her jeans. Aggressively. Not like Marlee at all.

Susie swam up from her drunkenness and managed to get one eye open. The other opened soon after. Her vision was blurred, but fear struck her heart when she realized it was Dirk on top of her, not Marlee. One of his hands continued to rub between her legs, and the other was pulling down the zipper of his pants.

"No," she squealed and tried to push him away. She was strong, but he was stronger. Using both hands, he pushed her flat on her back on the carpet. With his full weight on her, she couldn't move.

"Don't fight it, gorgeous. You liked it; I know you do." She could smell his sour breath, his face just inches from hers. "I just want to make you feel good."

He leaned down and covered her mouth with his. His tongue thrust through her lips repeatedly as if to show her what he was about to do to her body. She squirmed to get away but couldn't move because of his weight on her.

One of his hands reached down and popped open the button on her pants. Panic flooded her veins as he one-handedly tugged her zipper down. She used his distraction against him and threw her head at his. The sound of their skulls cracking together made her nauseous, but she ignored it as he howled and grabbed his head with both hands. She rolled out from under him and fought around the white-hot agony of her own pierced skull. Blinded by pain, she crawled away until she bumped into one of the recliners and pulled herself up to her feet. The room spun every which way, but she used the furniture to guide her to the walls, leading her to the front door. Once out of the house, she stumbled to the safety of her car.

Her head was pounding as she hit the lock button five times. Bile rose in her throat. She dug her keys out of her front pocket and started the car. She flung it into reverse and backed up. She then threw the gearshift into drive and punched the gas, hitting Karl's truck as she sped away.

Chapter Fourteen
No More

Susie's blood pumped like mad as she drove away from Alivia's house. She overshot the stop sign at C.R. 62 and was lucky there was no cross-traffic. She looked in the rearview mirror to make sure she wasn't being chased and then backed up off the main road. She hit the door locks again and took the briefest of moments to take a deep breath. She couldn't. It made her head pound even more. She reached up and gently rubbed the spot where her head had connected with his. She cringed as she thought of his body on hers, how she couldn't muscle him off of her. She'd always thought she would be able to defend herself against something like that. Her heart pounded at the realization that she might not have been able to.

After taking another shallow breath, she put on her turn signal and pulled onto C.R. 62. It wasn't long before a car beeped at her from behind. Adrenaline shot through her. Was it Dirk? A quick check in the mirror told her it wasn't. The driver kept beeping and waving his hands at her. What was the problem? She wasn't speeding, was she? A quick check of the speedometer told her the exact opposite. She wasn't even going thirty, and the speed limit was fifty-five. She hit the accelerator and willed her vision to stop fading in and out. The road was blurry in front of her, but she was able to make out the black surface with the painted lines on either side. If she stayed between the lines, she'd be good.

Apparently, her new speed wasn't good enough for the tailgater behind her, and he passed her over the double yellow. He reached his arm out of the driver's window and gave her the finger as he passed.

Susie didn't react beyond a groan. She didn't have the brain strength for it. A rhythmic click-click-click alerted her to a problem. She opened her eyes wide, trying to get them to focus. Once she realized the problem, her heart jumped. Her left tires were riding on the road reflectors separating the two lanes of traffic. She jerked the wheel to the right, only to have her right tires hit the reflectors on the shoulder.

"Stay on the road, idiot," Susie said to herself and managed to get the car in the middle of her lane. She opened her eyes wide again. They kept wanting to shut. "Yellow lines on the left. White lines on the right. Yellow on the left. White on the right," she said over and over as she struggled to navigate the road that led to Marlee.

She had been doing a stellar job, keeping her speed at about fifty-five when a sudden need arose. An urgent need. She had to pee. There was no way she could make it to Marlee's. Could she make it to the convenience mart just outside of Clarksonville? If she had the strength, she would have laughed at her ridiculous question. No, there was no way. As if sent from heaven, the sign for the parking area appeared. She could make that.

After a million years, the parking area finally materialized. Still on C.R. 62, she hit the brakes hard as the turn approached. She'd hit them so hard that her entire body jerked forward, and her face almost made contact with the steering wheel. Thank God no one had been behind her because they would have hit her. With a grunt, she pressed the gas pedal and jerked the car into the parking area. A metallic scraping sound assaulted her ears, but she ignored it as she zoomed toward an open spot in front of her. She threw the car in park and almost cried when she realized the parking area didn't have bathrooms. There wasn't even a single Porta-John. But she couldn't wait. There was a stand of woods a short distance from her car. That would have to do.

She grabbed a handful of McDonald's napkins from the center console, opened her car door, and stumbled out. The frigid North Country air hit her in the face like a physical object, causing her to stumble backward. She flailed at the still-open door so she wouldn't fall. Once fully upright, she made her way into the stand of trees and found a relatively private spot. When she reached down with her right hand to undo the button on her pants, reality hit her again. Her button was already undone. By Dirk. And her zipper was mostly down.

"Holy fucking shit," Susie muttered. With her heart pounding, she did her best to push those thoughts away and yanked her pants and underwear down. She was keenly aware that this was exactly what Dirk had wanted—her pants around her ankles. She couldn't help the tears as she squatted in the snow-covered leaves. Relief flooded her as she released her bladder. After cleaning up, then zipping and buttoning up, she made a half-hearted attempt to bury the evidence and then headed back to the safety of her car.

She looked up and couldn't believe what she saw. The driver's side door was wide open. Not only that, she'd left the car engine running.

Susie's heart clenched. There was no way she could go to Marlee's in the shape she was in. She ducked into her car and slammed the driver's door shut. She hit the locks and then hit them again, just to be sure. She left the engine running for the heater and tilted her seat back as far back as it would go. She checked the locks one more time and let herself drift off to sleep.

A piercing squeal woke her up. She opened both eyes in a panic, not sure where she was. Her heart was pounding. The parking area. Right. The high-pitch squeal of airbrakes sounded again. A cargo truck had pulled in. It was then that she remembered. Dirk. Her heart crushed itself into a thousand little pieces.

A sob escaped her throat as she pounded the steering wheel. "Why do I always cry in this mother-fucking goddamned parking area? Son of a bitch." Susie blew out a sigh. Her mouth tasted awful, but the mere thought of mouthwash or mints made her stomach churn.

She pulled her cell phone out of her pocket to check the time and saw that Marlee had left her five texts. Crap, what time was it? After five. How long had she been sleeping? Passed out was more like it. Marlee had been home for over an hour already.

Susie sent a quick text back that said, "On my way!" She didn't have the energy to find a smiley face emoji she usually sent with her texts.

She opened her window wide in an attempt to wake up. She felt like crap. Her head hurt, and her eyes were so blurry. What the hell was that all about?

She put on her seatbelt and slowly backed the car out of the spot. She navigated around the parked cargo truck and then waited for a long clear stretch of empty road before pulling out. On the way, she continued her chant, "Yellow on the left. White on the right."

A warm feeling overcame her when she finally pulled into Marlee's driveway. She was safe here. She started to cry when she saw Marlee outside chopping wood. Marlee was cute with her boyish blonde hair and sweet red-cheeked face. Susie loved the way Marlee's strong arms would wrap themselves around her. And her hands, Susie loved Marlee's hands. They were strong and calloused, and Susie loved to kiss the palm and then each and every finger in turn.

Marlee's face lit up at the sight of Susie's car, and she waved. Susie waved back, trying to get her tears under control. She pulled into her usual spot and took a couple of deep breaths, trying to get her emotions under control. Susie watched her girlfriend lift the wedge-shaped axe over her head with ease and then bring it down with so much force that the log split cleanly in two. Her heart melted at the sight. Susie took another breath and tried to find the peace that was hers when she was with Marlee.

Marlee put down the axe and headed toward Susie's car. She called over, "Are you getting out of that car any time today?"

Susie nodded and gave Marlee her best smile as if everything in her world was fine. Unfortunately, the motion sent a surge of nausea to her throat. She closed her eyes in an attempt to right the world. *Dios*, she couldn't let Marlee see how fucked up she was. Despite the pounding in her head, Susie pulled the key out of the ignition. She hoped the motion would hide the fact that she was trying not to get sick.

"Hey, woman," Marlee said as she reached the car. "It's cold out here. Where's your coat?" She opened Susie's door.

Amazingly, until that very moment, Susie hadn't realized that she'd left her coat at Alivia's. *Dios*, how fucked up was she? She hadn't even realized it when she'd walked into the woods to pee.

"Forgot it," Susie said, her voice unsteady.

"Aww, I'll get you one from the house. When I come back out, I'll split; you stack?"

Susie nodded despite the dizziness the motion created. She held her breath and tried not to recoil when Marlee leaned down to give her a quick kiss. If Susie breathed, then Marlee would smell the alcohol. Susie hadn't done her mouthwash/Tic-Tac/Altoid routine and knew she reeked. Marlee headed back toward the house. Unbidden, the memory of Dirk's sour breath and his mouth on hers assaulted her senses. She closed her eyes and shook her head as if to shake the memory from her brain.

The instant the kitchen door shut behind Marlee, Susie opened her car door. She had to get herself upright and steady before Marlee came back out. It was hard because her head was positively pounding. Maybe she should press a handful of snow on her head. She reached up and felt the growing lump. Yeah, that might help. She made sure to pocket her keys and shut the door before walking over to a nice-sized snowdrift against the garage. Unfortunately, to add to her misery, her stomach started protesting its own existence. An acid burp burned her throat. Only a burp. Thank God.

Doing her best to imitate a person who knew how to walk straight, Susie made her way to the snowdrift. The mere action of bending down to pick up a handful of snow sent her head spinning.

Her stomach heaved. She stumbled to the other side of the garage, out of sight of the house. She couldn't let Marlee see her. Reaching out with one hand, she finally found the garage wall. She pressed her hand against it to steady herself. The other hand held her rolling stomach. Every time it rolled, her head pounded even more. When her mouth filled with water, she knew exactly what that meant. Unfortunately, Marlee had chosen that exact moment to find her.

"Hey, where'd you go?" Marlee asked as she rounded the corner.

Susie couldn't answer as she leaned forward to spill the contents of her stomach all over the snow.

"Whoa, whoa," Marlee said.

Susie felt an arm go around her. She tried to pull away, not wanting Marlee to see her like that, but she hadn't the strength. Another wave hit, and her stomach let loose again.

"Oh, sweetie," Marlee rubbed her back.

Susie barely heard the words as she struggled to catch her breath between heaves. Eventually, they stopped. Susie reached up to stop her pounding head from spinning, and if it weren't for Marlee holding her up, she would have fallen.

"C'mon, Susie," Marlee said. "Let's get you in the house."

Susie grunted but let Marlee walk her away from the scene of her stomach upheaval. "Sorry." It was one word, the only one she could manage.

"You're okay, sweetie. You're okay." Marlee helped her walk. "That's it. One foot in front of the other."

When they got to the steps leading up to the kitchen door, Susie couldn't do it. Her leg simply would not lift itself up. Why was she so weak all of a sudden?

"Put your weight on this leg." Marlee tapped Susie's left calf.

Susie shifted her weight to the left, which freed up her right.

"Now lift this one." Another tap.

Susie lifted it up and onto the step. Marlee was so smart. She figured stuff out.

With careful instructions and a lot of strength from Marlee, they finally made it up the three steps into the kitchen. Marlee shut the door firmly behind them. Oh, yeah, the kitchen door. Susie loved that kitchen door. She loved pressing Marlee against it and teasing her with kisses.

"'Member that door?" Susie asked with a smirk. But even to her own ears, the words didn't sound like English. It sounded more like, "Mmmdor?"

"What?" Marlee adjusted her grip. "The door? I closed it. You'll be warm now."

"Uh, oh," Susie said as her world tilted and her stomach churned. She put one hand over her mouth and the other over her stomach.

Marlee practically carried Susie to the small bathroom just off the kitchen.

They got there just in time, and once inside, Susie fell to her knees and somehow found the toilet with her hands. Someone, probably Marlee, lifted the toilet seat, and Susie heaved. Nothing came out. Her stomach was empty.

"No more," Susie announced firmly and pointed to the bowl. She laid her head on the rim and closed her eyes.

"Oh, man," Marlee said. "Here, let me put a towel under your head."

Susie barely registered the softness that materialized under her cheek. She faded out of consciousness as she heard Marlee say, "Lisa? Can you come over? I need help."

Chapter Fifteen
I Don't Know

Susie woke to a throbbing headache and a testy stomach. The paste in her mouth was godawful, and she couldn't make any saliva to swallow. Her bedroom looked weird through her barely opened eyes. Her monster headache was probably clouding her judgment.

She groaned. *Dios*, why did she feel so bad?

"Water?"

Susie jumped at the voice in the darkness.

"Marlee? Why are you here?" Her voice sounded weak and gravelly.

"I live here," Marlee said with a laugh.

"In my room?"

"No, we're at my house."

"Your house?" Marlee's words made no sense. Susie pressed three fingertips to her right temple to ease the throbbing. It was then that she realized she was in Marlee's living room and that she had slept on the couch.

Marlee handed her an opened bottle of water. Susie took a tentative sip, grateful when her stomach didn't protest. Something furry rubbed against her arm. Despite her misery, Susie smiled. "Hi,

Patches." The mostly white calico cat sent up her friendly tail and purred.

"She's been with you all night," Marlee said with a soft smile.

"She has?"

"C'mon, you know whenever you're in the house, she wants nothing to do with me."

"Lesser women would be upset by that."

Marlee just smiled, and they sat in silence while Susie petted the cat.

"Susie, what do you remember?"

"Not much," Susie said but then thought for a minute. "*Aay*, outside the garage." She sucked air threw her teeth. "Sorry."

Marlee helped Susie sit up and then sat next to her. She stroked Susie's cheek. "What else do you remember?"

"You were chopping wood." Susie's expression softened. She looked at Marlee in the dim light. "You were so sexy."

"Chopping wood?" Marlee chuckled. "Okay, I'll take it." She reached for Susie's hands and held them. "What else?"

"Oh, wait. I had to pee so bad, so I ... " She was embarrassed and couldn't bring herself to relay the details about peeing in the woods. "Marlee, why am I here?"

The sympathetic expression on Marlee's face made Susie's heart melt. Marlee searched Susie's face as if trying to figure out a way to relay bad news.

"Marlee?" Marlee's mother appeared at the door to the living room. "Can I speak to you in the kitchen?" Her voice was not kind.

"Be right there, Mom."

Marlee turned back to Susie. "There's some aspirin right there and a bucket if you need to, uh, you know."

"Thanks."

"Do you need help getting to the bathroom?" There was a hardness to Marlee's voice that tore at Susie's heart.

"No."

Marlee stood up.

"Marlee?" Susie said.

"Yeah?"

"Whatever I did, I'm sorry. I'm sorry if I hurt you."

Marlee leaned down and kissed Susie on the forehead. "Yell if you need anything, okay?"

"Okay."

Susie watched Marlee's retreating back and wondered if she'd blown it. She scooched to the edge of the couch and grabbed the aspirin bottle. After taking two, she stood up. Unsteady on her feet, she made her way to the door and then to the bathroom. She relieved her bladder and then washed her hands and face. She pulled her toothbrush out of the medicine cabinet. Marlee had gotten it for her when they first started seeing each other way back in April. She used it to brush the fuzz off her tongue. Reaching back with the brush, she went too far and gagged. She grabbed her stomach and willed herself not to heave, especially with Marlee and her mother right down the hall in the kitchen. After a few quiet breaths, she settled down. She washed her face and then took a look in the mirror. She was shocked at what she saw. She looked like shit warmed over. Her skin was pale, and she had big dark circles under her eyes. And her hair? Forget about her hair. But that was the least of her worries. Her head—it hurt like gangbusters.

She opened the door to the bathroom, her sights set on laying back down on the couch and closing her eyes. Another sip of water might be good, too.

She stepped into the hallway but retreated when she heard Marlee's mother say, "I'm not happy with this."

"I know, Mom," Marlee said. "I'm not either. But I don't really know what happened yesterday."

"She showed up here drunk, Marlee. What's not to know? She drove drunk. She could have killed someone."

It was true, Susie thought. She flashbacked on trying to navigate the road—yellow on the left, white on the right.

"I can't have this, Marlee. I won't be able to live with it if she—"

"I know," Marlee interrupted, resignation in her voice. "I just have to—"

"I don't want you around that, either." It was Marlee's mother's turn to interrupt. Her voice had an edge to it that Susie had never heard before. "I can't forbid you to see her, but I wish you wouldn't."

Marlee made a small noise that Susie couldn't interpret. Marlee didn't respond to her mother's statement for so long that Susie began to worry, really worry.

"Marlee, I have to call her parents."

"No, Mom, you can't." There was a panicked urgency in Marlee's voice that Susie had never heard before. "Her parents are fighting a lot lately, and something like this might, I don't know, throw more fuel on the fire. Mom, I think they might be getting divorced."

Susie inhaled sharply at the words. Divorced? Why would Marlee say that? Her father was being an ass, sure, but that didn't mean divorce. She didn't want to hear anymore, so she scurried back to the safety of the couch and lay down with her back to the door. At the moment, she was choosing *not* to deal with any part of her life.

"Susie," Marlee's mother said from the doorway.

Susie looked over her shoulder. She was about to be thrown out. She rolled over and tried to sit up without getting too nauseous.

"I'm so sorry for this, Mrs. McAllister. I made a big mistake." Susie looked around for her shoes but couldn't find them.

"When you get home, I want you to tell your parents everything that happened. Please let me know when you do because I want to talk to them afterward."

"Yes, ma'am." Susie looked down. Marlee's mother was going to tell her parents in no uncertain terms that Susie was never to darken her daughter's doorstep again. Susie's heart tightened, and she couldn't help the sobs that escaped. The one place she had felt truly safe was closing in on her. She punched the couch cushion when she couldn't find her goddamned shoes. Fine, she'd go home without them. She stood up against the dizziness.

"Oh, honey," Marlee's mother said, her gentle hands guided Susie back down to the couch. "You don't have to go home right this second. Let Marlee take care of you for now."

"Okay." The words, *for now*, echoed in her brain. There was only now, right now. There would be no *later*.

Susie woke to the sounds of her friends talking.

"Hey, asswipe," Sam said to Susie. "It's ten o'clock in the morning. Are you finally awake now?"

Susie didn't answer right away. She was taking inventory. Her headache was still there, but it had lessened. Her stomach was absolutely in need of something, but she didn't know what.

"Hey," was all she managed to say back to her friend. She sat up and pressed her fingers to both temples.

Lisa sat on the couch next to her. "Headache?"

"Mm hmm," Susie nodded once. It was all she could manage.

Lisa was almost six feet tall and was intimidating on the softball field with her muscular frame and long black braid. She looked like an Amazon warrior heading into battle. But at the moment, she looked gentle and caring.

"We're going to take aspirin out of the mix since that's too acidic on your stomach," Lisa said. "We brought you ibuprofen, but I want to get something in your stomach first. Marlee's going to make you some ginger tea, and if you can keep that down, we'll try for a couple of saltine crackers, then toast, and if all is well, Marlee will make her famous chicken noodle soup."

"From the box?" Susie looked up at Marlee.

"Yep, from the box," Marlee said and then headed into the kitchen. Sam followed her in. She heard them talking in hushed voices but couldn't make out any of the words.

"In the meantime," Lisa said, "have a few sips of water."

"Okay."

With Lisa's help, Susie sat up and reached for the water bottle on the side table. She took a few tentative sips.

"Turn your back toward me. I want to give you some acupressure."

Susie turned and said, "I'm sorry, Lisa. Tell Marlee I'm sorry. And Sam. And Marlee's mother." Tears filled her eyes as the realization that she'd majorly messed up hit her again. "Oh, shit. My mother." She spun back around, making herself dizzy. "Where's my phone? I have to call my mother."

"Shh, shh, shh." Lisa put a reassuring hand on her shoulder. "We already did that. Last night. Marlee texted her with your phone. Your mother thinks you stayed here because it was too late to drive home last night."

"Did she yell?"

"In a text?"

"You obviously don't know my mother."

Lisa chuckled. "Turn back around."

Susie turned and then felt warm, strong hands on the back of her neck. Lisa's fingers gently massaged the base of Susie's skull, occasionally stilling to apply concentrated pressure before going back to massaging. There was nothing sexual in the way Lisa touched her. It was just wonderfully nurturing.

"Mmm. That feels good."

"Good, now let's loosen up your shoulders." Lisa moved down to Susie's shoulders and massaged the muscles there for a while. "Geez, Susie, you are tense." Lisa moved on to other muscles, and Susie let herself relax. Lisa ended by massaging the web of Susie's hands between her thumb and index finger.

"How did you learn to do that?" Susie asked. "My headache is almost gone."

"Sam's migraines. Seeing her in so much pain kills me, so I researched acupressure techniques."

150

"Do they help?"

"They do. I'm trying to get her off all those crap pills she takes."

Susie smiled at the love for Sam she saw in Lisa's eyes. She hoped she'd be able to see that look in Marlee's eyes again. If she hadn't blown it, that is. Then she remembered. Marlee's mother was going to banish her.

"Your tea, madam," Marlee said as she and Sam returned. She set it down on the side table.

"Thanks." Susie took a couple of tentative sips, surprised at how well it went down, and stayed down. She had never been so happy to have a cup of tea before in her life. "Thanks, Marlee." She locked eyes with her soon-to-be ex-girlfriend. "I'm sorry, *mi vida*." A hurt set of eyes looked back at her, but eventually, they softened, and Marlee nodded.

Sam pulled up a chair right in front of Susie, probably so she could see eye to eye with her friend who had royally fucked up. "You scared the shit out of all of us last night."

"You were here, too?"

Sam exchanged a glance with Marlee. "You don't remember?"

"No."

"Do you remember that Marlee slept on the floor right there? All night?"

"No." Susie turned to Marlee. "You did that?"

"I was worried."

Susie had no words.

"What *do* you remember?" Sam asked.

"I remember peeing in the woods." Susie looked down, embarrassed to be admitting something so base.

151

"Why did you do that?" Sam's expression was serious.

Susie looked away from Sam's penetrating eyes. Marlee's expression was one of concern. Lisa's expression was the most perplexing of all. There was no judgment, but there was no sympathy either. Lisa had a good poker face, that was for sure.

"Sus?" Sam said.

"Hmm?"

"Why did you pee in the woods? Why were you even *in* the woods?"

"I wasn't in the woods. I mean, I was, but only 'cuz I had to go. I wasn't going to make it to Marlee's."

"Why didn't you go before you left home?"

"I wasn't at home," Susie said.

"Where were you?"

It felt like one of those investigations you see on a cop show. But Susie knew she had no choice but to answer.

"Alivia's." Yes, that's right. Alivia and Karl were making out on the couch when she got there.

Sam looked perplexed. "And why were you at Alivia's?"

Susie smiled. "You'd make a good lawyer, Sam."

Her friends laughed, which broke the tension a little.

Why was she at Alivia's? Oh, yeah. She remembered. "I wanted to…"

"Wanted to what?"

She stalled by taking a few more sips of tea. After a deep sigh, she confessed, "I wanted to see if I could tell the difference between an ale and a lager."

"Beer?" Sam said simply. "Beer isn't the only thing causing your hangover."

"Oh, yeah. Karl made us, uh…" She snapped her fingers, trying to remember the name of the concoction Karl had made. "Boiler-something. You make it with whiskey. I think."

"Karl gave you whiskey?"

"Yeah. Alivia said they do it all the time and that I'd like it. She said it would take me where I needed to go."

"And where did you need to go, Susie?" Marlee said, her expression soft. Lisa stood up so Marlee could sit down next to her.

Susie turned to face Marlee. "Anywhere."

Marlee exchanged another glance with Sam. Marlee cleared her throat. "And is that all you did yesterday?" She seemed to be taking over the questioning. Maybe it was good-cop, bad-cop time.

"Yeah, that's it. Honest." Susie put her right hand up as if swearing on a bible. She beseeched her friends to believe her, mainly because it was true. "I mean, Dirk had pot in the kitchen, but—" Memories slammed into her head. Dirk's weight on her. His tongue thrusting in and out of her mouth, his hand rubbing her crotch and then and then—

She physically backed away from the memory by putting out both hands and backing up against the couch. "No, no, no, no, no," Susie cried. She couldn't find a way out of the room.

"Susie, Susie, Susie," Marlee put a hand on her arm, "you're okay. We're here. It's just us. What happened just now?"

Realizing there was no immediate threat, Susie worked to slow her heart rate. After a minute, she said, "I hit my head." She wouldn't elaborate when Marlee asked her how. "I hit my head," she said again.

153

She reached up and rubbed the spot, happy to find that the lump had lessened. "Can I have an ice pack?"

"Sure," Marlee said and got to her feet to go to the kitchen.

Susie whispered to Sam and Lisa, "Marlee's mom hates me. I need to apologize."

Sam answered first. "Marlee's mom does *not* hate you, Susie."

"And, besides, she's not home right now," Lisa added. "She's going to be gone all day with somebody named Bob. They went to Lake Placid."

"Oh, good." Susie felt momentary relief.

"Can I feel your head?" Lisa said.

"Yes." Susie reached up and found the spot for Lisa.

Lisa felt around, and Susie winced. "Sorry, Susie. That's quite a lump. How did you get that?"

Very clever, Lisa, Susie thought, but they weren't going to get that out of her. No way. She admitted to drinking with Karl and Alivia, but she was not going to acknowledge that other thing. Not now, not ever. In fact, she was going to forget it ever happened. And you know why? Because nothing really happened, she told herself firmly. Nothing.

She couldn't help the tears that started falling because it hadn't been *nothing.* It had definitely been something. She covered her face with both hands and wept into them. Lisa's strong arm went around her and pulled her close.

"Susie," Lisa's voice was soft, "whatever happened yesterday is over. You're okay. You're with us now."

Susie nodded behind her hands.

"And when you're ready to tell us what happened," Sam added, "we'll be here to listen."

Susie didn't move. To nod would mean that something had happened. And nothing had. Hearing Marlee approach, Susie wiped at her eyes. She hated that everyone had to see her like that.

"Your ice pack, madam." Marlee handed it to Susie.

"Get some rest, Sus," Sam said and stood up. "C'mon, Lisa, let's give them some room to talk." To Marlee, she said, "We're heading down to the basement. I'm going to tune up my violin but take your time."

Marlee nodded as they left the room.

Susie heard Sam say to Lisa once they were in the hallway, "One thing's for sure, I'm calling Alivia as soon as we get downstairs."

"No kidding," Lisa said. "Something happened over there. Or..."

"Or what?"

"Or maybe Susie got into an accident and hit her head on the windshield."

"You could be right. Come on, let's check out her car."

They could check out her car all they wanted, Susie thought. They were following a cold path, and that was fine with her. The further they veered from the truth, the better.

Marlee sat down on the far side of the couch. She swiveled so that her feet came to rest on the middle cushion. Susie did the same and touched Marlee's feet with hers.

"Do I look ridiculous with this ice pack on my head?"

Marlee shook her head, her smile thin-lipped. The smile never reached her eyes.

Susie caught her girlfriend's gaze and said, "I only went over there to have two beers, Marlee. Just two. I wasn't planning on getting blitzed. I wasn't. I promise."

"They held you down and poured whiskey down your throat?"

Susie tried not to blanch at Marlee's words. "No. I got caught up in their excitement. I just, I don't know, I just thought by hanging with those guys, I could forget what my father did and how hurt my mother sounded yesterday. Marlee, you didn't hear her. My mother feels so betrayed."

Just like I betrayed you, Susie thought as the memory of kissing Alivia came flooding back. She closed her eyes in shame.

"I'm sorry this is happening to you and your family, Susie." Susie's heart fluttered when Marlee rubbed one of Susie's bare feet with her own. "But drinking like that isn't going to help the situation."

"I know. I know. And believe me," Susie pointed to the ice pack, "I don't have any plans to drink again. Ever."

"You feel pretty shitty right now, don't you?"

Susie nodded.

"Remember this feeling when you get tempted again. Remember it when you want to escape reality. Life's tough, Susie, but you gotta find a better way to handle your shit."

Susie had never heard such harsh words from Marlee.

"I know. I know." Susie stood up and hurried toward the bathroom to hide an impending deluge of tears.

She had just put her hand on the bathroom doorknob when Sam burst back into the house, furious as hell.

"Susie Torres, what did you do? What the fuck happened to your car? Did you hit something? Did you get into an accident yesterday? Did you hurt someone, Susie? Did you?" Sam was nose-to-nose with Susie.

156

"No, I didn't." Susie put both hands up in defense. "I swear. I didn't have an accident."

"Oh, no? Then explain this." Sam thrust her phone in Susie's face. It was a picture of the passenger side of Susie's Toyota. A scrape about a foot high ran the entire length. The headlight was busted, too.

"I don't know. I don't know." *Dios*, what if she had hurt somebody? Susie got lightheaded and felt hands grab at her as she fell to the floor.

Chapter Sixteen
Nothing to Say

Susie was both bummed and excited when Monday rolled around. Mid-winter break was over, which meant softball was starting right after school in the upstairs gym. Susie hoped they could get out on the actual field soon because doing workouts inside sucked. She shuffled toward the cafeteria, not looking forward to seeing Alivia or Karl. She hadn't spoken to them since that fateful day. She was even dreading seeing Sam. She'd made a complete ass out of herself in front of Marlee, Sam, and Lisa by getting so blitzed and then so sick. The shame of that was like a tangible thing torturing her soul. Susie felt her friendships would survive unless Marlee's mother banned her from seeing Marlee. Susie didn't know if she would ever survive that.

And she still had no clue how her car had gotten so messed up. Sam went on Marlee's computer immediately after showing her the picture of the dents to her car. She searched police and hospital reports for any accidents on the route from Alivia's house to Marlee's. She didn't find anything. Thank God. Everyone, Susie most of all, had been relieved that Susie hadn't hurt anyone with her car. And her own mother, thankfully, hadn't seen the scrape yet. Miguel saw it and had a field day teasing her about it, but she threatened him with bodily harm if he said anything. Not that he took that threat seriously, but he'd understood it was in his own best interest that their mother not find out. In their mother's agitated state, there was no telling what would make her explode. And that was why she didn't do what Marlee's mother had asked her to. There was no way she was going to tell them she had driven drunk and wrecked her car. And there was definitely no way she was going to tell them or anyone, not even Marlee, that she had driven drunk to escape a man who had been trying to rape her. No way. If Marlee's mother called, well, then that's when she'd deal with her parents. But not before.

Susie was the first one at the lunch table and kept her head down, focusing all her attention on her lunch bag as she waited for her friends to arrive.

Sam threw her salad container on the table, "What's shakin', bacon?"

Susie mustered a smile and said, "Nothin'."

"How are you feeling?"

"*Dios*, so much better." Susie shook her head. "Thanks for..."

"No worries, Sus. We love you."

She exchanged a heartfelt glance with her friend. "Thanks. I don't know if I deserve it."

Susie wiped at the tears in her eyes, and thankfully Sam changed the subject, "Ronnie didn't make it to school today."

"Again?"

Sam shrugged. "I'm worried about him. He's missing so much school. Mr. Auerbach is getting ready to make our strings quintet into a quartet by eliminating Ronnie's double bass part."

"That's serious," Susie said. "Doesn't he realize he's only hurting himself?"

"I don't think he does. He's too engrossed in himself to think about anybody or anything else. It sucks."

Susie bit into her sandwich and almost choked when Alivia put a lingering hand on her shoulder.

"Hey, sweet thing," Alivia said. "You never texted me back. How was the rest of your break?"

"Good," Susie said, her mouth full. "But don't call me that."

Alivia sat down next to Susie, a little too close, but there was nothing Susie could do without drawing attention to it.

Karl sat on the other side of Alivia and said, "Hey, Susie, how was your hangover on Thursday?"

Susie shot a glance at Sam, but Sam vigorously shook her head to convey that she hadn't said anything to him.

"We all had massive hangovers," Alivia said and patted Susie's forearm. She rubbed her index finger back and forth over Susie's skin. As subtly as she could, Susie moved her arm under the table. "You should have seen Karl."

"Ugh," Karl said and blew out a sigh. "I couldn't even eat. Crackers, that was it."

Susie wanted to say, "Me, too," or "I know exactly how you felt," but she didn't because she didn't want comrades in her misery. She didn't want to bond over the stupid things they had done. She simply shrugged and said, "I'm fine now."

"Susie, you should have seen Dirk," Alivia said with a laugh. Susie closed her eyes at the mention of his name. "He said his head was splitting for two days."

"Oh, yeah," Karl said, "he wanted me to ask you something."

"Babe," Alivia scolded him, "I told you not to ask her. She has a girlfriend."

"I know that, but I have to tell Dirk I asked, or he'll give me shit."

"Ask her what?" Sam said.

Karl turned to Susie and said, "Dirk wants to ask you out. He said you were sending out signs or, what did he call it, babe?"

"Vibes," Alivia said, making air quotes. "Susie, Dirk said you were sending him vibes. Which I totally don't believe."

Vibes? Dirk? Susie's brain shut down. She couldn't listen anymore. Silently she stood up and picked up her backpack. Without making eye contact, without saying a word, she turned from the table and headed toward one of the cafeteria doors. Numb, she opened the door and closed it gently behind her. Blessedly, the hallway was empty. She thought about getting in her car and driving a thousand miles away. But she couldn't. She had softball.

"Fuck!" she muttered and headed toward her next class. Karl's words echoed in her head. *Dirk wants to ask you out.* Without thinking, Susie punched a bulletin board as she passed by. Pain shot up her hand, but she ignored it. Just like she was going to ignore Dirk's very existence.

The mere attempt *not* to think about something made it manifest. She relived his weight on her body, his hands rubbing her roughly, his tongue—

A sob escaped before she could stop it. She punched a locker and enjoyed the sound of the denting metal. Her hand throbbed delightfully.

"Whoa, Susie, are you okay?"

Damn. Ms. Armstrong had seen her punch the locker and now had a full view of sad-sack Susie desperately trying to keep her world right side up.

"Oh, my God, Susie," her AP Enviro teacher said, rushing over, "you're upset. Let's go to my office. Let's talk about it." She went back and held the door open to the science lab office.

When Susie hesitated, her teacher said, "It's okay. No one's in here. I was just heading over to set up for class, but we have time."

The last thing Susie wanted was to get yelled at by her teacher for hitting a locker.

"I'm okay. Thanks," she said and headed down the hallway.

"You're not okay, young lady," her teacher said. "C'mon, humor me." When Susie stopped walking, she added, "Really, I just want to know what that locker ever did to you."

Susie smiled.

"Atta girl, c'mon. Let's chat, shall we?"

Susie nodded and followed her teacher into the science department's lab office.

"Have a seat." Ms. Armstrong gestured toward her desk chair and went to sit in another teacher's chair.

Susie sat but said nothing. A text dinged on her phone. She glanced at it. Sam. Probably wanting to know where she was.

"What's up?" Ms. Armstrong prodded.

"Nothing." Susie folded her arms across her chest.

"Listen, you don't have to tell me anything, but something's got you upset. How's your mom doing? Didn't she have an accident recently?"

"She's fine," Susie said and looked away. But her mother wasn't fine, and neither were any of the people in her family. Her gaze took in the pictures on her teacher's desk. Ms. Armstrong and a dog. A college graduation photo of her teacher and two people that were probably her parents. No boyfriend, Susie thought. Interesting. Another text dinged. Alivia this time. She ignored that one, too.

"I'm glad your mom is fine. So why are you upset?"

Susie rolled her eyes and then closed them. She put her elbow on the desk and covered both eyes with a hand. "Nothing happened," Susie found herself saying. She looked up at her teacher. Ms. Armstrong nodded in encouragement. Susie continued. "This guy, he was drunk. I was drunk…"

"Susie, what happened?"

"Nothing happened. Nothing."

"You were both drunk…"

"Mm hmm." Her voice was high and tight. She didn't want to relive the details but, in between sobs, found herself spilling out every sordid one to her teacher.

"Susie, you have to press charges."

Susie bolted upright. "No, I don't. Nothing happened."

"Something very much happened, Susie. He touched you, and it was unwanted. That's called sexual assault. And actually, it sounds like attempted rape, too."

"You can't tell my mother."

Her teacher sighed and said, "That's the least of your worries, Susie."

"Nothing happened. And besides, I'm eighteen."

"Doesn't matter. You are an East Valley High School student, and you're in our care."

"It didn't happen on school property. He doesn't even go to this school. He doesn't go to any school."

Her teacher remained quiet, a concerned expression on her face. After a while, she said, "Softball starts today, doesn't it?"

Susie nodded.

"I know Coach Gellar," Ms. Armstrong said. "She's kind of serious about softball, isn't she?"

Susie laughed. "She's serious about a lot of things."

Ms. Armstrong laughed. "That is very true, Susie. Very true." She took a moment and then said, "Answer my next question honestly, okay? Is this guy in your life? Do you see him on a regular basis? I mean, will you be able to avoid him?"

"I think so."

"You think so, but you don't know so."

Susie hadn't thought about it. Dirk lived in East Valley.

"It's fine. I know how to avoid him." As the words came out of her mouth, she realized she had no idea how to avoid him. He could find her easily. He thought they had some kind of connection. An idea dawned on her. Maybe, yeah, maybe he was trying to cover his own ass. Make it seem like she'd led him on and initiated the whole thing. That realization made her even madder. Shit, she needed to get behind this thing. Now. Otherwise, no one, not even Marlee, would believe her.

"What happened just now?" her teacher asked. "Your face changed."

"I think I need help, Ms. Armstrong."

"Atta girl."

Her teacher made a phone call and, before long, said, "Okay, kid, you're on your way to see Dr. Austin."

"The school psychologist?"

Her teacher nodded.

"When?"

"I'm walking you over there right now."

"Now? But I have a class. I have *your* class."

"And this, Susie, is so much more important than that. I'll make sure Sam or Karl—"

"Not Karl."

"Okay, not Karl, but I'll make sure Sam gets you the notes."

Another text from Sam dinged on her phone, but Susie ignored it. She held down the power button and shut the phone off.

"Don't tell Sam where I am. Tell her, uh, tell her I wasn't feeling well and went to the nurse's office."

Susie was relieved when her teacher nodded.

They stood up and walked toward the guidance counselors' wing, and within minutes, Susie found herself shaking hands with Dr. Austin.

~~~

It was almost three o'clock, and there was only a half hour left to the first softball practice of the year. Susie's meeting with Dr. Austin had gone well, and not only was Susie relieved to get some of it off her chest, but the entire incident with Dirk was also officially on the record. And somehow, Dr. Austin got her to talk about her family

165

troubles. It felt good to vent about her father's infidelity and the effect on her and the rest of her family. The psychologist said that since Susie was eighteen, it was completely her own choice whether to press charges against the young man—that's what she kept calling him, the young man. Susie wanted her to call him the jerk, the asshole, the scourge of the earth, but she didn't. Dr. Austin said that if Susie wanted to talk again, her door was always open. Susie thanked the psychologist just as the bell rang to end sixth period, and she headed to her seventh-period Ethics class. Good. She hadn't had to see Karl or Sam during AP Enviro.

It was hard to avoid Sam at practice, so Susie gave her the Spark Notes version of her lie. She told Sam that she left the cafeteria because she didn't feel good and ran into Ms. Armstrong in the hallway, who then insisted she go to the nurse. She reassured Sam that she was fine, just tired.

Trying to get a decent workout in the gym was hard, but Coach Gellar did her best to keep the team moving and working hard. Susie's prediction about a zillion squats had been correct. Her leg muscles were already aching, and she was exhausted.

Sam and the infielders were on the bigger side of the partition, fielding ground balls off the gym floor, while Susie and the outfielders were hitting off the pitching machine in the smaller section. While Katie fed balls into the machine and Dara hit, Susie waited on the sidelines for her turn. This gave her lots of time to think. She couldn't stop her thoughts from going to her fake ID. She still hadn't used it, and there was this family-owned deli at the edge of town. It was kind of run down, and Karl said they didn't look at IDs very hard. Maybe she could stop there on her way home and replenish her supply of

Saranac Ale. Or maybe she'd try something new. Or, a little voice in her brain said, she could go directly home after practice.

"Your turn, Susie," Katie said.

Oh good, Susie thought. She didn't have to acknowledge that small voice in her head. After helping the other outfielders scoop up the rubber pitching machine balls and put them back into the feeder bin, Susie pulled her bat out of her bag and took a few practice swings. It felt good. She stepped into the makeshift batters' box made from masking tape on the gym floor. She tapped her helmet and made sure it fit snugly. She hadn't worn it since their last summer softball game.

From behind a screen, Katie held up a ball, so Susie could see it and then fed it into the machine. As it spit out toward her, the familiar whir of the ball livened Susie's soul. She stepped forward, swiveled her hips, and ripped the ball into the hanging partition.

"Yeah," she yelled, "that felt good." She nodded at Katie for another.

She had a singular focus—smashing the crap out of every ball Katie fed into that machine. She smashed ball after ball into the partition, making it vibrate.

A shrill sound of a whistle broke her reverie. Coach Gellar's big booming voice echoed in the gym, "Who's destroying my gym in here?"

"Who else?" Katie said with glee throwing Susie under the bus immediately. "Number seven, Susie Torres."

"It figures. Nice job, Torres," Coach Gellar said. She was old school with her red and black East Valley warm-up suit, a whistle around her neck, and the giant ring of keys on her belt loop. "How about going to right field for a while?" She pointed toward the cement

167

block wall on the opposite side of the gym. "That way, I can hear myself think on the other side."

"You got it, Coach." Susie turned back to her teammate and said, "Fire it up, Katie."

Katie fed Susie what she needed. The ability to take out her pent-up energy and unleash it on her surroundings felt so good she never wanted to stop. That poor concrete wall didn't know what hit it.

As she beat the hell out of the pitching machine balls, the small voice came back. It asked her if she thought she had a drinking problem. "No problem here," she muttered out loud. To herself, she said, "I'm hitting the shit out of these balls. If I had a drinking problem, I wouldn't be able to do that."

Coach Gellar's whistle blew to end the practice just as Katie fed the last ball into the machine. Susie dug deep and swung with everything she had, yelling, "I do *not* have a problem."

The small voice in her head had no response.

Chapter Seventeen
Take You Down with Them

Susie and her friends stood chatting in the lobby of Clarksonville Community College Student Union. Susie and Marlee held hands, and so far, everything between them seemed reasonably normal. Susie was on pins and needles, though, hoping Marlee wouldn't change her mind and break up with her. As each day went by, Susie had been resting easier, mainly because Marlee's mother still hadn't called her parents about driving drunk on that day she'd rather forget. Every day Susie held her breath when she got home from school, afraid that Marlee's mother had called. Then it wouldn't be a matter of *if* her own mother would crucify her, but how. Hopefully, tonight would not be that night.

Susie stood back and listened to her friends talk after the youth group meeting. This had been a good day. She got caught up in AP Enviro using Sam's notes, and Ronnie kept them laughing at lunchtime about a college visit over the weekend he'd taken with Jordan. Apparently, the students at Millson College, a small private college in New Hampshire, didn't know what to do with two guys holding hands on their campus. Leave it to Ronnie to escalate their discomfort by kissing Jordan every chance he got. Not that Jordan minded in the slightest. And softball that afternoon had been good, too. She'd felt strong and even managed to impress Coach Gellar with her sprints. Impressing Coach Gellar was a difficult thing to do. Many tried, few succeeded. But apparently, Susie had gotten faster since last year. And dinner at home had even been civil. Almost pleasant. Of course, her father wasn't home. He'd be home tomorrow. That's when life would be miserable again.

Marlee said to Ronnie, "I can't believe you guys are starting a choir."

"A *gay* choir, dearie!" Ronnie said.

"Filled with gay boys and gay girls," Jordan added. "You can be in it, Marlee."

"Nah, I don't think so. But Susie's a good singer."

Surprised to be dragged into the conversation, Susie blushed and denied any singing ability at all.

"She's being modest. She always sings with the radio, and she's really good." The look in Marlee's eye conveyed nothing but love. Susie blushed but shook her head, denying any truth to Marlee's words.

"Since we're all going off to college soon," Ronnie said, "we wanted to leave a legacy, you know?"

The gravity of his words must have hit everybody because their section of the lobby grew quiet. It was then that Susie realized they wouldn't have too many more of these moments with Ronnie and Jordan. As soon as they all graduated in June, except for Lisa, they'd be heading off in different directions. The thought was kind of sobering.

"Hey, listen, kids," Sam said, breaking the silence. "Lisa and I are going to take off. We're going off the grid for an hour."

"Ooh, hot lesbian love," Ronnie teased.

Sam had no comeback whatsoever because, apparently, that was precisely what their plans were. The blush on Lisa's face confirmed it. Susie understood their urgency because Lisa was the only one in the group with a hard curfew, so they didn't have much time. And when it was time for Lisa to go home, Marlee had to go too since they drove to the meetings together.

They said their goodbyes and headed to the parking lot together. Sam and Lisa drove off in Sam's sports car, and Susie and Marlee were about to get into Marlee's van when Susie said, "Hey, Ronnie."

"Yes, doll?" Susie smacked him on the arm good-naturedly. "What do you want me to call you? Butch? 'Cuz you are kind of butch with all those muscles."

Marlee rubbed Susie's arm over her coat, "Mmm, I love all these muscles."

"Aww," Jordan said, "you two are so cute. I'm glad you found each other."

Susie caught the love in Marlee's glance, and her heart melted. "Me, too," they said at the same time. Susie wanted to kiss Marlee senseless, but it would be sort of rude to do so in front of the guys, so she asked Ronnie the question she'd started to ask.

"So, are you going to Millson College?"

Ronnie burst out laughing. "God, no. They have a good theater arts program, but everyone's still in the closet there. Look, I already broke in one school as to the existence of lavender people, but I don't think I'm up for another. I just want to live."

Heads nodded in their group of four. "There was a little scandalous talk going around Clarksonville for a while," Marlee said.

171

"I think Lisa had it harder than I did. The bitches in the junior class are bad."

"Queen bitches?" Ronnie suggested with a laugh.

"Yeah, pretty much."

"Hey, Jordan," Susie said, rubbing her arms in the evening chill, "Where are you going to college? Or don't you know yet?"

"Sir Jordan is going to grace Cornell with his presence next year," Ronnie said.

"You are?" Marlee said, her interest clearly piqued.

"Yep. I got my acceptance yesterday."

"Hey, you guys?" Susie interrupted. "It's getting kind of cold out here. Why don't we move this party into the van? We can all fit in the back." She turned to Marlee. "Is that okay?"

Marlee nodded and hit the unlock button on her key.

"Awesome," Ronnie said. "My mother will be so pleased to hear I spent my evening with two lovely ladies."

Susie smacked him on the arm again. He didn't protest because he knew he deserved it.

"Hey," Jordan said, "let me just get my cooler from my car. We're doing Belgian Beats tonight."

"What're Belgian Beats?" Susie asked as she climbed into the back of the van behind Marlee.

"Belgian Wheat Ale. You'll like it, stud. You'll like it." Ronnie smacked her lightly on the arm and followed Jordan to his car.

Within minutes they climbed into the back of the van, lugging a huge cooler laden with iced-down bottles of beer. Dread spread across Susie's core. Here was temptation staring her right in the face. She watched with rapt attention as Ronnie popped the top off a beer and then plunked an orange slice in the bottle. Her brain warred with itself over whether to have one or to be a party pooper and abstain. The decision was made for her when Susie found her hand reaching for the bottle Ronnie offered. Susie didn't dare look at Marlee, afraid of the expression she'd see there.

Instead, Susie said, "Thanks, Ronnie. I'm going to have this one, and that's it. Just one." The last two words were pretty much a command to herself. "We have school tomorrow."

Ronnie raised an expressive eyebrow. "That never stops us, does it, sweet lips?"

Jordan leaned over and kissed Ronnie. "Nope."

"Isn't he cute?" Ronnie said. "I just love him." Ronnie pulled Jordan into a kiss so passionate it was almost embarrassing.

Susie covered Marlee's eyes with one hand and said, "Guys, you're blinding us."

The guys broke their kiss and laughed.

Ronnie popped open another beer and tucked an orange slice in it. "My princess," he said and handed the beer to Marlee.

"No thanks, Ronnie," Marlee said, making no move to grab the beer. "I'm driving." Her words had no overt judgment, but the message was there. Which one of them was driving? And which one of them shouldn't be drinking either?

"That's cool, my blonde goddess. That's cool." Ronnie handed the beer to Jordan and then made one for himself.

Knowing she had to make it last, Susie took the smallest of sips. The orange flavor on top of the wheat ale was positively delectable, refreshing even. "*Dios*, Ronnie, this is so good." The instant the words were out of her mouth, she regretted them. She'd told Marlee she had no plans ever to drink again, and here she was drinking less than a week after the worst hangover in her life.

"I know. Jordan's a master when it comes to finding good beers. Aren't you, my prince?"

"Mm hmm," Jordan said around the bottle at his lips.

Marlee cleared her throat and said, "So, Jordan, tell me about Cornell. Do you know what you want to major in?"

"Fine Arts," Jordan said. "They have an amazing program, and I plan to do a semester in Rome."

"With that red hair of yours, Jordan, you're going to send those Italian studs into a tailspin," Susie said with a wink.

"Unless I go with him," Ronnie said and linked arms with Jordan possessively. "They'll have to get through me first."

"As if that would be a hardship for you," Susie teased.

"Oh, it'd be hard, all right," Ronnie shot back.

"Ronnie, please," Susie scolded. "My ears are sensitive." She wasn't sure how comfortable Marlee was with Ronnie's sexual banter, so she said, "Marlee's thinking about Cornell, too." And as she heard her own words, she realized that if Jordan had already received his letter from Cornell, Marlee must have received one, too. She looked up at Marlee with a questioning expression.

But Marlee simply deflected the question in Susie's eyes and said, "Rockville University has a great engineering program, and I might be able to get a softball scholarship there. It might only be partial, but it'll help."

Her words spoke volumes. Money. Cornell would be out of reach for Marlee financially. It made Susie sad but happy at the same time.

She hoped to go to Rockville with both Marlee and Sam in the fall. If she got in, that is. If.

Jordan and Ronnie talked about their college plans, and then the conversation returned to the Youth Alliance choir they were trying to set up.

Susie picked up her beer and pressed the tip to her lips. She pretended to take a small sip as if nursing it. Truth be told, the delectable citrus-flavored wheat beer was long gone. Susie had devoured it in the first five minutes. Ronnie caught on to her little ruse and raised a questioning eyebrow. Susie simply shrugged and turned her attention back to Marlee, who was fully engaged in telling Jordan a story about playing the bass while Sam played the violin.

Ronnie plunked an orange slice in a newly opened bottle of beer and slid it behind Susie's leg when Marlee wasn't looking. Susie shot him a grateful look. Ronnie knew what she needed. It had been pure torture watching the guys drink freely while she couldn't.

For Susie, the evening turned into small sips when Marlee was watching and big gulps when she wasn't. Ronnie kept her set up, and she was feeling fine. Mighty fine. A beautiful blissful buzz took over her body. She could stay in this space all night. Her buzz kept back the realities of life, so she was free to feel the good things it had to offer.

"Ooh," Jordan said to Ronnie. "You've got a piece of orange pulp on your lip."

Ronnie reached to his lip. "Where?"

"I'll get it." Jordan waggled his eyebrows at Susie and Marlee and then practically leaped on top of Ronnie. Ronnie had no choice but to fall back, Jordan on top. Jordan kissed Ronnie passionately, and Ronnie responded with equal enthusiasm. Susie turned to Marlee and, seeing the passion reflected in her eyes, drew her into a kiss. Within moments, the sounds of their own kissing drowned out the passion of her friends a mere foot away.

Marlee responded feverishly to Susie's kisses and added a moan to the mix. Susie smiled as she kissed her luscious girlfriend. Marlee felt comfortable enough in front of the guys to let her desire show.

Clearly turned on, Marlee straddled Susie's lap and whispered, "I love you, Susie Torres."

"I love you back, Marlee McAllister."

Marlee nuzzled Susie's neck for a while, sending delicious swirls to every part of Susie's body. Susie groaned when the warmth of Marlee's lips moved away from her neck, but she was soon rewarded with Marlee's soft, eager lips on her own. Her tongue dipped between Susie's lips, eager but slow, exploring. "You taste like oranges," Marlee whispered. Susie let out a moan of her own and pulled Marlee closer to her. It sucked having to share space in the van. Marlee's hand reached under Susie's shirt. Susie moaned in encouragement.

Susie jumped when a fist pounded on the door she was leaning on.

"Hey, lovebirds," Sam said. "It's time to go."

A collective groan rose up from the four teenagers.

"Worst timing in the world, Samantha Rose," Ronnie said, sitting up.

"What're you guys doing in there?" Sam said with a laugh.

"Oh, geez," Lisa added. "Look at this. We could have just stayed here, eh?"

"No kidding." Sam pounded on the door again. "C'mon. Open up. Lisa has to go."

The gang moaned again but did as bidden. Cold air rushed into the van as Sam opened the sliding door.

"Holy shit, you guys," Sam said. "It smells like a brewery in here." She and Lisa took in the scene. Beer bottles lay everywhere in the van. Collectively the three of them had drunk more than a twelve pack. "You guys," she said again, clearly exasperated. "What did you do?"

"Lighten up, fiddler," Ronnie said, using the character name she'd had in a play they'd been in together. He smacked Jordan on the chest. "Hey, I have the best idea. It's brilliant. It came to me just now."

Susie grinned at how stinking drunk Ronnie was. She hadn't realized it until she saw how unsteady he seemed to be.

"What's this great idea?" Sam said, her arms folded across her chest.

"St. Patrick's Day party! My house. Two Saturdays from now," Ronnie nodded once to finalize the announcement.

Jordan pushed Ronnie in the chest, "Great idea, lover. We can have green beer. No, wait," he seemed to rethink it. "We can have beers in green bottles and cans. Like Heineken, Becks, Stella Artois."

"Dos Equis, Carlsburg, Rolling Rock," Ronnie added.

Jordan took up the list. "St. Pauli Girl."

"Good one," Ronnie said. "How about Mickey's Malt Liquor?"

"Genny Cream Ale," Susie offered, which earned her a glare from Sam.

"C'mon, you guys," Sam said. "Lisa has to get home. We *all* have to get home. School tomorrow?"

When they didn't move, Sam barked, "C'mon, clean up this van and get out, out, out!" She turned to Marlee. "You haven't been drinking, have you?"

"No, she has not," Susie said. "Don't be silly, Sam." She laughed, joined quickly by Ronnie and Jordan because they'd heard it, too. "Silly Sam. Did you hear that, Silly Sam? That's your name from now on."

A chorus of "Silly Sams" rose from the drunks in the van.

"Oh, my God, Sus." Sam's hands went to her hips. "I don't believe you. You're drunk, too." It wasn't a question.

"No-o," Susie singsonged the word. She snuck a peek at Marlee, whose face had fallen. They had truly pulled it off. Marlee had no clue that Susie had had more than one beer, and, honestly, Susie had no clue how many she'd actually had. Enough to make her words slur and her vision fuzzy, that was for sure.

Marlee glared at Susie. "I thought you were done with all this." She gestured to the empty bottles strewn all over her van. "It surprised me when you had one. You lied to me, Susie. You all did." The hurt expression on Marlee's face tore at Susie's heart.

"Sorry," Susie said and hung her head.

"Sorry ain't cuttin' it right now, Sus," Sam said. "Guys, get your acts together and get out of this van."

"Spoilsport," Ronnie said and closed the lid to the cooler when Susie dropped the last of her empties in it.

Sam said, "Marlee, I'm not sure what we're gonna do here. There's no way in heaven or hell that I'm letting either of these two fools drive. As far as that fool goes," she gestured to Susie, "she just might have to spend the night at my house. That'll solve the problem of her mother."

"Sam, how are we going to do this?" Lisa asked with a sigh. "I mean, your car is a two-seater. You can't fit more than one other person."

"I know. We have a problem. If I take you home, then even though Marlee has the room, I don't want her driving a bunch of drunks all the way to East Valley and then driving back home. She has to go to school tomorrow too, and this drinking jag?" Her eyes shot daggers at Susie. "This wasn't Marlee's fault; she shouldn't have to suffer because of it." Sam sighed and said, "I guess I could drive them all home in Jordan's car, but I don't want to leave my Mercedes here all night."

"And, Sam, why should *you* suffer?" Marlee chimed in. "Other people made bad choices, not you."

"Exactly," Sam said.

"Still here, girls?" a voice called out from the roadway.

"Uh, oh," Ronnie groaned loudly, voicing what Susie felt. Anne, the adult sponsor of the Rainbow Alliance Group, sat idling in her car.

"Hey, Anne," Sam said and walked over to Anne's car.

They spoke in hushed tones until Anne parked and walked up to the group. She took command immediately.

"So, here's how it's going to go. Marlee's driving Lisa home. No problem there. But boys? You're with me. I'm driving you both home and having an in-depth conversation with your parents. Jordan's car will be having a sleepover in the parking lot of Clarksonville CC tonight."

Ronnie and Jordan groaned. Marlee, Sam, and Lisa looked like they had no sympathy for either of them. Susie didn't know Jordan's home life that well, but it would probably be the first time Ronnie had ever had any kind of parental discipline. Susie had the feeling that Ronnie had his parents totally fooled as to his drinking ways.

"And, Susie," Anne continued, "you're with Sam for now, but I will be calling your parents as soon as I've taken care of these two. This," she twirled her finger around, indicating the van and the cooler of beers, "will never happen again. The entire youth group will be signing conduct agreements at our very next meeting." She glared at the three drunk teenagers. Her voice broke when she said, "Do you know how stupid this was?"

All three of them lowered their heads and said, "Yes, ma'am," kind of in unison. Susie felt like a child getting scolded. And it was immensely embarrassing in front of her friends.

"Ronnie, Jordan, Susie?" Anne looked at each one in turn. "I could lose my job over this." Anne looked directly at Susie when she spoke as if she expected more from her than the two guys. "You're better than this. You all are."

Susie's heart clenched. She hadn't even thought about anything like that. "I'm sorry, Anne. I just…" Susie wanted to explain how drinking sent her to a fuzzy place where she didn't have to deal with anything but knew she couldn't find the right words in her present state, so she simply apologized again.

"Sorry, Anne," Marlee said. "I didn't know how to get them to stop. I didn't realize it was getting so out of hand."

"Thank you, Marlee. You shouldn't have to police your friends. Just realize that when drinkers want to drink, they find a way. Don't let them take you down with them."

Susie felt so bad. Was she taking Marlee down with her? She sighed and let Sam help her out of the van and into the small Mercedes. Once seated with her seatbelt fastened, she realized Marlee hadn't kissed her goodbye.

Chapter Eighteen
Shattered

Susie groaned as she swam up from the abyss Wednesday morning. Sam was shaking her shoulder and telling her it was time to get up. Susie had to work around her headache and blurry vision to figure out where the hell she was. She didn't know if she was dragging ass because she'd slept on the stiff couch in Sam's living room all night or had too many beers in too short a time. Maybe it was the head-splitting screaming she'd endured from her mother over the phone after Anne had called to rat her out. No, that wasn't fair. Anne was a caring person and did what she had to do. Susie knew it was a miracle that her mother didn't make her go home last night. Sam probably had something to do with that. Sam knew how to talk to people. Sam had her back but maybe shouldn't.

No, Susie knew the real reason she was dragging ass. The Belgian Beats had gone down way too easily. But a small part of her was excited. She'd found a beer she could really sink her teeth into.

Walking to the cafeteria that afternoon with Sam was a cold silent affair. But that had been par for the course all day. Sam hadn't said more than two words to her that morning when she'd driven Susie home before school. Somehow Susie avoided her mother and was able to shower, change, and then drive herself to school in peace. She ended up parking near Sam in the senior lot. Sam was sitting in her car talking on the phone—to Lisa, no doubt. Sam got out of her car at the same time Susie did. Susie thought they'd at least walk into the school building together, but Sam had other ideas. She took off at a pace that left Susie far behind. Susie clamped her lips in irritation but knew she had absolutely no right to be upset. She had messed up and put Marlee, Sam, and Lisa in a difficult spot. And then when Anne showed up? That sucked, but at least it took the burden off her friends. Sam had said something the night before that stuck in Susie's mind. Sam had said something about "driving a bunch of drunks around." Drunks? Is that what she was? A drunk? She'd had a couple of beers, but she used to do that easy at Christy's parties. What was the big honkin' deal? Sam had overreacted. Plain and simple.

They headed through the doors to the cafeteria, and Susie said, "I have to buy today," and didn't wait for a reply. After picking up the greasiest cheeseburger she'd ever seen in the history of East Valley High School, she headed toward their usual table but stopped short to watch the drama unfold. Ronnie set his lunch bag on the table and sat next to Sam. Without a word, Sam stood up and moved to the extreme opposite side of the table. Apparently, Ronnie knew Sam well enough to keep his mouth shut. He simply hung his head and pulled an apple out of his bag.

Susie couldn't get her legs to move. How long was the silent treatment going to go on? As she stood there, she sensed someone move in behind her. She turned her head and smiled. Ahh, a friend.

Alivia smiled back and moved up to link elbows with her. "What's up, sweet thing?"

Susie frowned. She unwound Alivia's arm from her own and took a step away to create a reasonable amount of distance between them. "You can't call me that."

"I know. I just like to. What's up with them?" She pointed to Ronnie and Sam, sitting in stony silence.

"Sam hates us."

"Who? You and Ronnie? What'd you guys do?"

Susie gave her the summarized version of their fuck up from the night before.

"That youth group is so much fun," Alivia said. "Maybe I'll go with you guys next time, but for now, I'll sit next to you during lunch, okay?"

Susie turned to look at Alivia. Her friend may have been petite, but her friendship was huge at that moment. "Okay," Susie said as they headed to the table. Alivia sat next to Sam so Susie didn't have to. After a couple of minutes, Karl came to the table, set a lunch tray in front of Alivia, and then sat on the other side of Ronnie.

There wasn't much in the way of conversation. Alivia talked about some mundane things with Karl, but she couldn't get anybody else to join in. Nobody was in the mood. Susie shot her a grateful look for trying and got a hand on her thigh for it.

Susie had no idea what had gotten into Alivia's head, but she brushed Alivia's hand off and got a boo-boo face from Alivia for it. "Stop," Susie said under her breath, but loud enough for Alivia to hear. *Madre de Dios*, her head was pounding. Alivia's flirting was one more thing she didn't need. Susie moved her chair away and pulled her phone out to text Marlee.

Shit. What was she going to say? Knowing she'd never find the right words, she typed, "Sorry for being an idiot last night. I am not a drunk, like Sam said. I just like the taste of beer." She groaned and erased the last sentence. At a loss for how to make everything better, she added, "I love you, *mi vida*." She hit the send button and put her phone on the table face down. She didn't want anyone to see Marlee's reply because it might not have been kind.

She looked up to find Ronnie trying to catch her eye. With head gestures and facial expressions, they had an entire conversation conveying how royally pissed Sam was at them.

When the bell rang to end lunch, Susie checked her phone. No response from Marlee. She hadn't expected one. She didn't deserve one.

Ronnie and Susie let Sam storm off first, and then Ronnie burst, "Oh, my God. Why does that girl have so much power over us?"

Susie followed his gaze to Sam's retreating back. "It's in her blood. They're not the wealthy East Valley Paytons for nothing."

"Jesus, I've never felt more guilty in my life," Ronnie said as they walked out of the cafeteria. "I'm supposedly grounded for a week."

"Me, too, except I can drive myself to school and back after softball."

"For how long?" Ronnie said. They stopped outside Susie's AP Enviro class.

"The rest of my life, I think."

"Guess what?"

"What?"

"My parents still said I can have my St. Patrick's Day party."

"No way." Susie was amazed. Yeah, Ronnie got away with everything.

"I expect you and your lovely girlfriend to be there. Okay, stud?"

She didn't even punch him in the arm for calling her that. In fact, she kind of liked it. "I'll do my best," she told him. Even if her parents let her go to the party, Susie wasn't sure she would be able to convince Marlee to go.

Classes dragged by, and her energy waned. And if getting yelled at by Coach Gellar for two solid hours had been one of her life's goals, then her life would have been complete. Because she'd been dragging ass all day, she had absolutely no energy for softball. Coach Gellar was having none of it, though, saying Susie wasn't holding up her end of the co-captain position and earned herself extra laps after practice. Susie had no choice but to swallow her pride and take her punishment in front of her teammates. Sam didn't say a word and left without saying goodbye. No big surprise there.

Susie sat in her car after the practice, not wanting to back out because backing out meant she'd be heading home. Home was where her mother and father were. Home was where all hell broke loose on a regular basis and probably had already. Her heart clenched when she pictured Miguel retreating to his room. That was how he'd been handling things. A spark of thought entered Susie's brain, the part she'd recently given free rein to. Giving the thought merit, she backed the car up and headed to Manfredi's Deli on the older side of town. She found it right next to the Army recruiting station, just where Karl told her it would be.

She stood in front of the beer cooler and almost squealed with glee when she saw the twelve-pack of Belgian Beats. She opened her wallet and was vindicated when she saw she had more than enough money. Okay, she'd be dipping into her gas money, but that was okay. She'd figure something out.

She played it so cool at the checkout counter that the Academy should have handed her an Oscar. The clerk barely glanced at her fake ID and rang her up.

"Oh, wait," Susie said. "Do you have any oranges?"

The clerk pointed to a low cooler with yogurts, granola cups, and various fruit. Apparently, that was the morning commuters' breakfast cooler. She spotted a nice colorful orange and added it to her order.

"Thanks," Susie said, her confidence soaring. She was about to hide the twelve-pack in her trunk when that free-rein part of her brain told her to put it on the passenger seat instead.

She found herself on a dirt farm trail tucked just off C.R. 62. Susie's heart felt heavy when she remembered the fun times she and Marlee had had in this private spot. Susie sighed and pulled out her phone. Still no reply from Marlee. Resigned, she popped open a bottle. Before taking her first sip, she felt that now-familiar yearning for the calm that would overtake her. Instead of sipping, she took three big gulps as if trying to anesthetize herself instantly. There it is. On her empty stomach, the beer had an almost instant effect on her body as she relaxed. Her shoulders loosened up, and she heard herself sigh. The ale by itself tasted good, really good, even without an orange slice, but since she'd bought it, she decided to plunk in a slice anyway.

The first beer went down smoothly, and as darkness fell, so did her anxiety about going home. It would be the first time she'd see her parents after Anne's phone call. One more beer ought to do the trick, she thought and popped open a second one. This one was going down just as smoothly, but she decided to take more time with it. And at this point, her mother probably knew she hadn't come straight home from practice. Her mother was probably furious. So what else was new? Susie drained the second beer and debated popping open a third but didn't. She decided to be responsible and head home. She tossed the two empties into the field and then stashed the now ten-pack into her trunk. She'd go upstairs to her room, shower, and then put on her invisible battle gear to enter the house.

Pulling into the driveway, she drove past her father's car and parked with the dented side of her car away from the house. She opened the trunk for her backpack, and that free-rein part of her brain convinced her there was no harm in grabbing three more beers for her room.

The beer she drank in the shower was so refreshing she wondered why she hadn't thought of doing it before. Of course, her rendition of the title track from the musical Oklahoma had to be worth a Grammy, at least. Hmm, maybe Marlee was right. Maybe she should join that gay choir. Buzzing to beat the band, Susie toweled off and got dressed. Steeling her nerves, she walked down the stairs and across the driveway. She stood in front of the storm door for an entire minute before her hand finally reached for the latch. Once inside, her shoes came off in the mudroom, and she entered the house.

The soft voice of her father talking to Miguel hit her ears like a thing unknown. How could he just be here, pretending he wasn't being an A-class jerk by stepping out on her mother? How could he just talk to her brother as if everything was normal? The side of her fist pounded the wall.

"Susana, is that you?" her mother called.

"Yep." Susie tensed up, expecting the yelling to begin any second. "Help me with dinner."

"Yep."

Susie shuffled into the kitchen. Her mother had actually cooked. What a surprise. Her mother pulled the casserole out of the oven and told Susie to bring the salad to the table. Whoa, her mother had made her father's favorite Caesar's salad, anchovies and all. A small hopeful light turned on in her heart. Maybe they were on the mend.

Her greeting to her father was courteous but curt. She was not a fan of his at the moment. And he had probably heard about her getting drunk the night before, and he probably wasn't a fan of hers either.

There was no mention of her drinking or staying at Sam's, and after Susie's father said grace, her mother divvied up the salad to all the plates. Susie was hungry. She hadn't realized how much. She forced herself to slow down but then took too much on her fork, dropping the entire load down the front of her shirt and onto the table. No one saw it except her brother Miguel. On a normal night, he would have pointed and laughed at her. He would have made sure everyone had seen it. But nothing in his expression conveyed mirth. Instead, all she saw was concern, as if he wanted to ask what was wrong with her. She just grinned at him and thought, three beers after practice, that's what's wrong with me, *Jefe*.

Her father's fist hit the table. "What is this *mierda*?" He held up a forkful of the Caesar's salad. "It's cut too big. I can't eat this." He threw the salad down on his plate and reached for the casserole, scooping out a significant portion.

All eyes, except Susie's father's, went to her mother. If her mother had been a cartoon character, steam would have come out of both ears. Susie did a mental countdown to the explosion. Three, two, one!

"How dare you, Eduardo! How dare you! You don't appreciate anything anyone does for you. Not me, not your kids. I, at least, tried tonight. Oh, but you appreciate Vermont, don't you? But you know what? Vermont isn't here, is it?"

For Miguel's sake, Susie was glad her mother referred to her father's mistress as "Vermont" and "it." Susie's own heart was tearing up, and she hated to think what it was doing to Miguel.

"Goes both ways, doesn't it, Isabel?" her father roared back. "I've slaved to keep this family afloat, put food on this table, heat in the winter, cars for everyone. But do I ever get thanked? No. It's always, 'Eduardo, do this,' or 'Eduardo, do that.'"

"I work, too, Eduardo. I bring in almost as much money as you do. At least I don't leave my family to have an—"

Susie stood up so fast that her chair fell into the wall behind her. "Enough!" she yelled, dragging out the last syllable. Her fist hit the table like her father's had, causing the silverware to jump. Her outburst brought the silence her soul wanted. She didn't know if it was the beer talking or what when she pointed a finger at her father and said, "You have not a single leg to stand on, Papi. I know what you have in Vermont." His shocked expression was so terrifying that she turned to look at her mother. "I heard the voicemail, Mami. Yep, that one. The one that made you faint and got you sent to the hospital. No wonder no one could figure out what happened. It was too shameful to admit your husband could do that to you."

Susie was on a roll and kept going. "Your constant fighting, bickering, and downright disrespect for each other is affecting all of us. We try to ignore it, but I'm done, you guys. I'm done pretending your yelling doesn't cut my very soul. And Miguel, he's doing his best to hide it, too, but you don't see him the way I do. He's drowning in your hate, Mami. Papi, he looks up to you. Is this the kind of man you want him to be? One that leaves his family to go to *Vermont*?"

Knowing she had probably wasted her breath, she put both hands out as if to ward off any kind of verbal response they might have made. She backed away from the table and headed to the front door. Silence followed her. "I'm done," she said with finality and slammed the front door behind her. She grabbed her shoes and walked across the cold driveway barefoot. She made sure both the downstairs door and the door to her room were locked.

Once inside, she grabbed a beer she'd stashed in her closet. Without bothering with the orange slice, she chugged the whole thing down. Anger squeezed her very veins as she threw the empty bottle at the wall by the door. It smashed into a hundred pieces all over her hand weights. She leaped to her feet and reached for anything else she could find. When her fingers found her rock collection, she didn't hesitate. She threw rock after rock from her precious collection at the wall, watching them bounce off or break. Her fingers grabbed something smooth. Her rose quartz, the one her father had given her. Anger boiled up from the soles of her feet as she reached back for a mighty throw from deep left field to the catcher behind home plate. The quartz hit the wall with so much force that it shattered on impact. And then her heart shattered right along with it.

Chapter Nineteen
Too Angry to Cry

With great effort, Susie opened one eye. She slammed it shut instantly. Five-thirty? In the morning? What the hell? Why was she awake forty-five minutes before her alarm? Both eyes flew open when an urgent pounding on the downstairs door broke the morning stillness. An adrenaline spike made her head pound.

"Get up, Susana!" Susie's mother's voice was shrill. "Get down here now."

Susie tried to answer, but her mouth was pasted shut. She worked frantically to get saliva so she could speak.

"Yes, Mami," Susie finally yelled toward the stairs. She sat up and put a hand to her throbbing head. "I'm coming."

She opened the door to her room and peered down the stairs. Her mother stood in the darkness. "Move your car on the street to block the driveway."

"Okay, Mami. Let me find my keys."

"Do it now, Susana!" The door slammed shut before the last word had finished reaching Susie's ears.

Susie took a deep breath, trying to clear her head.

Block the driveway? Okay. You never questioned what Isabella Maria de Fatima Torres told you to do. You simply did it. Susie took about ten seconds to use the bathroom, take a sip of water, and slip shoes on. She found her coat thrown over the weight bench. Her keys would be in the pocket. She cried a little when she saw her rock collection smashed to pieces on the floor.

Her head pounded with every step she took down the stairs. *Dios*, her mouth tasted like fertilizer. Pasty fertilizer. Citrusy pasty fertilizer. Why hadn't she brushed her teeth? Gack.

Sadness ripped her heart open when she saw that her father's car was gone. Numb, she blindly did as her mother ordered. As she maneuvered the car, she realized what her mother was making her do—blocking her father from coming back. What was happening? Fully sober and wide awake now, Susie sat in the driver's seat, tempted to drive away and let her parents fight it out among themselves. How dare her mother use her this way? Susie just might have left if it wasn't for Miguel. With a frustrated sigh, she got out of her car and walked back to her room to brush her teeth and down two Advil. Since there was no chance of going back to sleep, she got dressed for school.

She ran a hand over Marlee's Clarksonville sweatshirt and put it on. It was her way of giving herself a much needed but completely undeserved hug from Marlee. She needed strength to face whatever she was about to endure in the house.

She almost panicked when she couldn't find her backpack. She wanted to stash it in her car for a potential speedy getaway. Where the hell was it? She always put it on or by her desk. Oh, right. She had completely blown off doing homework last night. Her bag lay unopened by the door, covered with shattered rocks.

She grabbed her pack, put her winter coat back on, and headed for her car. Serious thoughts of driving off gripped her, but she couldn't. That's precisely what her father had done—left without dealing with anything.

Susie put her backpack in the car and turned toward the house. A second-floor screen flew down and landed on the driveway. Thinking a gust of wind had knocked it loose, she walked over to pick it up and got pelted from above with a shower of clothes. Her father's clothes. Susie looked up just in time to see her mother getting ready to toss out another load. Susie scrambled out of the way just in time.

This shit was getting real. Her mother was either throwing her father out of the house, or he was leaving on his own. Either way, life as she'd known it was over.

Without bothering to take off her shoes, Susie headed into the house, trying to make as little noise as possible. She didn't want her mother to know she was there in case she was ordered to throw her father's stuff out the window or something. That she would not do. This feud was between them, and she wanted nothing to do with it. She went into stealth mode as she made her way to her brother's room. She knocked lightly, praying her mother didn't hear, and opened the door.

What she saw broke her heart. Miguel was sitting on the floor in the farthest corner of the room with his hands over his ears. She shut the door behind her and went to him. He whimpered when she touched his shoulder.

"It's just me, Miguel." Susie slid down the wall to sit next to him.

In the distance, they heard their mother muttering as she gathered anything associated with their father and tossed it out the window. "Good riddance," she bellowed, "out with the old."

The one that made Miguel whimper again was when their mother said, "I hope you rot in hell, Eduardo."

"Dude," Susie said to her brother, "we just have to ride out this storm."

A blare of a car horn sounded on the street. Susie's ears perked up. Shit, that must be her father. The Torres Family wasn't going to go down in flames quietly, was it? Nope, apparently, the entire North Country of New York State had to hear it.

"Miguel, I'm going to check on *Abuelita*, okay?" She patted him on the shoulder as she stood up.

He nodded and looked up at her with petrified eyes that seemed to ask her what was happening.

She had no answer for him. "You just hang here in your room for a while, okay? It's probably safest." This time he didn't nod. He simply hung his head and closed his eyes. He hadn't uttered a single word the entire time she had been in his room.

The door to her *abuelita's* bedroom was wide open. Was *Abuelita* as scared and confused as Miguel? She knocked on the open door, walked in, and gasped. Everything was gone. Susie threw open the closet door. Except for a few wire hangers, it was empty. The dresser revealed the same. There were no pictures, hairbrush, clock, or books on the bedside stand.

Susie sat down hard on the bed, her knees weak. Her headache re-announced itself like the beat of a bass drum as she took in the emptiness. She ran a hand over the comforter and realized the bed had been made as if her *abuelita* was going to come back. Tears choked her throat as she said, "*Abuelita*, where are you? Am I ever going to see you again?"

She struggled to get herself together. She had to be calm when she went in to tell Miguel that their *abuelita* was gone. She would rather be the bearer of that bad news than have him find out the way she did.

She inhaled to a count of seven, held it for the same, and exhaled. Resigned to her duty, she stood up and returned to his room. As she told him, he nodded that he understood.

Susie would have hunkered down with him for as long as the battle raged on outside his room, but her father was pounding on the front door. "Susie, get out here and move that car," he yelled for all of North America to hear.

With a sigh, she stood up and left her brother to himself. She'd left the front door unlocked. Why hadn't he just come in? It was probably right at that very moment, with all hell breaking loose around her, that she understood. Her father was leaving for good. He was a stranger here. He had no right to enter the house.

She opened the front door, and her father grabbed her by the arm and yanked her into the driveway.

"What the hell happened to your car?" he demanded, his eyes flashing in anger.

She looked at him, not knowing if he deserved an answer. The rented moving truck idling in the street told her everything she already knew. He was leaving. For good.

"Go to her, Eduardo," Susie's mother taunted from the upstairs window. "Go to your little whore in Vermont."

Her father closed his eyes in exasperation and then calmly demanded her keys.

Susie reached into her coat pocket and handed them over.

She watched him stomp up the driveway to her car and move it further down the street. He then jumped in the truck and backed it down the drive. He seemed calm as he moved around the yard, stuffing his clothes into plastic bags.

As much as Susie wanted to hide in Miguel's room with him, she couldn't take her eyes off her father as he calmly took things from the garage—his golf clubs, tools, tool chest, and a myriad of other things. He was moving out. Her numb brain tried to make sense of it but couldn't.

Her mother yelled from the open bedroom window, "Don't let him steal things, Susie. Go in there and watch him."

Susie didn't move.

"Move!" The sonic boom of her mother's voice made her feet move independently.

Once in the garage, she headed to the back wall so her mother couldn't see her from the upstairs bedroom window. She sat on her favorite garage stool and pressed her fingers at her temples to quiet her raging headache. She had absolutely no intention of getting involved with anything her father put in the truck. She took in her father's unshaven and haggard face. It looked as if he hadn't slept all night. And, it dawned on her that he probably hadn't. Maybe the yelling had gone on all night or something. She had basically passed out after she'd stormed out of the house. Ha. What luck. She hadn't heard a thing.

Maybe that's how he'd been able to move *Abuelita* out so fast. Poor Miguel, Susie thought, her heart breaking. His room was in between *Abuelita's* and the stairs. He must have heard everything all night long. No wonder he looked so traumatized.

Susie steeled her chin and glared at her father. Let him take anything he wanted. She had her car and could grab a few clothes to go live with Marlee or Sam, or she could live in her car in the high school parking lot. It didn't matter. She would figure out a way to take care of herself.

But why should she have to? Anger boiled inside her. How dare they take this away from her. They had no right. She leaped off the stool and grabbed the handles of the lawn mower. She wheeled it around the junk on the floor toward the moving truck. Her father intercepted her.

"No, Susie, no." He glanced at the window where her mother held court, tossing out occasional items. "You can't help me. Your mother will disown you. You know that's true. You're eighteen."

Susie's eyes glared at him, but she knew that he was probably one hundred percent right.

"I know you hate me right now, *Mariposita*, but this is something I have to do. I'll be back to see you. Both of you. You're my daughter, Susie. I want to see you grow up and ..."

"What a big man," Susie's mother yelled down. "Do it. Walk away from your commitments. Walk away from your family, from your children. Walk away from your promises, big stud."

He groaned and said softly, "You need this lawnmower here at the house, Susie. I'm not taking everything. I'm just taking what your mother would sell on eBay once I'm gone."

Susie softened her grip on the mower and then let go. Without a word, she looked away from him, picked her way out of the garage, and returned to her room.

Lying on the bed with the lights off, Susie said, "Mami? Papi? You didn't even try." She swallowed around the growing lump in her throat, too angry to cry.

Chapter Twenty
Going Under

Susie barely heard any of her teachers in her morning classes. Thank God none of them called on her because she would have answered each one with a blank stare. Her headache had lessened as the morning wore on, but her heartache had not. Before leaving for school, she lay on her bed and listened to her father pack the truck while her mother yelled insults at him. When he finally drove away, she craned her ears until she could no longer hear the sound of the rumbling truck. It was over. He was gone, and he hadn't even said goodbye. That hurt. He hadn't told her where *Abuelita* was, either. That hurt, too.

Once the coast was clear, Susie snuck back into the house and tiptoed her way up to Miguel's room. She told him to get dressed for school and be ready to leave in fifteen minutes. She wanted to drive him to school for two reasons, to get him away from their mother, and to make sure he was going to be okay. She had a feeling they would both be handling life one day at a time for a while.

She had pulled into the Mcdonalds' drive-thru on the way to the middle school and, even though he said he wasn't hungry, ordered him his usual Mickey D's breakfast anyway. When she pulled up to the drop-off, she handed him ten bucks for lunch. Knowing there wasn't much more she could do for him, she drove on to her own school.

Susie walked into the noisy cafeteria at lunchtime, grateful that she'd finally gotten her headache under control. Her stomach, well, that was another situation. She was kind of, maybe almost hungry, but the mere thought of a greasy hamburger or a chewy salad made her stomach protest. PB & J. That was the ticket. She headed to the sandwich station and asked the lunch lady to make her one on good old-fashioned white bread. Susie wasn't sure if she could even get that down, but she'd try.

Susie paid for the sandwich and then sat down at their usual table. Sam showed up a minute later, said, "Hey," and sat in the chair next to her.

"Hey," Susie said back. It was a start.

A not-exactly awkward but more like an uncomfortable silence followed until Sam said, "I'm sore from practice."

"Me, too," Susie said. "Too many freakin' squats."

"Yeah, I almost need help getting up out of a chair."

Susie laughed. "*Dios*! Me, too." Even though the conversation was basic and a bit strained, it felt good to know that her friend was there.

Alivia behaved herself during the lunch period and had hopefully gotten the message that Susie wasn't interested. Ronnie was nowhere to be found, and Susie didn't ask where he was.

Susie's afternoon classes went about the same as the morning classes. She tried her best to focus, not necessarily because she was interested in the material but because it was her best chance at keeping that morning's life-altering events at bay. Unfortunately, even though the National Geographic documentary Ms. Armstrong showed about plate tectonics was interesting, she couldn't concentrate on it. The dark classroom and returning headache had her closing her eyes. She slouched in her seat and moved behind Sam so her teacher couldn't see her.

Her free period at the end of the day was the hardest to get through because she wanted to walk right out the side door by the cafeteria, get in her dented car, and drive straight to Manfredi's deli. But she forced herself to go to the locker room to change for softball practice. There were two reasons she didn't leave. One was critical, the other practical. It was crucial for her to stay sober for her brother and have a clear and present head for him. The practical reason? She'd spent her last dollars on a peanut butter and jelly sandwich.

She opened her locker in the girls' varsity locker room and stashed her backpack. She pulled out her practice clothes and changed into sweats, a t-shirt, and sneakers for the gym floor. It was probably sacrilege to wear Marlee's Clarksonville sweatshirt to an East Valley practice, but she was going to do it anyway. She needed another hug from someone, anyone. She pulled out her glove and rubbed the leather pocket until her fingers got hot from the friction. It was soothing somehow. She sat there vegging on the locker room bench until Sam came in.

"Hey," Sam said. She put her backpack on the bench next to Susie and opened her locker.

Susie said, "Hey," back but didn't try for more small talk. It was too tiring.

The bell rang to end the period, and the locker room filled with the varsity basketball players whose season was close to finishing and the rest of Susie's varsity softball teammates. Susie stood up and headed for the gym to get out of the crowd. The only thing separating her from the aftermath at home was softball practice. And that was only two and a half hours. By five-thirty, she'd be on her way home. Or Manfredi's if she could bum some money off Sam or somebody. Of course, she still had some Belgian Beats in her trunk. That was the ticket.

As she looked at the gym floor, dread crept up her spine. What was she going to see when she got home? No trace of her father in the house? Pictures of him lying in a burning pile on the front lawn? Her mind imagined a dozen other possibilities.

The lump that had been in Susie's chest all day grew bigger and forced its way out in a choking sob. She covered her face and ran back into the locker room. She instinctively stumbled to a dark corner, put her back to the wall, and slid down until she was sitting on the cold floor. She put her hands over her face and gave into the sobs. They came from somewhere deep and dark inside of her.

A hand was on her shoulder in a matter of moments. Susie didn't look up to see who it was. She knew.

"Whoa, whoa, whoa, Sus." Sam sat down and put an arm around her friend. "What's happening here?"

Sam pulled her close and let Susie cry herself out.

"Okay, okay, Sus." Sam stroked Susie's back. "You're okay. I'm here. Tell me what's going on."

Keeping her eyes closed but pulling away from Sam, she said, "He left."

"Who left?"

"Papi."

There was silence for a moment. Sam was probably processing the information. "Your dad left?"

Susie nodded. "He moved out. This morning."

"Oh, shit."

"I think he's divorcing my mother," Susie said. "He has a girlfriend in Vermont. A lover. He has a *lover* in Vermont!" The words came tumbling out. "He had a moving truck and everything." She stopped to think about something for a second. "How the fuck did he rent a truck at five in the morning?"

"Five? Shit, Susie. That sucks."

"My mother went berserk. She lost her mind. Miguel is traumatized. And *mi abuelita…*"

The mere thought of maybe never seeing her *abuelita* again sent Susie into another crying jag, and she covered her face with her hands.

Sam rubbed Susie's leg and said, "That sucks, Susie. Can you tell me what happened?"

Susie tried to get control of her tears, but instead, she ended up hiccupping.

"God, Susie. This sucks. I wished you'd told me this morning."

Susie just shrugged. It had been such a shock that she was still processing it. She wouldn't have been able to talk about it earlier. She was barely able to talk about it now.

"Did you tell Marlee?"

Susie scoffed. "Marlee hates me. I haven't heard from her since the youth group fiasco."

"She does *not* hate you, Sus," Sam said softly. "She just feels, I don't know, betrayed or something that you lied. You need to call her."

"Humph," was all Susie could manage.

"Where are my co-captains?" Coach Gellar's voice boomed into the locker room.

"Shit," Sam said. "You stay right here. I'll handle this." Sam got up and left Susie to her misery.

Susie tried unsuccessfully to take a calming breath because the tears kept coming.

"Hey, kid," Coach Gellar said. She stood over Susie for a moment and then sat down on the locker room floor with a grunt. She chuckled and said, "See what you're making your old coach do?"

"Sorry," Susie wiped the tears off her face. "I just...I'll get up."

"Nah, kid. I'm already down. Let's just take a minute here. Sam's stretching out the team." They sat silently for a moment, and then Coach said, "Sam tells me you got dealt a pretty crappy hand this morning."

Susie nodded.

"Sorry, kid. That's a tough one. I know you've got a lot to deal with at home, and you know what?"

"What?"

"If it were anyone else, I'd tell them to forget about practice today and head home, but not you."

"No?" Susie was confused, but one thing she did know was that she did *not* want to go home. Not now, and not in two hours either.

"I know you, Torres, and the best thing for you is to put your mind to something else for a few hours. Sometimes you have to compartmentalize life. If there's nothing you can do about a situation at the present moment, then put it in a compartment to pull out later when you *can* deal with it."

Susie wanted to say that it was easier said than done but simply nodded that she understood.

"And I think right now that softball is the best way to get that other stuff off your mind. You know it'll be there waiting for you in two hours, right?"

Susie nodded.

"What do you say?" Coach Gellar nudged Susie with her shoulder. "Do you think you'll be able to keep it together if you stay?"

It sounded like her coach was giving her the choice to stay or to go home. Susie took a quick breath and let it out slowly. "I don't know. Maybe."

"Does your mom need you at home right now?"

"No."

"How about Baby Torres?"

"Miguel's fine. He should be at his friend Scott's house."

"Then you're in the clear," Coach Gellar said. Nothing in her body language said she was anxious to get back to the practice. She continued by saying, "My father always told me to 'worry as needs be.' In other words, if there's nothing you can do about a situation at this very moment, then stop fretting over it until you *can* do something." Coach Gellar patted her on the knee again and then stood up, grunting as she did so. "So, how about coming in to practice today? If you feel you're not up for it at any time, just let me know. And that goes for any time. Not just today."

"Okay, Coach," Susie said. "I'm just gonna take a minute to put myself back together, okay?"

"See you back inside."

Susie wiped at her face and then got to her feet. *Dios*, she was so tired. She went into the bathroom and splashed water on her face. It still looked like she'd been crying, but at least it didn't look too bad. The whole team had probably seen her colossal meltdown anyway.

Throughout the two-hour practice, Susie's mind commanded her body to do things it refused to do. Her arms were lead weights, and her legs felt like tree trunks as she tried to run. She was, once again, dead last in sprints. This time, though, Coach Gellar gave her encouragement instead of putdowns.

Susie dragged around in the locker room after practice. She didn't want to go home. Coach Gellar had told her to compartmentalize her troubles, and she sure as hell did not want to open the compartment that contained her mother. She changed leisurely, tossed her sweats and t-shirt into her softball bag, and then grabbed her backpack. After placing her sneakers neatly on the bottom of the locker, she stood up to put her coat on. She had stalled so long that she and Sam were the only ones left in the locker room.

"You have a phone call." Sam held her phone out to Susie.

"I do?"

"Just take it."

Susie took the phone and said, "Hello?"

"Hi," Marlee said.

"Hi." The relief in her voice was obvious even to her own ears. Her tense shoulders relaxed at the sound of Marlee's voice.

"Sam called me."

"She does that," Susie said, getting a chuckle from Marlee.

"She filled me in a little. Susie, what happened, and how are you holding up?"

"My father left us. He left, Marlee. He took all of his stuff. He doesn't live with us anymore. What does that even mean?" Susie said it all in a rush, but maybe she shouldn't have. She was probably upsetting Marlee because Marlee's father had left her suddenly, too, and she hadn't had the chance to say goodbye. But Marlee's father hadn't left voluntarily or willingly. He had died in a car accident. Susie's own father had gone willingly. He had just left them. He obviously didn't love them anymore. Had he ever?

"Sweetie?" Marlee said, her tone gentle.

"Yes?"

"I'm giving you a hug right now."

"You are, actually. I'm wearing your sweatshirt."

"Oh, I bet Coach Gellar had a fit with you wearing a Clarksonville sweatshirt."

Susie laughed. "She didn't say a word about it. She may not have even noticed. In fact, Coach Gellar didn't yell at me once today."

"Whoa, how did that happen?" Marlee asked. "Is it opposite day over there?"

"No," Susie said with a sigh and relayed her conversation with her coach.

"Hey, Susie?"

"Yeah?"

"I love you."

Susie couldn't speak with the tightness in her chest. "I know." Her voice was high and tight. Marlee had to know she was starting to cry. "Sorry, all I ever do is cry lately."

"Just keep your head above water, sweetie."

Out loud, she said, "I'll do my best." Inside she said, "Too late. I'm going under." Thank God she still had that beer in her car.

Chapter Twenty-One
It. Is. A. Secret.

When Susie woke up that Saturday morning, the morning of the big St. Patrick's Day party at Ronnie's, she'd had no plans to majorly fuck up her relationship with Marlee any more than she already had. Somehow it just happened.

In the week and a half leading up to that day, Susie dug in and worked hard at practice. She wasn't first in sprints, but she wasn't last, either. She didn't even let alternate-Susie drive to Manfredi's deli after she'd dumped the rest of the twelve-pack that had been hidden in her trunk. At the moment, there was no beer stashed anywhere in her room or car, and there was no leftover beer in the main house. Friday night, a full week and a day before the party, Susie was still grounded, so Marlee, Lisa, and Sam came over to hang out in her room. Her friends kept things light as they listened to music, played video games, and talked about their respective pre-season softball practices. At one point, Marlee stood up and reached down for Susie's hand.

"What's up, *mi vida*?" Susie said, taking the offered hand.

"Let's dance." A slow-tempo ballad had come on the radio.

Susie let herself be pulled into Marlee's strong arms. Once there, safe and secure, Susie felt herself relax. She hadn't known how tense she was.

"I'm checking in with you right now," Marlee said. "Tell me what's on your mind these days."

Susie rested her forehead on Marlee's and smiled. Marlee knew how to find her. "I don't want to drink to anesthetize my life anymore. I have to feel things instead of hide from them."

"So that means no drinking at Ronnie's party next week. Not even one. You know he'll have stuff there."

"I know. I know. I'll just have to be strong."

"I'll be strong with you," Marlee said and kissed her. "What else?"

"I'm just scared about what life will be like without my dad, and I'm scared for Miguel growing up without Papi. I'm older and can deal. I think. But he needs his father, you know?"

Marlee nodded. "Your father will still be in your life."

"I know."

Marlee spun her around the dance floor that used to be her bedroom floor. "I have an idea," Marlee said, stopping suddenly.

"What's that?"

"How about we take Miguel out somewhere? Maybe the rink or that new go-cart track that opened up."

"You'd do that?" Here was another of the many reasons Susie loved Marlee.

"Yeah, why not? And maybe we can watch a Mets spring-training game together one day on the weekend."

"He always watched the games with Papi," Susie said. "That would be good, Marlee. Thanks." She leaned forward and kissed her girlfriend. The kiss turned into a deep hug.

"And," Marlee continued, "how about right now we clean up that rock collection of yours that somehow got relocated to the far side of the room?"

"Yeah," Sam called from where she sat playing a video game with Lisa. "It's a pigsty in here."

"Shuddup, Sam," Susie said and then turned back to Marlee. "You'll help me?"

Marlee nodded and kissed Susie's forehead. It was a healing gesture, one that made Susie tear up a little. She blinked back the tears and let Marlee lead her to the rock collection, which lay scattered all over her hand weights and the floor. Susie had been ignoring them, not wanting to deal. Marlee found a large piece of the rose quartz and put it lovingly on the bookshelf where it had lived since Susie was in third grade.

After cleaning up, Sam suggested they turn the lights down low. Susie heartily agreed, and each couple found a private spot for some much needed make-out therapy. It didn't go much further than that because, well, two of her friends were in the same room.

And amazingly, the very next day, a week before the party, Susie's mother let her off the hook and suggested she visit Marlee in Clarksonville. Who knew what miracle had caused that to happen, but she wasn't going to question it. After checking in with her brother to make sure he was okay, she and Sam drove to Clarksonville and picked up their best girls. Sam had found a local bar in Clarksonville that was having a band. They let minors in, but they weren't allowed to drink, of course. That evening had been pure torture for Susie. The band was good but watching the bar patrons go up to the bar for full glasses of beer, all different colors, and the heads foaming up just so perfectly—that was torture. Pure torture. Susie felt that yearning in her core for a beer. Maybe she could grab somebody's abandoned beer off a table and drink it. Yeah, she could tell her friends she needed to go to the bathroom in the back of the bar. They were absorbed with the rock band on the makeshift stage anyway. Shit, she even had her fake ID on her and could order a beer and then chug it in the bathroom. But, no. What if the waitress asked her if she wanted another one? And, unfortunately, she *would* want one but wouldn't be able to. Her relationship with Marlee would probably go down in flames if she did. Once they finally left the bar, she got much needed relief, and the evening only got better when Lisa and Sam headed off by themselves for some private time, which left Susie and Marlee alone on the couch in Marlee's basement.

The rest of the week went by fairly quickly. Susie's mother even suggested that Susie go to Clarksonville to do homework with Marlee, and she did just that a couple of times after softball practice. Her mother's suggestion was completely out of character, but Susie didn't question it. She got the distinct feeling that her mother simply wanted to be alone and work things out in her head. That was fine because Susie was trying to work things out, too.

The evening of Ronnie's big Saint Patrick's Day party arrived, and Susie waited in the driveway for Sam to pick her up. Susie's heart sped up with she saw the Mercedes coming down the street. It was going to be a good evening.

"Hey, dork," Sam said as Susie got in the car.

"Hey. How'd the ten-month anniversary celebration go with Lisa on Wednesday?"

"I'm a happy girl. I can tell you that." Sam pulled out of the driveway and headed toward Ronnie's house.

"I bet Lisa's a happy girl, too." Susie smacked her friend on the arm.

Sam's face-splitting smile told the whole story.

"I'm working on another weekend at the lake house."

"Shit! No way." Susie pushed Sam in the arm. "When?"

"Soon. It has to be soon." Sam looked at Susie with a frustrated eye roll. "I can't take much more of this car."

"It's so freakin' small in here, Sam. First of all, I don't know how Lisa fits in this seat, and second, I have no idea how you guys manage to, uh, you know, in here."

"We get … creative," Sam said, her cheeks turning pink. "But now that she's got her driver's license, we can hang out in the Sebring."

"It's got a backseat!"

"Exactly."

Marlee and Lisa weren't at Ronnie's house yet, so they went inside to get out of the cold. Ronnie's parents were just getting ready to leave but were waiting to greet Sam and Susie.

"It's so good to see you girls again," Ronnie's mother gushed. "It's nice that Ronnie has so many friends."

Ronnie mouthed "female friends" behind his mother and then rolled his eyes. Susie did her best not to laugh at his antics.

Sam said, "Thanks, Mrs. Alessi. Enjoy your party."

"We will. Thanks. My husband, Ron, found an Irish pub in Southbridge, of all places."

"Sounds like fun," Sam said. "Happy St. Patrick's Day."

Susie could tell she wanted to tell them to be careful driving, but she closed her lips and took off her coat instead.

"Where?" Susie held up her winter coat.

"Back office," Ronnie said. "C'mon, I'll show you."

"Take mine," Sam said and handed her coat to Susie. "I need to talk to Dominique in my strings quintet." She headed into the living room, where a bunch of kids from Ronnie and Sam's strings class were talking. Susie noticed that each one had bottled water in their hands. That, she knew, would change as soon as Ronnie's parents left.

"C'mon," Ronnie said. "This way."

He led her through the kitchen, where it was dead silent. Karl, Alivia, and Jordan sat still, watching Ronnie's every move. Their eyes were expectant. Susie caught Alivia's eye, and Alivia's smile widened.

In true dramatic Ronnie fashion, he bellowed, "Let's drink!"

A cheer went up in the kitchen, and Susie blanched at the idea. She'd told Marlee she wouldn't. It wasn't long before Alivia handed her a Belgian Beat with a slice of orange. "Two little birdies told me this is your new favorite."

"You guys got this just for me?" Susie said.

"I did," Alivia said, her cheeks tingeing pink.

Susie, still holding the coats, wrestled with herself. She'd have one. Only one. She'd promised Marlee she wouldn't have any, but Marlee wouldn't have to know. She took a long pull from the bottle. Ahh, it was just what she needed. She'd gone over a week and a half without drinking. Trying to keep the cravings at bay was one of the hardest things she'd ever had to do. She didn't know why it had been so hard. She'd gone longer without a beer before in her life.

Ronnie showed her where to put the coats, and they headed back to the kitchen.

"Hey," Ronnie said, "everything's cool with Sam now, right?"

"Yeah, it's cool."

"Good. Now, let's go drink!"

Susie drained her Belgian Beat as they walked back to the kitchen. It had gone down smoothly, too smoothly. Ronnie grabbed her another one immediately. Since she hadn't felt any effect from the first one, she decided to have a second. But then that would be it. When half of that one was gone, she felt herself relax a little. The tension in her neck especially seemed to ease up.

"Jordan's making black and tans," Ronnie told her.

"What are black and tans?"

Jordan himself answered. "Watch. You can use any ale, but Bass Ale was the original. Pour it into the glass fast. That creates a good head so you can layer in the Guinness."

"I love good head," Ronnie said, earning him a smack in the chest from Susie. "Ow," he whimpered. "You got my nipple."

"You loved it." Susie rolled her eyes at him. "Then what, Jordan?"

"Then, using an upside-down spoon, gently pour the Guinness over it. You want it to just float on top." Susie was amazed at his technique. It created a perfect two-tone beer. Lighter on the bottom and darker on the top. "This one will be for you."

It was as if an alternate version of herself stepped forward and took the glass from Jordan. She heard this other self say, "Ooh, okay," and then chug the rest of the Belgian Beat. This monster inside her burped, causing her friends to burst out laughing.

Knowing it was wrong, Susie took a tentative sip of the black and tan. "This is really good." A round of cheering went up around the table.

Susie bargained with herself. She'd get the black and tan down fast, and Marlee would never know. She'd grab a coke from the fridge and have it ready to give Marlee when she got there. It would be a peace offering that Marlee wouldn't even know was needed.

"It's different, but it's good," she said to the table full of her friends.

After finishing the first, Jordan offered to make her another, but she declined. She was going to keep her promise to herself and to Marlee.

The promise lasted one minute if that. Alivia handed her another Belgian Beat, an orange slice already tucked inside. The alternate version of herself took it and sipped. And sipped again. *Yes, yes, this is what you want,* her alternate self told her. *This cushion. This numbness. This oblivion.*

Susie got lost in the tale Jordan told about why black and tans were a big no-no on St. Patrick's Day. He told them that back in the 1920s or something, the British Parliamentary forces sent in a militia to suppress Irish uprisings. This militia wore khaki-colored pants and dark shirts, and they were brutal, he told them. "To this day in Ireland," he said, "you don't order black and tans. It's an insult of the highest order."

Jordan helped himself to another of his creations and said, "In an ironic twist, I salute Ireland and all she's had to endure. To Ireland." He raised his glass.

Susie raised her bottle and, to her dismay, realized it was empty. She hadn't even realized she had drunk the whole thing.

Sam came into the kitchen just at that moment, and Susie thrust her empty into Alivia's hands. Alivia seemed to understand and stashed the bottle under the table.

"What's all the yelling in here?" Sam said to the group at the kitchen table. "It sounds like a revolution."

Not knowing that Susie was trying not to drink in front of Sam, Ronnie handed her another Belgian Beat.

Sam frowned. "Really?" She put her hands in the air in a what-the-hell gesture.

A war went on inside Susie's beer-muddled head. "Listen," alternate Susie said, "after living in my mother's madness this week, I deserve this beer."

"And the first four," Ronnie quipped.

Susie sighed. Who was Sam to harass her about it anyway? Susie had a delightful buzz going on, and she was hanging out with her friends and having a good time. "Look, Sam. It's okay. I'm not driving tonight. You are."

Sam looked doubtful.

"I'm okay. I really am." At Sam's doubtful expression, she said, "I'll walk a straight line for you." Susie stood up, but when she did, the room tilted on its axis momentarily, and she stumbled into Jordan.

"Oh, my God, Susie," Sam said. "You're drunk. And Marlee's not even here yet."

Just then, they heard the distinct sounds of Marlee and Lisa greeting some of the youth group kids in the living room.

"You'd better straighten up, Susie," Sam scolded, then put a smile on her face and turned around. "Hey, you guys." Sam hugged Lisa as she came into the kitchen. "You made it okay?"

"She's a good driver, Sam," Marlee said with a wink. Apparently, Lisa had driven them to East Valley in the Sebring. "No worries."

Since Susie was already standing, she walked over to Marlee, took her in her arms, and kissed her. She dipped Marlee back like in the movies and then smiled at the cheering crowd at the table.

"Is it getting hot in here or what?" Karl asked, fanning himself.

"Oh, yeah," Susie said and pulled Marlee back upright. She patted Marlee on the cheek and said, "This is my honey. Isn't she pretty, everybody?"

A chorus of agreement followed.

The frown on Marlee's face told Susie everything she didn't want to know. Marlee could tell that she'd been drinking. Shit, Susie had promised she wouldn't.

"Um," Marlee said, "I'm going to get some fresh air."

"I'll come with you," Susie said and grabbed for Marlee's hand.

Marlee pulled her hand away. "No, no. You stay right here. Enjoy your friends. I need some alone time."

Sam and Lisa exchanged a concerned glance and followed Marlee out of the kitchen. Alivia pulled Susie back to her chair.

"That's my girlfriend, you guys," Susie said again. "She's amazing. But I don't think she's talking to me right now!"

"Susie, you're wasted, girl," Ronnie said.

"Makes the world better, don'cha think, Ronald?" she said and then turned toward Jordan. "Right, Jordan? Jordan Warden. Huh, you should be in charge of a prison. You could be Warden Jordan."

Jordan laughed and patted her on the knee. Good thing he didn't pat the other knee because Alivia's fingers were massaging it slowly.

"Ivia," Susie said, knowing she'd somehow gotten the name wrong. Why had speaking become so difficult all of a sudden? "A-live-ee-uh!" Susie carefully pronounced. "You have to stop doing that." She purposefully reached down and pushed Alivia's hand off of her leg.

"Maybe you should slow down, Susie," Jordan said.

"Fuck that," Susie said. "Look, I can stop whenever I want. Everybody else at this table is having fun. Why should I join the prudes who aren't drinking?"

"Good point," Ronnie said. He raised his glass. "To prudes!"

A round of cheering went up from the table.

"Isn't a prude someone who won't have sex?" Alivia asked. Susie burst out laughing but then felt bad. Alivia's question had been sincere.

"Babe," Karl said, "a prude is a person who carries themselves with poise and dignity. They always use proper decorum in the way they dress and the way they speak. I just had this same conversation with Dirk the other day. He didn't know what it meant either."

Susie groaned as if punched in the stomach at the sound of Karl's cousin's name. She flew to her feet and knocked down the tower of Guinness cans Karl had been building with one sweep of her hand.

"Wrong," Susie said and punched her finger at his face. She turned from him and grabbed Jordan's beer from the table. Not knowing where to go, she headed for the bathroom. Without turning on the light, she did her business and then washed her hands. Her buzz had been killed by stupid Karl having to mention that asshole cousin of his.

Knowing she couldn't stay in the bathroom all night, she opened the door and weighed her options. She didn't know where Marlee was, but that didn't matter. Marlee didn't want anything to do with her, anyway. She definitely didn't want to go back into the kitchen, so she headed to the back office where her coat was. Once inside, she kept the lights off and sat in the luxurious office chair.

She took a few swigs from Jordan's beer and then spun the chair around a few times. She leaned it back as far as she could and discovered a sweet spot where she could tip the chair back and balance it midway. She had just gotten the hang of it when the door to the office opened. Briefly backlit by the hall light, Susie could tell it was Alivia. Alivia closed the door softly behind her and leaned against it.

"Are you okay, Susie?"

Susie nodded once. It was a lie, but Alivia didn't need to be dragged into her problems. Without losing eye contact, Alivia pushed off the door and headed toward her. Susie leaned the chair forward and put both feet on the ground. Without a word, Alivia straddled Susie's legs with her own. Facing Susie, she leaned forward. The chair tilted backward, and Susie wrapped her arms around Alivia so they wouldn't fall.

Once the chair stopped moving, they laughed for a moment, and then Susie locked eyes with Alivia. She continued to hold her tight.

"You know how to have fun, don't you?" Susie said.

Alivia nodded.

"You're not a prude, are you?"

Susie saw the heat simmering in Alivia's eyes. Alivia leaned forward slightly, but Susie didn't move. Alivia's need was clear. Soft lips met Susie's. A gentle moan escaped Alivia as the kiss deepened. Alivia pulled back and kissed Susie's forehead, her cheeks, her chin, her neck. She nipped at Susie's mouth and then caught Susie's lower lip in between her own. A gentle suck sent shivers through Susie. It was so sexy, so intimate, so…wrong. Susie whimpered, but not for the reason Alivia thought.

Alivia tried to deepen the kiss, but Susie pushed Alivia back by the shoulders. "No. I can't. I don't want this."

Susie felt Alivia tremble.

"I know." Alivia ran a gentle hand down Susie's face. "I can't do this to you. I can't do this to Marlee, but I want it…" She sighed and said, "Karl is hard." At Susie's raised eyebrow, Alivia said, "No, I didn't mean it that way. Oh, my God. I mean, he's a great guy, but he's not like you. You're a little bit hard." Alivia ran her hands over Susie's shoulders and biceps. "But you're soft, too." She leaned in and kissed Susie passionately on the lips. Susie gave in to the kiss because it felt like goodbye.

Alivia reached her hand up to Susie's mouth and wiped it. "I got lipstick on you." Alivia leaned back so the chair righted itself and climbed off Susie's lap. "You'd better wipe that off before you go back in there." Susie silently watched Alivia leave the room.

Knowing she had to go back out there at some point, she stood up and grabbed the beer. It only took a few more gulps to finish it. She opened the door to the office a crack and made sure the coast was clear before darting to the bathroom to clean up her face. Alivia's kisses had been, she searched for just the right word. Interesting. Yes, that was a good word. She couldn't deny it. And her ego had been stroked by the attention, but one thing was for sure, she had to avoid her friends in the kitchen, especially Karl, and find Marlee immediately. She went back to the office to get the coats and headed out to find her girlfriend.

Alivia had resumed her seat in the kitchen, but Susie just walked past them all without saying a word. Sam was coming back in the front door and lifted her chin at Susie's approach.

"Where's Marlee?" Susie asked.

"She and Lisa just left." Sam blocked the front door.

"Marlee left? I have to stop her."

Sam put her hands on Susie's shoulders and held her back.

"Move, Sam. I'm serious. I need to see Marlee. I have to say sorry."

"No," Sam said defiantly. "Look, Susie, I know things are tough for you right now, but you are royally and single-handedly fucking up your relationship. She is the best thing that's ever happened to you, and she needs a minute to digest all of this." Sam grabbed her coat that was draped over Susie's arm and put it on.

Susie just stood there, not knowing what to do. Marlee had left without saying goodbye or anything.

"Put your goddamned coat on, Susie. I'm taking you to my house, and I swear to God that this will be the very last time I save your ass like this." It looked like Sam wanted to say more, but she just pulled on Susie's elbow and led her out the front door.

Susie couldn't figure out how to get in Sam's small car.

"You are really hammered, Sus. Oh, my God. Come on, left leg in first," Sam instructed. "Good, now duck down and sit." With a laugh, Sam said, "Good girl. You're so talented."

Even Susie heard the sarcasm in Sam's voice. "Shuddup, Sam. You're stupid."

Sam strapped Susie in and then shut the door. Susie wiggled in the seat. "It's so small in here."

"It is," Sam said as she got in the driver's seat.

"Does Lisa fit?"

"Yep."

"You love her." Susie reached over and petted Sam on the arm.

"I do." Sam started the engine and pulled away from Ronnie's house.

"Hmm," Susie sighed and closed her eyes. "I love Marlee."

"I know."

"She hates me."

"And why does Marlee hate you, Susie?"

Susie opened her eyes to see Sam looking at her.

"She didn't say goodbye."

"No?"

"Nope, and she didn't even kiss me, Sam. And, you know what?" Susie poked Sam in the arm.

"What?"

Susie smacked her head back on the headrest, the motion of the car had kind of stirred up all the beer, and she was feeling light-headed. "Alivia keeps kissing me."

"Wh-what? Alivia?"

"I don't really like it."

"You don't like it when Alivia kisses you?"

"No. I. Don't." Susie poked her index finger on Sam's leg with each word. "I keep telling her to stop, but she doesn't."

"Um, when did she kiss you?"

"Just before," Susie said and closed her eyes again.

"Tonight?"

"Yep."

"Any other times?"

"At her house."

"Her house," Sam repeated. "Why did you let her kiss you?"

"No, no, no, I didn't *let* her. She just does it. Like Dirk. He's a jerk. No, he's an *asshole*. He's a *fucking* asshole."

"Dirk? Who's Dirk?" Sam asked.

"Karl's cousin. Dirk." Susie hacked, trying to get the taste of his name out of her mouth.

Sam pulled the car off on the side of the road. "Do you have to throw up?"

"No."

"What was that noise you made?" Sam said.

"Phht, Dirk's an asshole."

"Susie, what happened? Why is Dirk an asshole?" Sam took off her seatbelt and turned to face Susie.

Susie tried to turn and face Sam but couldn't move her upper body for some reason.

"Seatbelt," Sam said and reached over to unsnap Susie's seatbelt.

"Oh."

"What did Dirk do, Susie?"

"No, no, no." Susie shook her head from side to side. "I don't want to…"

"What did he do, Susie?" Sam's tone was more insistent. Susie had heard that tone from Sam before, and she didn't like it.

"Blah, blah, blah," Susie babbled. "It. Is. A. Secret. Sam."

"I know lots of secrets about you, Susie."

"No, you don't."

"Alivia kisses you."

"Oh, yeah." Susie inhaled sharply. "Don't tell Marlee, 'kay?"

"I won't," Sam said. "But *you* should."

"No, no, no." Susie leaned forward and poked Sam on the arm.

"What did Dirk do, Susie? Tell me."

Susie pounded her head on the headrest until Sam physically stopped her by grabbing her head.

"Susie, stop. Stop."

"He laid on top of me. I didn't want him to do that. I couldn't move. He rubbed me there." She pointed to her crotch. "He was rough. I didn't like it. He rubbed me here, too." She reached up and rubbed her own breasts. "Wanna know the worst part?" she whispered and leaned closer to Sam.

"Okay."

In a rush, she told Sam about his tongue in her mouth, his zipper going down, and then his hand pulling her zipper down. "He told me not to fight it. I was scared, Sam. So scared." She started crying, and Sam reached over and pulled her into a hug.

"Shh, shh, shh, Sus." Sam rubbed Susie's back. "You're okay. I'm here. You're okay now."

Susie hiccupped as she cried in Sam's arms. She felt herself drift off to sleep as Sam let her go and then pulled the car back on the road.

Chapter Twenty-Two
Not Today

Susie opened her eyes and stretched her arms overhead. The now-familiar ache of a morning headache greeted her. She blinked her eyes a few times to figure out where she was. Sam's? Again? She groaned as she stood up. *Dios*, if this were going to be a regular thing, Sam would have to get a more comfortable sleeping couch.

The curtains were closed, so Susie had no idea what time it was. She had to pee something fierce, so she got up and knocked lightly on the door to Sam's bedroom. Receiving no answer, she opened it slowly.

"Sam?" Susie said softly. "I'm just going to use the bathroom, okay?" She opened the door and was assaulted with bright sunlight streaming through the uncovered windows.

"Whoa, whoa, whoa," Susie cried as she covered her eyes. After the initial shock wore off, she peeked out from under her hand. Sam was already up, judging by the fact that her bed was made.

Susie went into the bathroom and found a brand new toothbrush on the countertop. Sam's note read, "New toothbrush, towel, washcloth, hairbrush for you. Shower if you want. Borrow clothes if you want. I am downstairs in the conservatory practicing."

Susie's heart clenched. Sam was still looking out for her. Setting out the brushes and towels was a small thing, but Susie wasn't sure she deserved Sam's kindness. She vaguely remembered Sam helping her out of the car and then to the garden around the fountain to throw up. *Dios*, Susie groaned. Sam's mother had won prizes for her gardens, and Susie just—No, she wouldn't dwell on that. She remembered Sam shushing her as they went into the house. Susie wanted to sing, but Sam didn't. Oh, yeah, Sam kept saying they'd sing tomorrow in the light of day. Susie remembered her drunken self trying to make sense of that. She had asked Sam if singing sounded better in daylight, maybe because of the sun's electromagnetic radiation. Sam had called her a science geek at that point, and Susie responded by saying, "Thank you very much." Susie shook her head, embarrassed at her own drunkenness. Sam had taken care of her, even though she had no reason to.

"And Marlee hates me, too," Susie said out loud. She took in her reflection in the bathroom mirror. "This—" Susie waved a hand around her face, "is *not* what you signed up for, *mi vida*." Her face was puffy and pale, and those stupid dark circles were back. Okay, the circles had never really left. "But *she* left. And my father left before that." Susie stared at her reflection. She was numb. She was too numb to cry.

Susie washed her face trying to scrub off the memory of Alivia's kisses all over her face. That was definitely not what she wanted. Guilt clenched her heart. Shit, did she tell Sam about that last night? Even if Marlee didn't take her back, she still didn't want Marlee to find out about Alivia. Ever.

A shower. That's what she needed. She stepped in and took a hot soaking shower hoping the water would help her body hydrate. Once she toweled off, she felt a little better. Instead of burdening Sam by borrowing her clothes, Susie just put on the clothes she'd worn the day before. Yep, the same ones she'd slept in. She downed a couple of Advil she found in Sam's medicine cabinet and then made sure the bathroom was relatively cleaned up. She took one step into the living room and stopped.

Marlee stood up. "Sam said you and I need to talk."

"Talk?" Susie took another tentative step.

"She texted me late last night and said I should come here this morning. I've been here since seven o'clock."

"Seven?" What did Sam want them to talk about? Alivia? Shit. It had to be. Marlee was about to break up with her for good. "What time is it now?"

"Eleven."

Shit, she'd slept that late? "You've been here for four hours?" Four hours of waiting to break up with me. Well, at least Marlee was doing it in person. She would. She was considerate and thoughtful and kind.

Marlee nodded and sat back down on the chair. "Sam kept coming up here to check on you. When she heard the shower running, she knew you were finally up. And so here I am."

Susie walked to the couch with tentative steps. She sat down and folded her arms. Do it gently, Marlee, Susie pleaded in her head.

Marlee stood up and picked up a tray Susie hadn't seen before. "I made you ginger tea and toast." She set the tray down on the low table in front of the couch. "Here's a bottled water, too, in case the tea doesn't sit right. So, do you need an Advil or something?"

She shook her head and reached for the cup of tea. "Thank you."

Dios, Marlee was going to kill her with kindness before putting the knife in her heart to kill her again. Susie drank in Marlee's sweet and innocent face, knowing that it might be the last time she ever saw it.

Susie's face scrunched up as her heart broke through the numbness. She tried to get her tears under control. She didn't want Marlee to feel bad about breaking up with her.

Marlee moved to the couch and pulled Susie into her arms. "C'mere, c'mere, c'mere, sweetie."

"You called me sweetie," Susie said as she tried to stop crying.

"Of course. You're my girlfriend. I get to call you that." Marlee kissed Susie's face as if trying to kiss the tears away.

"I still am? I'm still your girlfriend?"

Marlee pulled back and said, "How can you doubt that? Look, I have to admit that I was mad and confused by you being drunk last night, but—no, no, let me finish. But I should *not* have left you. Your father did that to you, and then I left just because the situation was uncomfortable. It wasn't my best moment, Susie, and I'm sorry. I should have been there for you, and I wasn't. Something is going on with you, and you need to tell me. You need to trust me."

"I haven't been dealing with shit lately."

"So tell me. Tell me about your, um," Marlee grinned, "shit."

Susie would have grinned back if the whole thing hadn't been so tragic. Susie couldn't figure out where to start. Her father leaving them, just leaving? Her mother so hurt by her father's actions that she had turned into more of a lunatic than she already was? Poor Miguel, too young to have to deal with something this serious? Dirk assaulting her? Alivia harassing her? She took a shaky breath.

Marlee cleared her throat and said, "You're drinking to drown out your feelings. Tuesday in the van after the youth group meeting? That was so unfair, Susie. You said right to my face that you were only going to have one. But that was a lie. Last Saturday, in your room, you told me you wouldn't ever drink again. And you did. And it was a lot by Sam's accounting."

There was silence for a moment and Marlee said, "Susie, there has to be trust between us. Trust." When Susie didn't respond, Marlee sighed and said, "Drink your tea."

Susie immediately raised the cup to her lips. Anything Marlee wanted her to do, she would do.

Marlee took a breath and sighed. "Look, I have to tell you the truth. I did get into Cornell, but I didn't want to tell you. And that wasn't being honest with you. And truthfully, I'm still not sure what I'm going to do next year for college. I mean, the plan was that if we both got into Rockville, then that's where I would go. I can always try for Cornell for graduate school or something. But now…" She paused as if searching for the right words. "After last night, I'm not sure what I want to do. Susie, in all honesty, I'm not sure I want to be with a person who lies right to my face. That doesn't feel good. And I'm not sure I like the person you become when you're drunk. I'm not sure that's the person I want to be with." She looked up at the ceiling, trying to blink back her tears. "Our eleventh-month anniversary is in four days, which means we're working on being together for almost a whole year. An entire year. We've had our ups and downs. And, in my opinion, we're in a real down right now, but we're not out. My head has been doing a lot of talking, Susie, but my heart knows what it wants."

Susie looked up expectantly.

Marlee nodded. "It wants you, Susie. I want you. I want to help you deal with your family and all the crap that's going on in your life. I want to be your rock, your foundation. If you'll let me. You don't need to drink—that just pushes all the shit in your life away momentarily. But it doesn't last, does it?"

Susie shook her head.

"It all comes flooding back to you once you're sober, doesn't it?"

Susie nodded. She shifted her gaze to the cup of tea she was holding. "I don't know how to deal."

"Talk to me. Tell me things, Susie. I'll drive right over to East Valley to see you. I'm scared as hell of your mother, but I'll take her on if it means I'm helping you."

"Wow, those are some strong words, Marlee. To be honest, I don't like the way I feel after drinking," Susie confessed. "I don't like how I feel after the third or fourth beer, but for some reason, I keep going. I want to get numb, I think. I want to hide from reality."

"Susie?" Marlee's voice was stern.

"Yes?"

"I'm part of that reality." Marlee's cheeks were tinged red from emotion. Normally that would have been endearing, but Susie knew it was partly from anger. Anger directed straight at her. It sucked. "Susie, let me help you. Okay?"

Susie searched Marlee's eyes for what she knew she'd find there. Compassion, commitment. Love. Susie nodded.

Marlee pulled Susie into a long hug and, when she pulled back, said, "Now drink that tea and have some toast because we're not done talking."

"We're not?" Oh, shit, Susie thought. Marlee's going to bring up Alivia.

Marlee held Susie's hand while Susie ate a slice of toast. One slice was all she could handle at the moment. She drained the teacup and reached for her water bottle. She had to be hydrated for what was coming next.

Marlee kissed Susie on her forehead and then said, "I am going to say a name, okay?"

"Okay." And that name will be Alivia, Susie thought with one hundred percent certainty.

"Ready?"

"Yes." Do it already.

"Dirk."

Susie recoiled and took a sharp intake of breath. She closed her eyes and fought the pain in her chest. She didn't want Marlee to know about that. Ever. A numbness overtook her brain, and she put a hand up as if to stop the memories from assaulting her again.

"Susie?" There was compassion in Marlee's tone. "Open your eyes. Talk to me."

Susie opened her eyes but said, "No, I'm never talking about that day again. Ever. It's done. Over. Complete. It's in the books, and I'm shuttin' it down."

"But you can't, Susie." Marlee took her hands. "Unfortunately, this will always be part of you, part of your life story."

"Sam told you, didn't she?"

"Yes."

"Marlee, please don't make me."

"Susie, I know it's hard. Look, I tried to bury my feelings when my father died. My mom couldn't get me to talk about it. As far as I was concerned, it was done, finished, and 'in the books.' I tried to deny that it had ever happened, but it kept coming back up. Susie, you have to meet this head on and deal with it in whatever way you're going to deal with it, but deal with it. I'm here to help you."

Susie frowned. But she knew that Marlee was right. "Okay."

"Tell me what happened."

It took more than a full minute for Susie to punch past the block she'd placed in her brain, but she finally found the words, and the tale spilled out in all its sordid glory.

Tears fell down Marlee's face as she listened, but she didn't interrupt. Susie let the words tumble out, and, oddly, it felt freeing to tell someone. To tell Marlee. To feel safe.

Marlee reached out and held her without words for a while.

"Do you think he'll bother you again?"

Susie shrugged.

"We need to know," Marlee said. "Karl doesn't know his cousin did this, does he?"

"I don't think so."

"Karl needs to know."

Susie groaned but knew it was true. "Maybe Sam can help me tell him tomorrow at school."

"That would work."

"You know, a few days after it happened, I saw the school psychologist about it," Susie offered after a moment.

"You did?"

Susie nodded. "I wasn't going to go back to her. I didn't want to talk about it anymore, but maybe I can. Maybe I'll make another appointment."

"Good idea." Marlee looked down for a moment and then said, "I think you should press charges against him."

Susie squeezed her eyes shut. That would make it all so public, and everyone would know. All she wanted to do was put that steel-reinforced block back in place. To appease Marlee, she said, "Maybe."

Marlee held her tight for a few quiet minutes. A quick memory of Alivia standing at the office door at Ronnie's house sent a shot of guilt to Susie's entire soul.

"Marlee?"

"Hmm?"

"This will be a deal breaker, I know, but I have to tell you something."

"Uh, oh, now you've got me scared."

Susie sat up. "Go sit over there. It'll be easier for you to be mad at me after I say it."

"It can't be that bad," Marlee said.

"Please?"

"No, I won't. I'm staying right here." Marlee rubbed her right shoulder with her left hand.

"What's wrong?" Susie asked.

"Nothing. Just tension, I think." Marlee's smile made Susie's heart melt. This whole thing was just as hard on Marlee as it was on her. "That and softball. Coach is killing us."

"Us, too," Susie said.

Marlee held both of Susie's hands in hers. Susie couldn't look at Marlee. A few seconds ticked by, and then Marlee said, "Susie? What's going on?"

Susie took a short breath and let it out. Now was the time. It had to be now because if Marlee found out from someone else, it would definitely be over between them. Susie said, "Please know that I love you, Marlee. I take this ring seriously." She squeezed Marlee's hands and then held up the hand with the gold plastic ring on her finger. "I know it's only a toy, but this means something to me."

"Me, too." Marlee held up the matching plastic ring she wore on her own hand. She brought the hand back down and gently stroked Susie's wrist.

"This is hard for me to say." Susie looked down. She couldn't look at Marlee when she blurted, "I kissed Alivia."

The hand stopped stroking. "What?"

"I know you heard me," Susie said weakly. "But that's not even right. I mean, Alivia kissed *me* the first time."

"The *first* time?" Marlee pulled her hands away and stood up.

Susie's heart pounded in her chest. "I mean, Alivia started it, and as soon as I realized what was happening, I pushed her away."

Marlee folded her arms across her chest. "How many times were there?" Marlee's scowl made Susie's chest tighten. She was the cause of that pain.

"Only two. Just two times." *Dios* that sounded so bad. Marlee was going to throw the ring at her any second.

"Just two," Marlee repeated.

The pain etched in Marlee's face made Susie's throat tighten with tears. She didn't even try to stop the flood. She nodded and said, "I'm sorry. It didn't mean anything. I swear."

Marlee put a hand up to stop Susie from talking further and stabbed at the tears on either side of her face.

"When?"

Susie told her about both times.

"Last night?" Marlee's eyes flashed. "When last night? After I left?"

Shame radiated through Susie as she shook her head no.

"Before I got there?"

More shame with another shake of her head.

"While I was there?" The almost-hysterical pitch to Marlee's voice launched Susie to her feet. Marlee put out a hand as if to keep Susie back. "You fucking kissed her while I was still at the party?"

Susie's eyes smashed themselves shut as she tried to keep the pain away. "I'm sorry. Throw your ring at me. I don't deserve you."

"Just stop talking for a minute, Susie." There was silence for a moment. Susie knew her fate was being decided by the girl she loved standing six feet away. Marlee dropped her arms and lifted her head high. "Why did you let it happen a second time?"

"You pushed me away." Susie's voice was meek even to her own ears. "In Ronnie's kitchen. And I, I don't know, I felt rejected."

"You're blaming *me*? I didn't throw her at you." Marlee's anger lanced Susie's heart.

"I know." Susie hung her head down in shame. "I didn't mean it like that. I was drunk when she threw herself at me in the back room. I know, that's no excuse, but okay, you want honesty, right?" Susie stood up taller. "Both times, I was drunk. The first time was, like, two seconds, and I pretty much pushed her off me once I realized what was happening. The second time? I'm not proud of this, but I think I was trying to get back at you for rejecting me. This was how my drunk mind reasoned it out. You were mad at me for being drunk, but being drunk helps me cope with the shithole life I have at home now, and it felt like you weren't supporting me. I know. It doesn't make sense, and I take full responsibility for the bad decision to let Alivia kiss me again, but Marlee, I shut that down, too. Alivia even said she couldn't do this to you, so she stopped. She cried, too. I think she's searching for something, Marlee, and I had to tell her that I wasn't it. I told her I had you, and you were all I wanted."

"You told her that?" Marlee's arms were folded across her chest again.

"Yeah, I did."

"Last night?"

"Yes. It won't happen again. I won't let it." Susie held Marlee's gaze.

Marlee reached up and rubbed her neck and shoulder again.

"I hope you'll forgive me one day," Susie said, hearing the defeated tone in her own voice.

Marlee studied Susie's face, stubbornly wiping at her tears. She turned toward the door but then turned back. "One day, maybe." Marlee shook her head and dismissed Susie with a vigorous wave of her hand. "But that day, Susie Torres, that fucking day is *not* today." Marlee turned on her heels and stormed out Sam's door without looking back.

Chapter Twenty-Three
See Ya Later

Susie hid out at Sam's for the rest of that fateful Sunday after Marlee walked out on her. She'd have to go home soon enough and face her mother's wrath, but she decided to put it off for as long as possible. Sam did her best to help Susie see how hurt and betrayed Marlee felt, and together they tried to brainstorm ways to get Susie out of the ditch she'd dug for herself. Damage control, Sam had called it. The one thing she and Sam agreed on was that Susie had to tell Karl about his cousin. The sooner, the better.

Ronnie and Jordan called to see how she was doing. That was sweet, except that their call had some business attached. Apparently, Anne wanted the three of them to develop a conduct agreement to present to the youth group at the meeting in two days. Anne wanted a copy to look over by Monday evening, so the four of them, Susie, Sam, Ronnie, and Jordan, video-called each other and hammered out a conduct agreement. Susie thought it was pretty good and wished she'd been presented with one to sign two months ago before she tried to ruin her own life single-handedly. Ronnie and Jordan sent Anne the conduct agreement that day, and she wholeheartedly approved it and said she couldn't wait to see them present it to the group.

It was now Monday afternoon. Susie walked into the cafeteria and headed toward their usual table. She stopped short when she saw Karl already sitting there. Susie felt bad. Her life was for shit, and now she was about to ruin Karl's.

A gentle hand reached around her arm and held on.

Susie yanked her arm away. "You can't keep doing that. It's bordering on harassment."

"I know," Alivia said. "I just like to."

"Well, stop liking it," Susie growled. "Marlee might break up with me because of it."

"Oh, no," Alivia said. A truly pained expression settled on her face. "I never meant to hurt anyone."

"Just stop." Susie sighed. It was a frustrated breathy sigh.

Sam walked up and put her tray down right next to Ronnie.

"I broke up with Karl last night," Alivia said matter-of-factly.

Susie turned to look at Alivia. "What? Why?"

"I love him, but I'm not *in love* with him."

"I'm sorry, Alivia. I didn't know."

"Can I sit next to you today?"

Susie raised an eyebrow and frowned.

"No funny stuff. I already promised you."

Susie took a deep breath to gather strength. "Yeah. Come on."

Sam, Karl, and Ronnie had their heads together. Sam was doing all the talking. Karl stood up so fast that his chair fell back and clattered on the floor. Ronnie held his head in his hand.

Susie felt her pulse quicken. Did Sam tell him already?

They stopped talking when she approached.

241

"Is it true?" Karl said, his tone aggressive. He must have realized how he sounded and softened his voice. "Susie, is it true?"

Susie questioned Sam with her eyes.

"I didn't want you to relive it, Sus."

"Relive what, Susie?" Alivia said.

Susie sighed and said to Karl, "Yes, it's true."

"Son of a bitch. He is a dead man." He pounded the table with a fist, making Sam's lunch tray bounce. He looked back at Susie and said, "I'm sorry that happened, Susie. Nothing I do can change that for you, but I'm going to kill him."

He smacked Ronnie in the chest with the back of his hand. "Back me up?"

"Let's go," Ronnie said. He pulled out his phone and hit a couple of buttons. "Jordan, meet us at the Stewart's on 62 in East Valley. We've got something important to do. I'll call you from the car."

The guys lit out of the cafeteria so fast Susie didn't even have a chance to process what was happening. She sat down hard on the chair.

"Susie?" Alivia asked quietly. "What's going on?"

Sam wiped the tears in her eyes and gestured for Susie to tell her.

Amazingly, Susie found her voice and told Alivia a short version of what had happened in her house.

Alivia burst into tears and threw her arms around Susie. "I didn't know. I didn't know. I'm so sorry."

Susie found herself comforting Alivia, and it was oddly cathartic, healing even.

Alivia checked herself and pulled away. "Sorry, Susie. I hung on too long. I meant nothing by it. Nothing." She smoothed out the sleeve of Susie's sweater. "Sorry."

"Sam, what are those guys about to do?"

Sam searched Susie's face and said, "Your friends love you, Susie. I think they're going to get you justice. They're going to give you back your power."

"Yeah," Alivia said and punched a fist in the air.

Susie's phone dinged as a text came in. She hoped it was finally a text from Marlee. Maybe she was sending her good luck telling Karl. Her mouth dropped open when she saw it was a text from her father.

"*Mariposita*, can you meet me at the East Valley Diner after your softball practice?"

Susie blew out a sigh.

"You okay, Sus?" Sam said, looking toward the phone.

She nodded and showed Sam the text. "Should I say, 'yes'?"

Sam frowned. "Of course, you should. He's still your father. Now you have a chance to ask him all your questions."

"Okay. I will. I can't think straight lately."

Sam reached for one of Susie's hands and squeezed, conveying her support and friendship.

When Sam let go, Susie texted her father back. "Yes, I'll see you around five-fifteen." She wanted to add so much more but couldn't. She had to get her thoughts together.

~~~

After softball practice, she threw her softball bag and backpack in the trunk. Sam gave her a big hug and sent her on her way. A million questions ran through her head as she headed to the diner, but one stood out in front of all the rest. Why? Why did he leave?

She pulled into a parking space but didn't see his car. Maybe he wasn't there yet. She took a deep breath to steel her nerves and headed inside the diner. She spotted him immediately, his dark skin, black mustache, and bushy eyebrows. His handsome face lit up when he saw her. He stood up, and she watched his smile turn into tears as she approached.

She ran the last few steps and flew into his arms, "Papi." She cried on his shoulder until they both realized they were standing in the middle of the diner crying in each other's arms.

"C'mon, *Mariposita*. Sit." He gestured for her to sit on the other side of the booth.

She slid in, and before she could ask him how he was, a waitress stopped by for her drink order.

"Just water, please."

Her heart was beating so fast; she was sure her father could tell. When the waitress left, she looked out the window at her piece of shit car. It anchored her somehow, and she turned back and blurted. "Papi, why did you leave us?"

"You always go right for the heart, don't you?" He smiled, and Susie softened at the familiar twinkle in his eye.

"Why?" She wasn't going to let him off the hook.

"Let's eat first." He blew out a sigh. "I don't know how much room I have, though. I took your brother out for ice cream this afternoon."

244

"You saw Miguel?"

He nodded. "I wanted to see you both separately."

Her antennae went up. "Is he okay?" She didn't like the idea of her father getting to Miguel without her there.

"You're a good sister, Susana. Protective. That's good." He smiled at her.

The waitress brought her water and then took their order. Susie's stomach was in a knot, but she ordered a cheeseburger and fries anyway. He asked her how school was going, and they made small talk until the food came. She picked at the fries, unable to eat much more than a few.

She pushed her plate away and looked at her father.

"Susie, I had to leave."

"Why, Papi, why?" She couldn't look at him and, instead, restacked the sugar packets neatly in the metal caddy. The assorted jelly packets were next.

"*Tu* Mami and I had grown apart. We haven't seen eye to eye for a long time. I lost myself somewhere, Susie. I don't expect you to understand, but I'm only forty-two years old, and it felt like my life was over." His words came out in a tumble. "I couldn't be my own man with the hold your mother had on me and you kids. I couldn't do what I wanted and wasn't allowed to feel what I felt."

"When did all of this start?"

"When Miguel was a baby."

"Miguel is fourteen, Papi. You've been miserable for that long?"

"I had made a commitment, Susie. I didn't take that lightly. I wanted to watch you kids grow up. And I still want to be there for you. I want to see you become a woman, go to college, find a career, marry a life partner, and have children, maybe?" He smiled at her, and she couldn't help but smile back. "I'm so glad I was still here to see you find your first love. Marlee is good for you."

"Yes, she is," Susie said. Too bad that situation was fucked up royally, she thought.

"We're still *familia*, Susana. My decision has been a long time coming. And please know that I won't be one of those deadbeat dads. I'll be at as many softball games as I can. And Miguel's soccer games, too. He's going into high school next year, and big changes are coming for him. I don't want to miss that. And one day, I want you to meet Lauren."

"No, Papi. I can't."

"It's too soon. I know."

"How long?"

"About eleven months."

Susie realized that her father had started stepping out on her mother at about the same time she had started seeing Marlee.

"I did love your mother, Susie. Know that. For a long time. But people change. We both changed. Your mother knew that, too, I think, but she just wasn't ever going to bend with me. It's always her way—"

"Or no way."

Susie realized something huge at that moment. It wasn't that her father had "changed the natural order of things." No, he had simply removed himself from a toxic situation. He had to do what was right for him.

"Papi?"

"Yes?"

"Where's *Abuelita*?"

"She's in Vermont with me. She's fine and told me she loves you and misses you and Miguel terribly."

"I miss her, too. Tell her that, okay?"

"I will."

Susie chuckled. "The house isn't the same without her TV blaring all the time."

Her father laughed. "We've got that taken care of at Lauren's. *Tu abuelita* has her own section of the house with a bedroom, living room, bathroom, and kitchenette."

"Wow. Really?" Just how big was this house he was moving into?

Her father nodded. "Lauren's house has what's called a mother-in-law apartment. The garage was converted years ago. Her mother-in-law lived there for a little while but moved into an assisted living facility about a year ago."

"Papi, is she married?" Susie was dreading the answer. She hoped he wasn't taking someone's mother away from a family. She couldn't bring herself to say the name of her father's new love interest. The one that took him from her.

"She's a widow. For a couple of years now. Cancer took her husband."

"I'm sorry about that. That must have been hard."

"She's still grieving, I think, but I understand he was a big part of her life, and I'm not going to replace him. We're just moving into a new phase of our lives."

"Is she white?"

He nodded. *Dios*, her mother was going to hate that.

"Does she have children, Papi?"

Barbara L. Clanton

"No, they couldn't."

"Are you divorcing Mami?"

He nodded.

Susie's heart dropped. It was true. She cleared her throat and said, "Does she know about Miguel and me?" Does she know that she single-handedly destroyed our family? The last part, she did not speak out loud.

"She knows and is very excited to meet you and Miguel."

Meeting Lauren would be an astronomical betrayal to her mother.

"I told her that you two were coconuts," Susie's father said with a grin.

"Coconuts?"

Her father nodded. "Brown on the outside, white on the inside."

Susie wasn't sure what to make of that, so instead, she said, "I have a question."

"Shoot."

"The day you packed up and left. How did you rent a moving truck at five in the morning?"

"I rented it the night before."

"Hmm," Susie said. That explained a lot. "You already knew you were leaving, didn't you?"

"Yes. After dinner, I brought *tu abuelita* and all her things to Señora Diaz's house. I used my car to make that trip. She didn't have that much left. I had been moving her things out a little at a time."

"So she knew she was leaving that night, too?"

He nodded. "Then I rented the truck and returned in the morning to finish getting my things. Susie, I had been moving out

248

slowly over the past few weeks, so your mother wouldn't notice, but I think she did."

Susie looked down at her hands and picked at the cuticles. No wonder her mother had blown up the way she did. She had seen it coming and knew she couldn't do anything about it.

"And then," her father continued, "your mother had to go and make my favorite salad—which was so good, by the way. I could tell she was giving in an inch, but it was too late."

"So why did you pick a fight? "Susie asked the question, but then it dawned on her. "You wanted her to hate you."

"Yes. To make it easier. She had to hate me to let me go."

"Will there be anything else?"

Susie jumped when the waitress spoke. She hadn't even seen her approach.

"Nothing for me," Susie said.

"I would like some coffee, a box for her meal, and the check."

Susie's heart sank. Paying the check meant her visit with him was almost over.

"We're probably going to be sitting here for a while talking," her father added.

Susie's heart lightened.

"You got it," the waitress said. "I'll be right back with your coffee."

Just then, Susie's phone dinged. She snuck a quick peek and noticed it was Karl, and he had sent a video attachment. "Oh, no."

"Everything okay?" her father asked.

"Yeah," she lied. "I have to go to the restroom. I'll be right back." She stood up and stashed the phone in her front pocket. She turned back to her father and said, "Don't go anywhere."

He smiled. "I won't. We have the matter of your car to talk about."

"Oh, no," she said again, but this time for a different reason.

Susie waited until she was in the restroom to open the text from Karl. Thankfully the handicapped stall had been unoccupied. It gave her room to pace.

"Dirk won't bother you ever again," Karl's text read. "Somehow, the police got wind that he was dealing pot. They arrested him for possession and intent to sell. They also got him for the production of fake IDs. He's going away for a long time. Watch the video. I hope it helps."

She clicked the video link and watched as two police officers led Dirk out of a house in handcuffs. The video zoomed in on his face. Susie grimaced. Dirk's lip was split, and his right eye was swollen shut. Karl's handiwork, no doubt. Her hands shook as she watched it.

She couldn't help reliving the assault at Alivia's, but it didn't seem to affect her as much this time. She had been so alcohol-impaired that she had no clue how she was able to get away from him and then drive all the way to Marlee's house. A sudden memory popped up in her head. Her car. She had hit Karl's truck. And there was something else. She was pulling into the parking area. Yes, that was it. She had hit the guardrail on the way in. That was the scraping sound she'd heard but ignored because she had to pee so badly. Relief flooded her. She had been petrified that she had truly done serious damage to someone or something with her car that day.

And as far as what Karl, Ronnie, and Jordan had done to Dirk, she wasn't sure how she felt about it. One thing she did know, though, was when her friends said they had her back—they did. She took a breath, tucked her phone in her back pocket, and headed back to the table.

"Everything okay?" her father asked.

"Yeah, I think it is now." She meant it.

"Let's talk about your car. What happened to it?"

Even though he had moved out, he was still her father. He, apparently, still had all the rights, privileges, and power. Susie looked him in the eye and said honestly, "I messed up." She was too ashamed to tell him the true reason why but added, "I hit a guard rail."

"Were you speeding?"

"Actually, no." She remembered how she just couldn't think straight that day. She had come to a complete stop on C.R. 62 and then turned into the parking area. "I wasn't going fast at all. I guess I just didn't realize how close the guardrail was. I'm sorry, Papi. I'll pay for it."

"Can you even get the passenger door open?"

She shook her head.

"I have a solution, if you're amenable," he said.

"What's that?" She was afraid the answer would be for her to become an indentured servant for the rest of her life. A sudden thought came to her. "Papi, am I going to be able to go to college? Now that you moved out? Do I have to get a job or go into the Army?"

"The Army?" He laughed and said, "We have a nice fund set aside for college for both of you, Susie. There is no way I would ever jeopardize your future that way."

"Thanks, Papi. That's good to know."

"So, about your car—I think it's time to scrap it."

Susie's eyes widened. "Scrap it?"

He nodded. "Do you see that black Honda CR-V?" He pointed to a car parked in the lot.

"Yeah."

"It's yours if you want it."

"Wh-what? Why?"

"That was Lauren's husband's car. It's just been sitting in her garage, and when I told her about the damage to your car, she wanted you to have it."

"Have it? Not pay for it? Absolutely not, Papi. I'll make monthly payments for it. I don't know what I can afford, but I'll pay."

"She knew you would say that."

"How does she know what I would say? I've never met her."

Her father chuckled. "I talk about you kids. A lot. She's excited to meet you both. Anyway, she wants you to have it because she knows there will be much more on your plate now."

Who was this woman? Susie couldn't help but think that Marlee would have done the same thing if she had been in a similar situation. Maybe Lauren felt guilty, and this was her way of making herself feel better.

"I told her I didn't think you would just take the car as a gift, so together, you and I will make monthly payments. We'll work out the details later. What d'ya say, Susie?" Her father's voice was soft but expectant.

"How can I turn it down?"

"Good." He reached into a folder she hadn't seen before and pulled out an envelope. "She's already signed the title over to you. All you need to do is go to the DMV and get one in your name."

"*My* name? Really, Papi? It'll be mine, for real?"

"*Sí, mi mariposita.* Your mother is going to have a fit, but you can lie and tell her Sam gave it to you."

Susie groaned. And just when she was trying to get lying out of her life. "I'll think of something."

"And here's your insurance card. I'll keep that up for you until you graduate from college. How does that sound?"

"Amazing."

"And I think we're just going to have to scrap your car. It's too old and not worth fixing."

The excitement of a new car, a fancy SUV at that, didn't overpower her sense of loss for her current car. She and Marlee had had some nice times in that little brown rusty Toyota. All things change, though, don't they? You have to be ready to adapt. She hoped her mother would adapt. Her mother had to start bending a little, or she was going to break. Susie was desperately trying not to break, but she had to find a way to reach Marlee. She had to reassure her that Alivia meant nothing.

Her father paid the bill, and they headed outside. A flatbed truck was parked in front of her car.

"You knew I'd say, 'yes,' didn't you?"

"You'd be crazy not to." They walked over to her car. "Go ahead and get your stuff out."

With her father's help, she moved all her stuff to the new car. She made sure she checked every compartment, visor, seat, and floorboard for any and everything. Thank God she didn't have a twelve-pack stashed in the trunk. *Dios*, she hoped those days were behind her.

The new car was in mint condition, and it was big. The interior looked showroom new. "Papi, are you sure she wants to give this up?" She hopped into the driver's seat and grabbed the steering wheel.

"Yes, she's sure. You're going to have more responsibilities now, Susie. Especially when your mother's at work. Miguel is playing soccer at school, and you may have to be his chauffeur. Scott's parents have already helped out, but we can't abuse their generosity."

Susie nodded and checked out the console. There were so many buttons and knobs that it would take a while before she figured it all out. Ooh, there was a CD player, too.

"Susie?"

"Yes?" She adjusted the rearview mirror and breathed in the new car smell.

"I'm sorry. I truly am sorry."

"Papi, don't." She didn't really know what to say, but she now understood why he had left. "Just make sure we get to see you sometimes."

"I will. Count on it."

With sadness in her heart, she watched her little rust bucket get put on the flatbed. She took a picture with her phone and was tempted to tease her friends by sharing the photo with them without explanation. But that would only make them panic, and she was, hopefully, done testing their limits.

She drove her father to Señora Diaz's, her mother's card-playing friend, and dropped him off. His Camry was parked in the driveway.

Before he got into his car, he looked up at the March sky. Susie followed his gaze.

"Bright blue today," Susie said.

"With a dash of cumulus," he added.

"Vermont isn't that far away, Papi."

"You're right. It's not, so let's just say, 'See ya later,' instead of 'Goodbye.'"

"See you later, Papi. I love you."

"I love you, too, Susie. Take care of your brother. And, please, take care of your mother, too. She will need you. She may not know it, but she will. You have to be the strong one." He wrapped her in a hug and then wiped at the tears in his eyes as he headed to his car.

Susie wiped the tears in her eyes as she watched him drive away.

Chapter Twenty-Four

Just in Time

"Youth group tonight," Sam said to Susie on their way to the cafeteria. "Are you guys ready to present your conduct agreement thingy?"

"Yeah, I think so," Susie said. "It's more like a safety and well-being contract."

"Hey, slow down, you guys," Alivia said from behind them. "I'm going to that youth group thing tonight. Are you going?"

"We were just talking about that," Sam said. "Susie's driving me in her new car."

"Saw the car. Love it," Alivia said. "Can I sit next to you at lunch?"

"No," Susie said as they approached the table. "I'm going to see Dr. Austin right now."

"The school psychologist?" Alivia asked. Her eyebrows scrunched up in concern.

"Yep."

"To talk about, you know, what happened?" Alivia asked quietly.

"Yep. And other stuff." Susie knew that Alivia felt somewhat responsible for what had happened with Dirk that day, mainly because it had happened at her house. "It wasn't your fault, Alivia."

"I know, but…"

"It wasn't your fault," Susie said again softly.

Karl set his lunch bag on the table. Even though they had broken up, Karl and Alivia were still sitting at the same table for lunch but on opposite sides. Susie excused herself from Alivia.

"Hey, Karl?" Susie said. "Can I talk to you?"

"Sure." He stood up, and they walked a short distance away so they wouldn't be overheard.

"I don't know who did what," Susie held her phone up to indicate her meaning, "and I don't think I want to know, but thank you."

"He had it coming," Karl said, his expression stern. "Nobody does that to my friend. He's not my cousin anymore, as far as I'm concerned."

"I'm glad I have you as a friend." Susie hugged him. "Thank you."

"No worries."

"And Karl?"

"Yeah?"

"I think I hit your truck that day."

"That was you?"

Susie nodded. "Not my best moment."

"It was just a busted taillight, Susie. I already got it fixed."

"I have to pay you for it," Susie said.

Karl scoffed. "Not on your life, Susie. It didn't cost much to fix, and I'd rather be done with that day altogether if you don't mind."

"You got it." She hugged him again.

She said goodbye to her friends and headed out of the cafeteria to the administration wing of the school. Dr. Austin was going to get an earful today because Susie had a lot to talk about.

After her meeting with Dr. Austin, which went amazingly well, Susie made it to her AP Enviro class just in time to hold the door open for her classmates. She waited for every single one of them to go through before going in herself. The late bell rang before she got both feet in the room.

"You're late, Ms. Torres," Ms. Armstrong said with a grin.

Susie smiled back. On her way to her seat, she patted Sam on the shoulder. It was her way of letting Sam know that her session had gone well and that she was okay. Karl patted her shoulder from his seat behind her when she sat down. She turned and smiled at him. Karl was one of the good ones.

Ms. Armstrong flicked the lights off and then on, indicating the start of class. "Let's take a few minutes upfront to hand in your papers. You know the drill. Make sure your names are on the front page and put them in the bin here." She held up the in-box that always sat on her desk.

Susie groaned. With all the shit going on in her life, she hadn't paid much attention to homework. She had completely forgotten that the paper was due today. All she had was a quasi-topic—humans destroy the natural order. But she hadn't developed any kind of thesis statement.

When Sam and Karl returned to their seats after handing in their papers, they both threw her an inquisitive look. Susie felt her cheeks get warm.

"I forgot," she whispered.

Sam's eyes got big, and she grimaced for Susie's sake. Susie looked away. She was kind of embarrassed that she had completely forgotten about the assignment. Susie prided herself on being a good student who did her homework and studied for tests. Something like this was unheard of in her world.

Susie took diligent notes as the class went on and vowed to make up all the work she had slacked off on. One thing was for sure, if Marlee ever talked to her again, Susie would beg her for help with AP Calculus. She would even pay. As for her other classes, she'd figure something out.

When the bell rang to end the class, Susie leaped to her feet and hustled to her teacher's desk.

Ms. Armstrong turned around after putting a board marker back on the tray and jumped. "Ooh, Susie. You scared me. What's up?" She pushed her glasses back up the bridge of her nose.

"I, um, just wanted to let you know that I didn't turn in my paper today because I didn't do it yet." Susie swallowed against the nervous lump developing in her throat. At the beginning of the class period, she'd only had a topic, but by the end, a clear thesis had come to mind. The basic premise was that species, including humans, had to adapt to their surroundings and situations or die. They had to evolve or perish. Just like her father had done. Just like she and Miguel were doing. She hoped one day that her mother would be able to do the same. "No excuses, but with everything going on, I didn't put in much time. You can still give me a zero, but I *will turn the paper in as soon as possible*. I want to do the work."

"I think we can make some allowances, Susie. Just get it to me as soon as you can, though. Okay?" Her teacher patted her on the arm. "Everything okay?"

"Working on it," Susie said.

"Good. Let me know if there's anything I can do to help you."

Once the last student had funneled out of the room, Susie felt more free to talk. "I had another session with Dr. Austin today."

"Oh, you did? I'm glad."

"Every Tuesday at lunch from now on. Thanks for forcing me to go that first time."

Ms. Armstrong smiled. It was a sympathetic smile. "Your well-being should always come first, Susie. Don't forget that. And, hey, you'd better get going. I don't want you to be late for your next class."

"Okay. Thanks, Ms. Armstrong."

Susie hustled back to her seat to grab her backpack and flew out the door. She stepped inside her Ethics class just as the late bell rang.

"You made it just in time, Ms. Torres," her Ethics teacher said with a smile.

Chapter Twenty-Five
Forgiving Mood

Susie was lost in thought as she drove to Clarksonville that evening for the youth group meeting. It would be the first time she'd see Marlee since she'd walked out of Sam's room on Sunday. Susie had texted her every day, telling her about the contract Anne asked her to write with Ronnie and Jordan, telling her again how sorry she was to have been so selfish, and telling her how sorry she was that she had lost Marlee's trust and respect.

"They're already there," Sam said from the passenger seat after reading a text from Lisa.

"Marlee wanted to get there early, so I couldn't get her alone to beg her to take me back. That's it, isn't it?" Susie glanced over from the driver's seat.

"Maybe. Lisa didn't say," Sam said. "Marlee may not be in a forgiving mood, Sus."

Susie groaned. "I know."

"This whole thing sucks," Sam said. "Your parents splitting up, that shit that went down with Alivia, that deviant Dirk, you getting drunk every time you turned around."

"I know. I'm sorry, Sam."

"Stop saying you're sorry." The irritation in Sam's voice was loud and clear. "Look, I'm an ally, okay? I've known you a lot longer than Marlee or Lisa, and I know you're hurting. And I also know that there's a good person inside you. A person who wouldn't cheat on her girlfriend, but what sucks the most is that Marlee might not ever forgive you."

"And it will be all my fault." Susie took a slow breath. "*All* my fault."

When they walked inside the youth group room, Lisa's eyes lit up when she saw Sam. Marlee had her back to the door, so although Susie wanted to make eye contact to see her mood, she couldn't. Susie couldn't tell whether she still wore her ring or not. Sam took off running and leaped into Lisa's arms. A twirl and a long kiss was Sam's greeting. Once Lisa set Sam down, Marlee greeted Sam with a big hug. She never did turn around to look for Susie.

Resigned to her cold fate, Susie powwowed with Ronnie, Jordan, and Anne about how they would present the conduct agreement to the group. Once Anne seemed satisfied they were going to be serious about their presentation, she went over to welcome a group of newcomers.

"Oh, by the way," Susie said to Ronnie and Jordan, "I saw the video." She held up her cell phone. "Thank you."

Both guys nodded but were uncharacteristically quiet until Ronnie said, "That was all Karl." He pointed to her phone.

"That Dirk guy didn't stand a chance," Jordan added.

She gave each one an overlong hug and told them she loved them. And she meant it. They settled in behind a long table with three chairs. It felt to Susie like they were being lined up before a firing squad. But she knew they had earned this assignment and didn't grumble.

Susie turned to look at her friends. A flutter swirled through her and settled low in her belly as she watched Marlee tell Sam a story about wacky Eddie, a guy she worked with at the auto repair shop. She was very animated, her arms and hands telling a lot of the story. Susie's heart clenched. Marlee wasn't wearing the ring. Marlee laughed at something Sam said, and Susie couldn't help but smile. By some miracle, Marlee turned as if sensing Susie watching her. A shy smile crept up Marlee's face. Susie's smile broadened.

"She'll say, 'yes,'" Ronnie said softly in her ear.

"What are you talking about?" Susie didn't take her eyes off Marlee. Marlee looked down as if embarrassed.

"When you beg her to take you back."

"She'll say, 'yes,'" Jordan echoed.

"I hope so," Susie said almost under her breath. She looked at the guys and said, "To be honest, I don't know if she's ready to talk to me yet."

"With that look she just gave you," Ronnie said, "you two will be doing a lot more than talking once she gets you alone."

"Shuddup, Ronnie," Susie said good-naturedly. From her seat of exile, Susie wistfully watched Lisa tell a story about one of her sisters who had stolen the show at a recent violin recital. Apparently, no one believed she'd only been playing for two months. Sam stood next to Lisa gushing with pride because Sam had been the one to buy her the violin and had been the one to teach her, too. Susie wished she could be over there hanging with her friends.

"Uh, oh," Ronnie said. "Incoming."

Rushing into the room was a flustered Alivia.

"Hi guys, I lost track of time. What did I miss?" Alivia was a little out of breath.

"Nothing yet," Ronnie said. "We're doing our spiel first, and then we're going to organize the choir."

"Ooh," Alivia gushed. "We're having a choir. Sign me up."

"Will do," Ronnie said.

"Good luck, you guys," Alivia said and started to walk away. Abruptly she stopped in her tracks and gasped. "Who is that?" Alivia whispered to Ronnie. She pointed to someone across the room near the windows.

"That's Jessica," Ronnie said. "You've seen her before, Alivia. She was here for the debates."

"Jessica?" was all Alivia seemed to register.

"Jessica Myers," Susie said, even though she didn't want Marlee to see her talking to Alivia. "She plays basketball at Clarksonville."

"She's an athlete?" Without waiting for a response, Alivia said, "Excuse me. I have to, uh, I have to put my coat…"

Alivia never finished her sentence and floated toward the coat table. Susie exchanged an uh-oh glance with Ronnie and Jordan as they watched Alivia throw her coat on top of the pile and then glide toward Jessica and her friends.

"*Dios mio*," Susie said, shaking her head.

"Jessica doesn't stand a chance," Ronnie added.

In a matter of minutes, Anne called the group to order and introduced Susie, Ronnie, and Jordan.

Most of the kids in the group had heard about them getting drunk after the last meeting, so the series of catcalls and sarcastic applause was no surprise. Ronnie waited for the din to die down and said, "We never thought we'd be up here tonight delivering a 'Safety and Well-being Conduct Agreement' to you guys. We messed up a couple of weeks ago. Actually, to be fair, we got *caught* a couple of weeks ago, but each of us has been messing up for a long time. In fact, I even had a party at my house on Saturday, which many of you were there for. And many of you were also there when my parents came home early. They were livid."

"To say the least," Jordan added.

Susie looked at Ronnie. He seemed genuinely remorseful that his behavior had hurt his parents.

"It made Jordy and me realize that we were majorly messing up. I am majorly grounded, probably for the first time in my life. The only exception was to come to this youth group. That was an amazing concession on my parents' part."

"Probably because I told them about this conduct agreement you three were writing," Anne said. The expression on her face was serious.

It was only the second time Susie had seen a blush on Ronnie's face. The first time was when he'd just met Jordan at the Gay Pride Festival last October.

"The three of us," Jordan said, "have been partying a little too hard lately."

"Obviously, it's cost us," Susie added. "I drove while impaired. I lied to everyone in my life—my parents, myself." She had to stop to swallow past the emotional knot forming in her throat. "And I lied to the love of my life. I regret that deeply. I'm ashamed that I humiliated her that way."

"So, tonight," Jordan continued when Susie couldn't, "we want to present a 'Safety and Well-being Conduct Agreement' contract to you. The purpose of this contract is to hold ourselves and each other accountable for our actions. We're open to suggestions for improvement, of course, but by the end of the evening, we hope to have something printed and ready for every member of the Rainbow Alliance to sign. We have thirty-four 'I will' or 'I understand' statements. We've broken these up into four main categories."

Jordan turned on the projector and shined the conduct agreement on the screen.

Ronnie pointed to the four headers using one of his dad's laser pointers. "Drugs and Alcohol, Driving, Mental Health, and General Safety."

Having found her voice, Susie said, "Under Drugs and Alcohol— you can read them for yourselves—but collectively, they say that you won't buy or drink alcohol, do drugs, or smoke cigarettes. Cigarettes are legal if you're eighteen or over, but not if you give them to someone underage."

Sam said, "Seems pretty straightforward, you guys."

"Okay," Jordan said, "under the Driving category, it says that you won't drive while impaired or get in a car with someone that is impaired. And this part is interesting, too. It says you also won't let someone else drive impaired."

"It's hard to police your friends," Ronnie said, "but you might just save their lives."

Jordan nodded and added, "It also says you'll wear a seatbelt, stay in the car if you break down, and by no means will you get into a stranger's car."

One of the Southbridge girls recommended a wording edit on one of the lines; after that, there were no more suggestions.

Ronnie summed up the Mental Health section, which basically said that you would seek help if someone was harming you mentally or physically or if you yourself had self-harming or suicidal thoughts. There were no suggestions for changes.

Ronnie looked over at Susie, and she nodded. Yep, she was ready to bare her soul on the last category. He handed her the laser pointer. She took a breath and let it out slowly. "General safety is kind of broad in scope. This first line says, 'I will be aware of my surroundings at all times and remove myself from a potentially dangerous situation.'" She cleared her throat, trying to keep her voice steady. "I didn't do that." She looked down at the tabletop, not wanting to make eye contact with anyone, especially not Alivia. "I went to a friend's house and had a few beers and some whiskey, but there was a guy there that I didn't know well. I did *not* feel comfortable around him. He gave me the heebie-jeebies, actually." The room had gotten stock still as she spoke. "My two other friends went to find a private spot to be alone, leaving me alone with him. I'm not blaming my friends; I'm just telling you the facts. In my alcohol-induced haze, I wasn't aware that I was in danger."

Tears fell down her cheeks, but her voice remained strong. "I will spare myself and you the details, but suffice it to say, this man sexually assaulted me. It was a miracle I wasn't raped. How I got out of there, I'll never know." Alivia's soft crying filled the quiet space. "But, apparently, I wasn't done trying to harm myself because as blitzed as I was, I drove all the way to Clarksonville from East Valley. Forty minutes away." A few heads turned to look at Marlee. "On the

267

way, I hit a friend's car. Then I hit a guardrail. Thank God it wasn't a child or a family that I hit. I could have killed someone. I could be in prison right now because I was stupid and let drinking be the most important thing in my life." Emotion closed her throat, so she handed the laser pointer to Ronnie. She hid her eyes behind her hands and cried at all the stupid things happening in her life and all the stupid things she'd done that made her lose Marlee. Marlee was the only good thing she had, and she'd fucked that up completely.

Ronnie put an arm around her. Jordan took just the right amount of time to let her compose herself and then said, "These general safety points aren't just for the girls here, you know. We guys have to be aware all the time, too. Gay-bashing is still alive and well." His statement was greeted with groans of agreement from the group. After reading the rest of the General Safety points, he concluded by saying, "I know we sometimes feel invincible, that all those statistics don't apply to us. But you know what? They do." He took a breath and said, "Okay, if there are no other changes or suggestions, I'll polish this up and print out enough for everyone here tonight."

Anne began a round of applause. Susie blanched at the standing ovation they received from their peers. Susie didn't feel they deserved any praise and was more than embarrassed by the attention.

"You three surpassed any expectation I had of this," Anne said. She was positively beaming. "Okay, let's take a short break while we print the contracts. After signing, anyone interested in the choir stays. Everyone else can stay and watch or can take off. It's fine either way, but remember to sign the conduct agreement before you leave."

"They're printing now," Jordan said. The soft whir of a laser printer could be heard on the far side of the room. He and Ronnie stood up and headed over to it.

Susie pushed her chair back and stood up slowly.

Anne said quietly, "Susie, I didn't know. I'm sorry that happened to you."

"Thanks," Susie said. She smiled, knowing the smile didn't reach her eyes.

"Are you okay?"

"Yep."

"Really?" Anne frowned.

"I'm working on it. I'm talking to a counselor at school, and I'm not drinking anymore. I'm trying to get my life together."

Anne nodded. "That's going to take a lot of fortitude, kid. And if you need to talk, call me, okay?"

"Thank you, Anne." This time Susie's smile was genuine. She looked down and then turned toward her friends.

"Ahh," Anne said, following her gaze, "still trying to make repairs, I see."

"Yeah."

"Good luck. Just be honest with her and with yourself." Anne patted her on the shoulder and walked away.

Susie took a deep breath for courage and then headed toward her friends. Hopefully, Marlee would talk to her. Sam stepped back so Susie could move in between her and Marlee. Marlee smiled at her with closed lips; her cheeks tinged red—hopefully, that was a good sign. There was still no ring on her finger. That was a bad sign.

Sam hugged Susie and said, "That was great, Susie. You really put yourself out there."

"Thanks," Susie said.

Lisa said, "That was brave, Susie. I've got to give you that."

Susie nodded but detected something unspoken in Lisa's comment. It was as if Lisa was going to give her this one thing but not something else. Susie was keenly aware of what that was. Lisa was deeply protective of Marlee, and Susie had hurt Marlee.

Sam looked at Marlee, who hadn't spoken yet. "What did you think, Marlee?"

"I think I need to see Susie in the hallway." Marlee took two steps toward the door and turned to see if Susie was following. The look on her face was unreadable, but Susie had once vowed to follow Marlee wherever she led, so she did.

Once in the hallway, Marlee brought them to a secluded dark corner near a back stairwell. Marlee stopped and turned. She leaned against the painted cinder block wall. Susie waited. Marlee studied her face as if trying to come to a decision. Without warning, Marlee lurched forward and grabbed both sides of Susie's face. She crushed her lips to Susie's. The kiss was both passionate and desperate. Marlee half-moaned and half-groaned as if she didn't really want to kiss Susie but couldn't help it.

Marlee pulled back suddenly and said, "I'm still pissed at you. I'm still confused. But one thing I know for sure, Susie Torres, is that I love you." She sighed a deep half-groan, half-sigh as if resigning herself to her fate.

"I love you, too, Marlee McAllister. I've never stopped." Susie's heart clenched. "I'm sorry I'm such a fuck up."

Marlee pulled her closer. It seemed like she wanted to say something else but let out another frustrated groan and kissed Susie again. This time the kiss deepened to the point where Marlee pulled her closer and navigated one of Susie's thighs between hers. "I wish we weren't here right now."

"*Dios*, me, too."

Susie nipped at Marlee's lips and caught the lower lip in her mouth. She lightly sucked as she stroked Marlee's face. Marlee's moan was music to her ears. And never in a million jillion years would Susie ever tell Marlee who she'd learned that little move from.

Marlee pulled back breathless. "Tell you what," she said, "Let's go back, sign that conduct agreement, and get out of here."

"Really?"

"Really."

Susie let herself be led by the hand toward the meeting room. As they approached, Susie heard a familiar five-foot-two East Valley senior moan from a different dark corner of the hallway. Her eyes widened at the sight. Marlee put her hand over her mouth to hide a growing smirk. Petite Alivia had tall butch Jessica Myers pressed up against the wall, but Jessica didn't seem to be protesting. Not one bit. They were locked at the lips.

Susie and Marlee slunk back out of sight of the two girls kissing passionately just as Ronnie popped his head out the meeting room door. "Anybody for the choir needs to come back in now." He disappeared back into the room.

Alivia appeared around the corner first, pulling Jessica by the hand. Susie smiled at Jessica's embarrassed expression at seeing Susie and Marlee in the hallway. Alivia and Jessica headed into the room, hands still clasped together.

Marlee started to follow, but Susie grabbed her hand. "I'm not joining that choir," Susie said.

"Why not? I thought you wanted to sing."

"Alivia's joining it, and I'd rather not sing with her. I'd rather sing with you. Privately, *mi vida.*"

Marlee leaned forward and kissed Susie deeply. Susie's toes curled from the emotion of it.

Marlee pulled away first, much to Susie's dismay, but then Marlee wrapped a possessive arm around her waist. Susie wrapped her own arm around Marlee's waist and joined at the hip, they went back into the room. An explosion of cheers and applause greeted them.

"Thank God," Sam said to Lisa but loud enough for the entire room full of people to hear.

"And all is right with the world," Ronnie proclaimed to the room. He beamed at them.

Susie blanched at Lisa's scowl, her own smile evaporating under Lisa's withering gaze. Susie dropped her eyes. Obviously, there were more relationships to repair than just the one with Marlee.

"C'mon, you guys," Sam said. "This is the line for the conduct agreement forms."

Susie and Marlee got behind Sam and Lisa.

"Nice development here," Sam said with a grin. "I like it."

"Me, too." Susie's relieved expression made Sam smile.

"Me, three," Marlee added.

There was no response from Lisa.

"Hey, Marlee?" Susie said, her tone less serious.

"Yeah?"

"Can you tutor me in Calculus?"

"Ooh, you say the sexiest things. Of course, I can."

The crowd in front of the table finally cleared, and they each grabbed a conduct agreement form and a pen. They found seats and started initialing each item.

"Hey, Susie," Marlee said without looking up, "guess what happened yesterday."

"Uh, I don't know."

"Basketball season ended."

"Okay. So, what?"

"Hey, Susie," Marlee said again, "guess what happened *today*?"

"Bowling season started?" Susie shrugged at Sam's questioning face.

"Jessica Myers tried out for the softball team," Lisa answered evenly. There was no mirth to her voice.

"Jessica?" Susie looked over to where Jessica sat with a petite Alivia in her lap, arms wrapped around Jessica's neck.

"Yes. All-star basketball player, elite athlete, strong-as-shit Jessica Myers is playing softball," Marlee said. The excitement in Marlee's voice was almost tangible. "She throws hard and runs fast. Coach Speers thinks we found our replacement for Jeri in center field."

"Oh, no," Susie cried. "Clarksonville's gonna kick our ass this year, Sam."

"Tell me something I don't know." Everyone laughed, and then Sam added, "My only goal is to get a hit off of Marlee this season. Just one."

"Setting your goals pretty high there, baby?" Lisa teased, a smile finally lighting her face. "And somehow, I don't know how, but Marlee's pitches are faster and moving more."

"I know how," Sam said.

"How?" Marlee asked. "Even I don't know how this miracle is happening."

Sam started humming a twelve-bar blues bass line, one of Marlee's favorites.

"Oh, my God, Sam," Lisa said. "You're right. The bass guitar. Her wrist and fingers are stronger."

"And that guitar weighs, like, eleven pounds or something," Sam added. "That's a lot of weight to hold up. Her back, shoulders, and neck have all been getting stronger."

"What did you do?" Susie reached over and smacked Sam in the arm. "You single-handedly made the enemy stronger. Treason!" Susie accused with a laugh.

"I wasn't thinking, Sus. I wasn't thinking." Sam hung her head in mock shame. "All right, I'm done." She put the cap back on the pen. "What are you guys gonna do now?"

"Marlee?" Susie said.

"Hmm?"

"Is your mom home?"

"Now?" Marlee looked up from her form.

Susie nodded.

"Yeah, she should be. Why?"

"I want to talk to her," Susie said. Repairing other relationships was long overdue. "I need to explain myself. I need to reassure her that I'm not a creep or a bad influence."

"Ha!" Sam burst out. "Good luck with that."

Sam's outburst earned her a light backhanded tap from Lisa. "She's trying," Lisa said. "Give her that."

Susie nodded in gratitude toward Lisa. Maybe Lisa had it in her heart somewhere to forgive her, too.

"Sorry, Sus," Sam said. "I didn't really mean that. I was just trying to be funny, but I think it's a great idea. Do you want moral support?"

"Would you?"

Sam nodded. "We'll be your character references."

Susie looked expectantly at Lisa.

Lisa must have seen the silent plea in Susie's eyes because she said, "I'm willing to listen to what you have to say."

Susie nodded. That was fair.

"All right, then," Marlee said. "Let me text my mom and tell her you're all coming over. But Susie?"

"Yeah?"

"My mom may not be in a forgiving mood."

Susie's sense of purpose deflated a little. "I know, *mi vida*, I know."

Chapter Twenty-Six
Rising Up

"I love teacher workdays," Marlee said from the passenger seat of Susie's new SUV.

"With a Friday afternoon road trip to the lake house," Susie added. "No school. No practice." She flashed a grin at Marlee and then melted when she saw that the gold plastic ring had reappeared on Marlee's finger. A slow-moving Cadillac had somehow gotten in front of her on the two-lane road to Watertown. She had to keep checking her speed, so she didn't get too close. She was dying to find a good place to pass.

"Sam and Lisa are waiting for us at the house?" Marlee asked.

"Yep. As soon as Sam shows us the ropes, they're heading to Syracuse to meet her parents for some big classical music concert. They're all staying overnight at some swanky hotel down there. Sam said we could join them if we wanted to."

Marlee burst out laughing. "As if."

"It'll be nice to have the lake house to ourselves, won't it? At least for the first night." Susie shot Marlee what she hoped was a sizzling look. Judging by the blush quickly spreading across Marlee's face, it was.

"Ooh," Susie said, "I can finally pass your ass." They had just crossed over the Watertown line, and the highway opened up from two lanes to four. She pulled into the fast lane and sped up, finally feeling like she was getting somewhere. "Bye bye, sucker," she said to the driver of the slow-moving Cadillac.

"Aww, it's a grandma," Marlee said as they passed.

Susie felt bad instantly. Not that her own *abuelita* drove, but she'd hate for someone to be rude to her for any reason. A pang of loneliness hit her unexpectedly. She missed her *abuelita*. The house had been so quiet without her. Susie never realized how much love the house had with her in it. Somehow, she had to get to Vermont for a visit. But that meant meeting her father's new girlfriend, and Susie hadn't wrapped her mind around that whole concept yet.

"Oh, no, Susie," Marlee cried. "I think that was the turn." She pointed to the street passing them by on their right.

"Yep, it was. Sorry. I was so set on passing that grandma that I missed it. Shoot." Susie looked ahead and saw a nearly empty parking lot. "I'll turn around in there." She changed lanes, and then she saw it. A small rainbow flag was hanging outside the front door. She pulled into the parking lot.

"Oh, man," Marlee pointed to the flag. "Do you see that?"

"Yeah, I think it's a gay bar. The Pride Pub," she read off the sign. She exchanged a glance with Marlee. "Who knew Watertown was so progressive?"

"Yeah, really."

"Let me turn around." A way too familiar yearning gripped her chest as she took in the Coors Light sign hanging in the bar window. Her imagination tempted her. Inside the pub would be kindred spirits—gay people who drank. In there, she could kiss Marlee, and no one would care. In there, she could have as many beers as she wanted, and those people wouldn't think anything of it. She closed her eyes for a moment and breathed in slowly.

"Are you okay, Susie?"

"Yeah, I'm just tired. I'll be okay." She melted at the compassion she saw in Marlee's eyes.

After righting her mistake, Susie found her way to the house and pulled into the driveway. Sam's Mercedes sat pointed toward the street, ready to make a speedy getaway.

"Here they are," Sam said from the front door. "Good trip?"

"Oh, yeah," Susie said. "Except for one teeny tiny missed turn, we made it just fine."

Sam and Lisa came out to help them bring their luggage inside and up the stairs.

"Classic Susie," Sam said to Lisa with a groan. "I'm almost sorry she got an SUV. Now she has room to bring more shit."

"Sorry," Susie said, not sorry at all. "I need things."

"You're only staying two nights, Dingus. God, I'm going to get a hernia," Sam teased as she dragged the smallest of Susie's three suitcases into the house.

"Thanks, Sam," Susie said hoarsely.

"For what?"

"For letting us, you know, stay here."

Out of earshot of the other two, Sam said to Susie, "I think you and Marlee need this."

Susie nodded and fought back tears.

"Hey," Sam said louder when Marlee and Lisa came back outside, "did you know my parents said okay to use the lake house right away? I didn't even have to beg."

"They don't care that your nanny isn't here to supervise?" Marlee said, lugging Susie's medium-sized suitcase inside.

"Aww, I wish Helene was here, but nope. I guess they figured I'm eighteen now and can make big-girl decisions."

Susie burst out laughing. "Wow, you've got them fooled."

"Shuddup, Torres," Sam said good-naturedly. "Okay, is that the last of it?"

Susie nodded. She pulled her biggest suitcase through the doorway and dropped it by the stairs.

"Good, now for the care and feeding of the house." Sam headed into the kitchen. "Follow me, kids."

After giving Susie and Marlee a twenty-minute run down of everything they might ever possibly need to deal with, Sam and Lisa got ready to head out.

"You have all the emergency numbers, and you can call Randy, the handyman, if you need anything," Sam said. "He's really good and can be here in fifteen minutes. But, Sus?"

"Yeah?"

"You won't need him, so don't worry."

"Cool," Susie said. She hoped not. "Hey, you guys, guess what miracle happened this morning."

"What happened?" Marlee asked, grabbing Susie's hand in hers.

"Miguel cleaned out the dishwasher."

Sam and Marlee gasped.

"Without being told," Susie added.

"Another opposite day in East Valley," Marlee said with a grin.

"That *is* a miracle," Sam said. "Hey, Sus?"

"Yeah?"

"I'm glad you pressed charges against that asshole Dirk."

Susie blew out a sigh. "Yeah. My parents went with me to the police station, and I filed charges yesterday. Papi still wants to kill him, but they actually had a civil conversation for once. Of course, when I told them about drinking and then driving, they teamed up and were pretty pissed at me. It's a miracle they let me go on this trip. I think they saw that I needed a break or something."

"You finally told them?" Lisa asked. A mixture of disbelief and admiration crossed over her face.

Susie nodded and then looked at Marlee. "Marlee's mother convinced me to do the right thing. She told me she didn't call my parents herself because she was hoping I would finally take ownership of my actions."

Marlee threw her arms around her. "You're so brave, sweetie."

Lisa tapped Marlee on the shoulder. "May I cut in?"

Marlee stepped back.

Susie braced herself, not sure what Lisa was going to do.

Lisa reached out her long arms and pulled Susie into a hug. "I'm proud of you," Lisa said. She held on and whispered in Susie's ear, "But if you hurt Marlee again..."

Lisa pulled away and wiped at the tears in her eyes.

"I won't," Susie said. "I promise. I won't."

No one seemed to know what to say after that.

"Oh, my God, Lisa," Marlee said, breaking the sudden silence, "we almost forgot to give them the Jessica update."

"Oh, yeah," Lisa said.

"So, get this," Marlee said. "Jessica told us Wednesday that she'd been attracted to Alivia since she first laid eyes on her."

"That would have been during the youth group debates three months ago, right?" Susie asked.

"Yeah," Lisa said. "How did Jessica phrase it, Marlee? Something like she '*definitely*' noticed Alivia?"

"No, no, no," Marlee said. "Jessica said she '*totally*' noticed Alivia back then."

"She dragged out the word really slow, like this—'toe-tuh-lee,'" Lisa said with a laugh.

Sam teased, "And Alivia 'toe-tuh-lee' likes Jessica. That's for sure."

"No kidding," Marlee said. "Jessica's got a bad case of the Alivias. She was so surprised when Alivia flirted with her on Tuesday. She said she thought Alivia was straight."

"We all did," Susie said and rolled her eyes for her friends' benefit.

It was a slightly awkward moment, but Sam jumped in and said, "For the past two days at lunch, Alivia hasn't stopped talking about Jessica. It's Jessica this and Jessica that. Karl, poor guy, had to get up and move to another table yesterday. That was kind of sad."

"Okay, on that downer, Sam," Lisa said, "we should probably get going so we're not late meeting your parents."

"All right, kids," Sam opened the front door for Lisa, "be good, but if you can't be good, have fun!"

"Same to you, Dork," Susie said.

"Sunset is in about an hour," Sam called back to them as she got into her car. "Don't miss it."

After taking another self-guided tour of the house, Susie and Marlee rooted around the kitchen so Susie could come up with a menu for dinner. Marlee got to work slicing potatoes for her famous Petrov potatoes, a yummy baked potato recipe with butter—a *lot* of butter apparently—and parmesan cheese that she'd learned from her neighbors, The Petrovs. Susie got busy grilling steaks on the outside grill on the wrap-around deck. Much to Marlee's dismay, Susie grilled asparagus to complete the meal. "C'mon," Susie said, "you were the one that called them glorified green beans."

Marlee sighed. "I know. I know. It's fine." Although Marlee said the words, they weren't very convincing. Susie just shrugged and couldn't help thinking that Sam had pulled out a bottle of wine the last time they'd been at the lake house. *Dios*, how nice that would be to have some wine with Marlee and get buzzed, go upstairs, and make love all freakin' night long.

"Mmm," Susie said out loud.

"That was an interesting moan," Marlee said, giving Susie a hug from behind. "A precursor for things to come later, I hope?"

Susie turned and pulled Marlee into her arms. She kissed her gently, wanting it to turn into something more, but it was too dang cold on the outside deck. Susie broke the kiss, much to Marlee's dismay, but said, "Yes, that was a foreshadowing of things to come." She tossed the steaks on a plate, grabbed the potatoes and asparagus off the grill, and they headed inside.

They ate their meal off TV trays in the living room to have the best view of the sun setting over the trees surrounding Lake

Bonaparte. After eating their filling meal and then cleaning up, Susie turned down the lights and turned on the gas fireplace.

"Mmm, that's cozy." Marlee patted the spot next to her on the loveseat in invitation.

Susie jumped on the couch, bouncing Marlee up a little. She turned to Marlee and pulled her close. There was no doubt in either of their minds what the order of business was for the evening.

"Happy eleven-month anniversary, Marlee." Susie brushed her lips against Marlee's, breathing her in. Their kisses morphed into something fervent as they fed off each other's needs.

Marlee pulled back momentarily, probably in need of air, and said, "Happy anniversary, sweetie."

Locking eyes with Marlee, Susie reached for Marlee's hand. She kissed each knuckle in turn. "You know that gay bar we passed on the way here?"

"The Pride Pub?"

"Yeah. The rainbow flag got my attention, but do you know what else got my attention?"

"What?"

"The Coors Light sign." Susie hadn't planned on sharing her feelings, but she felt safe. "Marlee, there's this pull. This yearning, maybe that's a better word. I feel a hunger to go in and have a beer, to throw back a cold one and get that relaxed and mellow feeling all over." She resisted the urge to close her eyes and sigh.

Marlee pulled her into a healing hug.

"Marlee, I think I need help." She reached into her back pocket and pulled out her wallet. "Inside here is my fake ID—the one that makes me twenty-one and able to buy beer. I thought about this in the pub parking lot. I need you to save me from myself. Take this fake ID from me, Marlee." She handed her unopened wallet to her girlfriend.

Marlee didn't take it. "You need to be the one to do it, Susie."

"This pull is so freakin' strong sometimes. I don't think you know this, but I've been drinking ever since Christy discovered she could steal her father's beer. She was fifteen. I was fourteen. We drank practically every weekend and sometimes during the week after softball games. I only stopped when you showed up in my life. That first night when you and Jeri came to one of Christy's parties, and you didn't take the beer Christy offered you, I figured I had to stop if I wanted any chance with you."

Marlee's eyes softened as she said, "So the other day, you told me you were going to quit drinking."

"And I have."

"I know. Even around friends and at parties, right? You're done with that?"

"Yep."

"This is going to be hard for you, really hard, but Susie, I don't have any idea how hard."

"Dr. Austin suggested I join this Alcoholics Anonymous group for teenagers. I'm thinking about that."

Marlee's eyebrows raised. "That would probably be good for you." She pulled Susie into another quick hug. "And, in a show of solidarity, I'm going to quit something, too."

Susie furrowed her eyebrows in disbelief. "Have you been living a secret life or something? What do you have to quit?"

"Sugar. Sodas. Candy."

Susie smiled. Marlee was so cute.

"I know," Marlee said. "I can see it in your eyes that you don't think it'll be a hard thing. But the mere thought of actually doing it, Susie, makes me nervous. Really, really nervous. No, wait. Hear me out." Marlee adjusted so she could face Susie. "I have a Coke every morning with breakfast. I usually have one with lunch and a third after practice on my way home. I put one in my softball bag so that I'll have one. I drink it even if it's warm. I bet you didn't know that. And then there's the candy bar at lunch. Every day. To top that, I have this secret ritual at night while doing homework. I line up three candy bars. Usually, it's a Hershey's Almond bar, a Nestlé's Chunky bar, and Nestlé's 100 Grand bar. Sometimes I'll sub in M&Ms or Milky Ways or Snickers. Oh, and Twix, too. Twix are good 'cuz they're like two candy bars instead of one. It might even be a Baby Ruth, Butterfinger, Kit Kat, Nestlé's Crunch, Reese's Pieces—"

"Marlee?" Susie looked at Marlee with concern, her smile long since faded.

"Sorry. I got carried away. My point is that it's a well-thought-out plan. I have candy stashed everywhere: my room, the basement, and my locker at school. The only reason I don't have a stash in the van is that I'm afraid you'll find it and ask me why. I get antsy if I don't have my candy at night." Marlee sighed and said. "I know it's stupid, but it is what it is."

"*Mi vida*," Susie reached over for Marlee's hand, "All that sugar is not good for you. I think you really do have an addiction."

"I know. I've been having some headaches recently. I thought they were from, you know."

"The stress of having to deal with me."

Marlee sighed. "Something like that." She smiled softly. "But I think it might have to do with how I eat. I think it's time to listen to you and my mother and eat better finally. I have to do something now before I start to get health problems, you know? And since you're trying to overcome something hard, I thought I would do it too, not only because it's time for me but because I want to know what you're going through. I want to have perspective."

"Are you sure, Marlee? That sounds like it's going to be tough."

"No kidding," Marlee said. "And did you know there are six sixteen-ounce Cokes in the refrigerator right now, and every single gosh-darn one is calling my name? I am seriously jonesing for some sugar right now. I haven't had a single soda, candy bar, or anything all day. Last night after practice was my last soda."

"It's like a thirst," Susie concurred. "Not necessarily a literal one but a deep soul-sucking thirst for the chemicals, the euphoria, the mood change."

"Exactly. And Coca-Cola and soda advertising is everywhere, Susie. Ev-ver-ee-where."

"Should we ignore them, or should we make a game of counting how many we see in a day?"

"I don't know." Marlee ran a hand threw her hair. "I'd hate to do the wrong thing." Marlee was so cute when she was nervous.

"You know what?" Susie said. "Dr. Austin says I need to acknowledge my feelings. She said I have to meet them head on and deal with them. So here's what we do. Every time we see a sign for Coke or something sugary, we count it. Every time we see a beer sign, we count that. If we see more sugar signs in a day, then I have to give you a back rub. More beer signs? Then you give me a back rub."

"Ooh, sounds like a win-win to me." Marlee waggled her eyebrows.

They sat in an agreeable silence for a moment, and then Susie dropped her eyes. She opened the wallet she still held in her hand and pulled out the fake ID. She held it out for Marlee to take. "Do something with this."

Without taking it, Marlee stood up abruptly.

"Hey, where are you going?" Susie said.

"I'll be right back." Marlee headed into the kitchen, and Susie heard one of the kitchen drawers open. Marlee came back with the kitchen garbage can and a pair of scissors. She handed the scissors to Susie.

"Okay," Susie heard herself say. She cut the ID card into the tiniest bits she could manage while Marlee watched.

"That was good, sweetie." Marlee took the scissors from Susie, picked up the garbage can, and headed back to the kitchen.

Susie then heard the distinct sound of the refrigerator door opening. "One, two, three, four, five, six Coca-Cola labels," Marlee called out. "I'm winning six to one." Marlee stood in the kitchen doorway and said, "So where will you be giving me this backrub? Here in the living room or…" She shifted her gaze up the stairs toward their assigned bedroom.

Wordlessly Susie stood up and hit the switch to turn off the fireplace. She waited until the flames sputtered out and then headed toward Marlee, standing at the bottom of the stairs with her hand outstretched. Waiting.

Once inside the bedroom, Marlee made the first move. She fell to the bed pulling Susie on top of her. Her lips brushed Susie's lightly.

Marlee's strong hands maneuvered Susie's thigh right where she needed it. The points of contact between them were intoxicating.

Susie drank in the heat of Marlee's light blue eyes peering back at her.

"I want to feel you," Marlee said and tugged on Susie's shirt. Susie let Marlee pull the shirt all the way off and then worked on the bra. Susie returned the favor and then held herself above Marlee, teasing her obvious need. Wanting to extend the enticement, Susie reached back and grabbed one of Marlee's hands. She brought the fingers to her lips and kissed each fingertip lightly. In a rush, she pulled one finger into her mouth and sucked. She thrust the finger in and out, causing Marlee to moan and squirm underneath her. Marlee's legs wrapped tightly around one of Susie's thighs.

Marlee caught the finger gently with her teeth and growled. "C'mere." She leaned forward. After a searing kiss, Marlee pushed Susie up and away from her.

"Susie, I'm so in love with you. I feel, I don't know, alive with you." Susie kissed Marlee in answer, lingering in the kiss. Marlee groaned and let out an exasperated sigh when Susie pulled away.

"And, you," Susie said, "you have this hold on me. Even across the miles that separate us every day. Even when I'm acting like an idiot, I feel the tug of you. I drove to you after..." She couldn't bring up his name. "After what happened at Alivia's. I try to be strong and invincible to the world, but I don't need to be that way with you." Marlee's love held her up, so she continued. "Marlee, I've never wanted someone, something so much. Together we're bigger than just two parts. My soul is crushed when you're not with me."

"Looks like there's nothing we can do but be together," Marlee said. "Be *with* each other, *for* each other."

"With you, I belong somewhere." Susie ran her hand over Marlee's cheek. "I believe I owe you a backrub, *mi amor*."

"Later," Marlee said, a little breathless. "We have all night."

Susie growled in agreement and pressed her thigh down harder. Marlee arched up into Susie, her head tilting back, her eyes closing with desire. Susie's own desire enflamed her. She knew Marlee was desperate for her touch, but her need was just as great. She heard her own labored breathing as she rolled off Marlee and lay on her side. Marlee scooched closer, and they lay face-to-face, but Marlee didn't wait. She lunged forward and crushed Susie in a fervent kiss. Marlee's tongue glided over Susie's lips, urging them to open. Marlee's insistence was gentle but urgent. Marlee's exploration of her mouth turned Susie to absolute jelly. The exploration turned into a deep kiss which Marlee cut way too short when she moved on to explore more of Susie's body.

Oh, yes, Marlee knew what Susie wanted. She knew what Susie needed.

Susie gave in to the sensations. With Marlee, Susie knew she would go higher, not only right there in the bedroom, but in spirit and soul for the rest of their lives. She was a Phoenix, rising from the ashes.

~~~ The End ~~~

Helpful Resources:

Overcoming Alcohol Addiction: How to Stop Drinking and Start Recovery
https://www.helpguide.org/articles/addictions/overcoming-alcohol-addiction.htm

Teens Health from Nemours
https://kidshealth.org/en/teens

Newsletter Signup

Sign up for Barbara L. Clanton's newsletter to stay on top of new (and revised) releases. She also likes to provide writing tips for newbie (or oldbie) writers in addition to recommendations for books to read (other than her own, of course).

Sign Up on Barbara L. Clanton's Official Website:

www.BLClanton.com

About the Author

Barbara L. Clanton

Barbara L. Clanton is a native New Yorker who left those "New York minutes" for a slower-paced life in central Florida. While in middle and high schools, she played any sport she could find—softball, volleyball, basketball, and field hockey. She could even be found in the upstairs gym playing handball with her friends during high school. She played softball at Princeton University and was the team captain during their Ivy-league championship senior year.

Her career has been spent teaching mathematics at college preparatory schools in both New York and Florida. She also coached softball and basketball in both states as well. She was inducted into the ASANA's (Amateur Sports Alliance of North America) Hall of Fame as an amateur softball player.

Somewhere in adulthood, she picked up a new hobby. "Dr. Barb" plays the bass guitar and has been in several pop-rock bands, playing such notable events as Gay Days Orlando.

When asked why she started writing, she said she was writing the books she wished she had in high school to help her make sense of her (supposed) "differentness." Although the world is evolving, it's still not easy to come out to yourself or the world. She hopes her books will help.

Barbara L. Clanton's Website:
http://www.blclanton.com

Barbara L. Clanton's Instagram:
https://www.instagram.com/barbara.clanton14

Barbara L. Clanton's Facebook:
https://www.facebook.com/BassGuitarGirl

Barbara L. Clanton's Goodreads Page:
https://www.goodreads.com/author/show/3072442.Barbara_L_Clanton

Barbara L. Clanton's Author Page on Amazon:
https://www.amazon.com/Barbara-L-Clanton

Books by Barbara L. Clanton

THE CLARKSONVILLE SERIES (Young Adult)

The Clarksonville Series follows four high school girls in upstate New York as they maneuver the difficult process of coming out to themselves, each other, and their families. And it doesn't always go well. The four friends have a mutual love of softball which helps them bond and find love. Each book is from a different character's point of view, but all four main characters are present in each book. There are currently eight books in the series.

Out of Left Field: Marlee's Story
(Book One in the Clarksonville Series)

High school junior Marlee McAllister lives and breathes softball. She's the pitcher for the Clarksonville Cougars in the North Country of upstate New York. With the season opener approaching, Marlee and her best friend, Jeri D'Amico, go to scout their rivals, the East Valley Panthers. The Panthers' star pitcher, Christy Loveland, took the All-county pitching title the preceding year. It is a title Marlee covets. Marlee and Jeri settle in for the game, but as the Panthers take the field, Marlee finds herself staring at Susie Torres, the Panther left fielder. For reasons Marlee doesn't understand, she's drawn to Susie. Over the next few weeks, Marlee and Susie will slowly act on their mutual attraction. But suddenly, Susie pulls away without explanation, and Marlee realizes it has to do with Christy. Susie won't explain the bond she and Christy share, but whatever it is, it threatens Marlee's burgeoning relationship with Susie. Struggling to maintain her grades, dealing with the ever-increasing estrangement from her best friend Jeri, and handling the pressures of the All-county pitching competition, Marlee also has to confront the bittersweet realities of what it might mean to be gay.

ISBN: 978-1-953734-04-4 (eBook)
ISBN: 978-1-953734-16-7 (Paperback)

Tools of Ignorance: Lisa's Story
(Book Two in the Clarksonville Series)

Lisa Brown is the starting catcher for the Clarksonville Cougars High School softball team, and she has a major crush on her pitcher Marlee. Lisa continues to carry her torch for Marlee, even when Sam, a rival softball player, flirts sweetly. However, Lisa becomes more confused than ever when Tara, the first girl she ever kissed and the first girl who ever broke her heart, resurfaces. Since Marlee doesn't know Lisa's alive, should Lisa give up on her once and for all?

Sam seems to have secrets of her own, but Lisa wonders if she should overlook them and allow her fledging attraction to grow for the pretty blonde, or should she fan the tiny flame still burning in her heart for Tara? Lisa faces these problems and deals with society's tools of ignorance in her quest for love and acceptance.

ISBN: 978-1-953734-06-8 (eBook)
ISBN: 978-1-953734-17-4 (Paperback)

Going, Going, Gone: Susie's Story
(Book Three in the Clarksonville Series)

Susie Torres planned to spend most of the summer before her senior year of high school with her girlfriend, Marlee McAllister, but that's proving to be quite challenging. Marlee works at D'Amico's restaurant, and Susie babysits for Mrs. Johnson, her mother's boss. Susie hates the job because she not only works like a slave but almost gets paid like one. Susie is desperate to take her physical relationship with Marlee further, but she knows she has to go at Marlee's slower pace. Complicating things is the attention that a pretty blonde softball player from another team shows Marlee, and Susie falls into a funk when Marlee seems to enjoy it.

On top of that, nothing she does seems to be good enough for her summer softball coach. Frustrated with life, Susie accidentally, on purpose, comes out to her mother. It would be an understatement to say that her mother didn't take it well. Can Susie deal with a girlfriend whose head has possibly been turned by another, an employer who treats her like dirt, a coach who doesn't respect her, and a mother who tells her she is unnatural? Can she get her life back on track before senior year starts?

ISBN: 978-1-953734-05-1 (eBook)
ISBN: 978-1-953734-18-1 (Paperback)

Stealing Second: Sam's Story
(Book Four in the Clarksonville Series)

Samantha Rose Payton likes girls, but her parents don't know that. And Sam would like to keep it that way because her parents are ultra-conservative Republicans. They live in a mansion and have servants and chauffeurs. However, instead of playing the dutiful debutante who plays the violin and still has a nanny at age seventeen, Sam would rather watch ice hockey on TV and play second base on her summer softball team. Having to hide her relationship with her girlfriend, Lisa, from her parents is becoming an agonizing struggle. Not only are her friends pressuring her to come out to her parents, but they are also trying to convince her to attend a very public gay pride festival at the local college.

At least she has her nanny Helene to confide in, but for how much longer? Sam is acutely aware that the time for Helene to move on may be fast approaching. And if that isn't enough, Sam's summer softball coach gives her no end of grief after an error-filled game and isn't afraid of making an example out of her. Will Sam remain the perfect princess her parents expect? Will her beloved nanny leave her forever? Will her girlfriend get fed up about being kept hidden? Will her friends continue to pressure her about coming out? Will Coach Greer make her life miserable? All of these questions are answered in Stealing Second: Sam's Story.

ISBN: 978-1-953734-07-5 (eBook)
ISBN: 978-1-953734-19-8 (Paperback)

Out at Home
(Book Five in the Clarksonville Series)

Marlee McAllister just wants to fit in. She didn't know she didn't fit in until Kate and Rita—the prettiest girls in the senior class—pointed it out. Even Marlee's grandmother declared that Marlee's too old for "this tomboy nonsense." All the other girls at school have long hair except Marlee. All the other girls wear something other than jeans, a t-shirt, and sneakers to school every day. Except for Marlee. All the other girls fit in except Marlee.

Marlee decides to grow out her short hair, buy femmy girly clothes, and pretend she has a boyfriend named Ronnie. Really, though? She has the most amazing girlfriend in Susie Torres. Susie is everything Marlee hoped for—sweet, sexy, kind, athletic, pretty. And best of all? She loves Marlee as much as Marlee loves her. Although their parents know about their relationship, not many other people do.

Marlee is out at home but not to anyone else. And if anyone else finds out she's into girls, Kate and Rita especially, the entire school and her grandparents will know within a day. Life as she knows it will be over.

Out at Home is the story of Marlee McAllister's life-altering struggle to fit in.

ISBN: 978-1-953734-20-4 (eBook)
ISBN: 978-1-953734-24-2 (Paperback)

Tools of the Devil
(Book Six in the Clarksonville Series)

Seventeen-year-old Lisa Brown loved going to church. Oh sure, sometimes she'd rather sleep in, but she liked the calming and empowering strength of her faith. Sundays revitalized her spirit when she thanked God for the wonderful things in her life, like her loving family and amazing girlfriend, Samantha Rose. One day she hoped to marry Sam, have a house and yard, and have babies together. One day.

But then it happened. That fateful Sunday, the guest preacher stepped behind the pulpit and spoke four words that would change Lisa's world forever. "Homosexuality is a sin," he said. Had she heard him right? When her mother put a hand on her forearm, she knew she had. Every muscle in her body tensed, and she forgot to breathe. What was happening?

The church she'd been baptized in, grown up in, and wanted to get married in had, in one instant, turned against her. Still not quite believing what she'd heard, she mumbled, "Ignorance is a sin, Reverend." Never one to back down from a challenge, she scanned the congregation but didn't find a single soul who looked upset by his statement. On the contrary, many nodded in agreement. Under her breath, she muttered, "Game on, people. Game on."

ISBN: 978-1-953734-21-1 (eBook)
ISBN: 978-1-953734-25-9 (Paperback)

Going Under
(Book Seven in the Clarksonville Series)

Susie Torres is a second-semester senior with devoted friends and an amazing girlfriend in Marlee McAllister. Susie's father has the kind of job that takes him away from home on frequent business trips, but lately, his trips seem to be longer and more frequent. Tensions rise at home when Susie's mother challenges him about that. At first, Susie and her younger brother Miguel hide in her room when their parents' frequent squabbles elevate to out-and-out yelling matches. But as her parents' war escalates further, Susie finds other ways to escape the tension.

A fake ID becomes a clear and easy way to anesthetize herself with alcohol. Her crumbling home life becomes momentarily forgotten whenever she swims in a sea of peaceful drunken bliss. Unfortunately, Susie doesn't realize that she is alienating everyone around her with her attempts to cope with her parents' possible divorce. Including Marlee. Her best friend Sam tries to warn her that her excessive drinking is driving away all of her friends, but Sam's well-meaning advice isn't heard. Will Susie finally realize that it is her own actions that are making her life fall apart around her? That her new love of drinking is getting in the way of everything good in her life? That her amazingly patient girlfriend isn't going to put up with much more?

ISBN: 978-1-953734-22-8 (eBook)
ISBN: 978-1-953734-26-6 (Paperback)

Stealing Hope
(Book Eight in the Clarksonville Series)

Sam Payton is a high school senior with a bit of an identity crisis. Raised in a well-to-do family, she dutifully plays the role of Samantha Rose Payton, the wealthy debutante. Now, almost one full year into her life-changing relationship with Lisa Brown, Sam is hit with many life-challenging events. Her best friend, Susie Torres, struggles with alcohol addiction and a wrecked home life as her parents go through a bitter divorce, and Sam tries to help her friend keep her head above water. In another struggle, two friends cross the line between friendship and intimacy—a line that should not have been approached. Sam finds herself trying to make them see how incredibly egregious the transgressions are for all involved. And to top it all off, Sam's mother is diagnosed with a serious illness.

Through the love of her parents and her girlfriend, Sam navigates these challenges the best way she can, all while trying to fulfill everyone's varying expectations of her. Sam struggles to break free of the preconceived roles she seems to be bound by to figure out who she really is. It ultimately comes down to whether Sam can make everyone see that she is both a softball-playing ice-hockey-loving lesbian named Sam as well as a classically-music-trained debutante named Samantha Rose.

ISBN: 978-1-953734-23-5 (eBook)
ISBN: 978-1-953734-27-3 (Paperback)

THE WHICKETT SERIES (Young Adult)

Art for Art's Sake: Meredith's Story
(Book One in the Whickett Series)

High school senior Meredith Bedford is a social outcast. Her family recently moved from the Catskill Mountains to the sprawling suburbs of Albany, the capital of New York State. Shy and self-conscious about her acne scars, she stays to herself and tries to remain invisible. Her twelve-year-old brother, Mikey, has Down Syndrome, and she tries hard not to blame her troubles on him. Despite verbal and sometimes physical harassment, she survives because she has her art. She was selected to be part of the elite Advanced Placement art class and is quite good at capturing the emotions of her subjects in her portraits. Besides her family, art is the one thing that helps her cope with her outcast status.

One day, at a senior class meeting, she sees Dani Lassiter (president of the senior class and captain of the lacrosse team) and knows that she must paint this enigmatic young woman. One class period later, Dani manipulates things to have Meredith as her partner for a history project. Meredith is suspicious of Dani's motives but takes a chance. And it pays off. Meredith slowly sheds her invisibility cloak and allows Dani in—a little at a time. They explore an old Victorian house for their history project and become close with Esther and Millie, the two older women who own the house and who've lived together for about forty years. But, when Dani reveals to Meredith that she is gay, Meredith simply can't deal with the news. How had she not known? What is it that won't allow her to come to terms with this unexpected news? Will Meredith control her own homophobia, or will she reject the one person who had taken a chance on her and made her feel human?

Dani's Story
(Book Two in the Whickett Series)
< Coming Soon >

THE GRASSE RIVER SERIES (Young Adult)

Quite an Undertaking: Devon's Story
(Book One in the Grasse River Series)

Devon Raines, a sixteen-year-old journalism nerd, was happily minding her own business when wham, her life was turned upside down. She struggled with grief when her grandmother died from a sudden heart attack. But it was at her grandmother's wake that she locked eyes with the most beautiful black girl she'd ever seen. No, Rebecca Washington was the most beautiful *girl* she'd ever seen, period. Would this beautiful dancer freak out if she knew Devon was gay and attracted?

Enter Jessie Crowler, Rebecca's basketball-playing best friend. Or were they only friends? Devon tried to hide her attraction for the ebony dancer, but would fate allow Rebecca to look her way? Would Jessie get in the way? Would the difference in skin color keep them apart? All this adds up to quite an undertaking in Devon's formerly quiet existence.

Rebecca's Story
(Book Two in the Grasse River Series)
< Coming Soon >

THE GIRLS' SPORTS SERIES (Children's Books Ages 9-12)

Bases Loaded

Sixth-grader Mackenzie Kelly's first love was soccer until her best friend talked her into playing summer softball. Now Mack is eager to be on her school's softball team and dreams of playing in the Olympics with her idol, Cat Osterman. But first, she needs to bring up her failing English grade to stay on the team. When she learns softball has been cut from the Olympics, she's determined somehow to get it back into the Olympic Games so she can fulfill her dream.

"I just wanted to let you know I received the book and I think it is FANTASTIC!"
— Jessica Mendoza, *US Olympic Softball Team*

ASIN: B0094IT3RK (eBook)
ISBN 978-1-934452-79-0 (Paperback)

Side Out

Seventh-grader Dina Jacobs feels like she's landed on another planet when her family moves from Long Island, New York to Indiana. She tries out for the seventh-grade volleyball team, and her new friend, Christine, introduces her to Olympic volleyball. Now Dina dreams of playing in the Olympics like her newfound idol, Logan Tom. Indiana doesn't seem so bad until Dina's Jewish faith crashes against her coach's win-at-all-costs attitude. Miserable, Dina is torn between staying true to her religious customs or putting them aside to play the game she loves.

ASIN: B005HM9CUU (eBook)
ISBN 978-1-934452-65-3 (Paperback)

Live, Love, Lacrosse

Addie Coleburn, fresh out of the sixth grade, is spending the summer at her grandmother's house in Syracuse with her mother and brother. Kimi Takahashi, a girl who lives up the street, invites Addie to go to the park and play lacrosse. Addie hasn't the first clue what lacrosse is and would rather sit on Grandma's front porch eating potato chips, drinking sodas, and reading books. But then again, spending the summer dealing with her younger brother isn't that appealing, either, so she goes to the park with Kimi. Within a week, she's hooked on lacrosse. She's overweight and can't keep up with the faster, stronger girls. She has to find a way to lose her excess weight quickly or risk getting cut from the team.

ASIN: B09GPYMHDK (eBook)
ISBN 978-1-943837-50-2 (Paperback)

www.ingramcontent.com/pod-product-compliance
Lightning Source LLC
Chambersburg PA
CBHW070807180626
46818CB00001B/141